ONLY WITH
A COWBOY

Books by P.J. Mellor

PLEASURE BEACH

GIVE ME MORE

MAKE ME SCREAM

THE COWBOY
(with Vonna Harper, Nelissa Donovan and Nikki Alton)

THE FIREFIGHTER
(with Susan Lyons and Alyssa Brooks)

NAUGHTY, NAUGHTY
(with Melissa MacNeal and Valerie Martinez)

Books by Melissa MacNeal

ALL NIGHT LONG

HOT FOR IT

NAUGHTY, NAUGHTY
(with P.J. Mellor and Valerie Martinez)

THE HAREM
(with Noelle Mack, Emma Leigh and Celia May Hart)

Books by Vonna Harper

ROPED HEAT

SURRENDER

THE COWBOY
(with P.J. Mellor, Nelissa Donovan and Nikki Alton)

BOUND TO ECSTASY
(with P.F. Kozak and Lisa G. Riley)

Published by Kensington Publishing Corporation

ONLY WITH A COWBOY

P.J. MELLOR
VONNA HARPER
MELISSA MACNEAL

APHRODISIA
KENSINGTON BOOKS
http://www.kensingtonbooks.com

APHRODISIA BOOKS are published by

Kensington Publishing Corp.
850 Third Avenue
New York, NY 10022

All Kensington Titles, Imprints, and Distributed Lines are available at special quantity discounts for bulk purchases for sales promotions, premiums, fund-raising, and educational or institutional use.

Special book excerpts or customized printings can also be created to fit specific needs. For details, write or phone the office of the Kensington special sales manager: Kensington Publishing Corp., 850 Third Avenue, New York, NY 10022, attn: Special Sales Department, Phone: 1-800-221-2647.

Aphrodisia and the A logo Reg. U.S. Pat & TM Off

ISBN-13: 978-0-7582-2027-1
ISBN-10: 0-7582-2027-8

First Trade Paperback Printing: May 2008

10 9 8 7 6 5 4 3 2 1

Printed in the United States of America

CONTENTS

HARD IN THE SADDLE

P.J. MELLOR

Acknowledgment

Special thanks to Jody Payne from Evensong Farms for her extensive knowledge of horse breeding. Any mistakes were totally mine.

1

Madison St. Claire feigned sleep, listening as her fiancé, Alan, moved about their darkened hotel room. If he knew she was awake, he might want to have sex again. The thought clenched her stomach.

In hindsight, agreeing to marry Alan Hunsinger was not one of her brighter ideas. Their lackluster love life proved it. She planned to discuss their hasty engagement with him as soon as they returned to Detroit. When he'd encouraged her to leave her engagement ring at home while they traveled to set up a new business in the little po-dunk town of Slippery Rock, Texas, she had hoped Alan was having the same misgivings.

Unfortunately, they had been stuck in *Hooterville* for almost three weeks now and, quite frankly, she smelled a rat.

And she was increasingly concerned she may be engaged to it.

The door clicked shut and she breathed a sigh of relief, snuggling down farther under the blankets. Thanks to the sleeping aid she'd taken, her mind drifted. Who knew when they would be able to go home? She'd discuss everything with Alan when he returned.

* * *

Loud knocking on the door of her room awoke her. Before she'd done much more than open her eyes, blinding light filled the room through the open doorway.

The silhouette of a woman stood framed against the sunlight. "Sorry!" The woman's twangy accent set Madison's teeth on edge. "I said housekeepin' before usin' the pass key. I thought the room was empty."

Madison struggled through the sleep-induced fog, silently cursing Alan for convincing her to take the sleep aid the night before. "Well, obviously that's not the case."

The maid visibly cringed and Madison immediately regretted snapping at her. But before she could apologize, the maid was gone, closing the door on her way out.

Battling the sheet, Madison got to her feet and walked to throw the privacy bolt to ensure her shower would not be interrupted.

As she turned to make her way to the bathroom, something white on the floor caught her eye. She bent and picked up the paper. Walking to the bedside table, she flipped on the lamp and sank to the mattress to read the motel bill.

Evidently she and Alan had checked out: obviously a mistake. From what she'd seen of Slippery Rock business practices, mistakes happened all the time. Why would the motel be any different?

The front desk picked up on the first ring.

"Hello, this is Madison St. Claire in room 302. Yes, I received the summary, but there must be a mistake. He did? Well, why didn't you just put it on the card we used when we checked in? Oh. That's not possible. I—" She listened for a few moments, jaw clenched, then said, "I understand. What do you mean my room has been reserved? Yes, I know hunters make reservations in advance. Yes, I'll be down soon and give you another card. Sorry for the inconvenience."

What was Alan up to?

* * *

After her shower, she packed her bags and loaded them into the car, then headed to the office to straighten out her bill. With the opening of hunting season, it might be difficult to find another motel room. Bad enough Alan had dragged her to the tiny town in deep southern Texas, but for him to have taken off and left her there was unconscionable. As soon as she paid their bill, she was going to call him and find out where he was and what he thought he was doing.

The old man at the counter looked up from his paper at the sound of the door chime.

"I'm Madison St. Claire, room 302."

"I know who you are." He took a sip from a mug emblazoned with the slogan HOT GRANDPA. His hazel gaze was hostile, at best. "Ran your card again. Denied. Again. Called the company. Card is canceled."

"That's not possible. There must be some sort of misunderstanding. My company will look into it. I—"

"Called them, too. Said you don't work for them anymore."

"What? That's ridiculous!" As soon as she paid her bill, she would call Hunsinger Properties and get everything straightened out. The old man was obviously mistaken. What a surprise. She rummaged around in her purse. "I must have left my card case in the room. I'll be right back with another card."

"Take your time. I'll be here."

With a withering glance, she stomped out of the tiny office and up the stairs to her room.

Once inside, she literally turned the place inside out, tossing bed linens, towels, and papers, moving furniture, opening drawers—all to no avail.

Her mind flashed to Alan slinking around under cover of darkness. At the time she'd thought he was being considerate. Now she knew better.

She checked her wallet.

The rat had not only abandoned her, he'd taken all of her cash as well as her credit cards.

Swiping at the wetness on her cheeks, she paced the length of the room several times, attempting to calm down and formulate some kind of a plan. What was wrong with her? She always had a plan. Why, then, couldn't she wrap her mind around a course of action for this horrible scenario? The only thought she could come up with was to go back to Detroit and strangle Alan with her bare hands. And even that would not be enough.

Sinking to the edge of the unmade king-size bed, she reached for a tissue and sniffed. What was she doing? She never cried. Never.

She'd obviously lost her touch. By getting involved with Alan the Rat Hunsinger, she'd dropped her guard, become lax.

Darkness descended while she sat there, wracking her brain for a plan. She was a woman of action. Women of action . . . acted.

She retrieved her briefcase and opened her laptop, only to cuss a few seconds later when she was denied access to the corporate Web site of Hunsinger Properties. What was going on? After trying a few more times, she logged out and back in as Alan. Just as she'd suspected, he'd neglected to change his password. She clicked on the Projects file.

"Son of a bitch!" Flopping back against the pillows, she ground her teeth, blinking back fresh tears. Damn. It was even worse than she'd expected. There was no Slippery Rock project. No construction bonds to sell.

She'd been set up. A few more clicks to various files confirmed it.

A glance at the digital clock surprised her. Boy, it was really dark for four-fifteen P.M. The clock was obviously wrong.

She shoved back the sleeve of her raw silk suit to check the gold watch strapped to her wrist. The clock was correct.

Thunder rumbled, vibrating the bed.

It was past checkout time. What was she going to do? Where was she going to go? She flipped open her cell phone and punched the speed dial button. The phone emitted a chime. She squinted in the darkness to read the letters on the screen.

No Service.

"Stupid building probably has tons of crap insulating it, blocking my signal." Stalking to the door, she stepped onto the balcony and tried again.

Chirp. No Service.

Fat raindrops dotted the pavement of the parking lot, splattered the steps leading to her floor.

She had to get out of there. The manager would soon be looking for her, wanting his money. Money she didn't have.

Damn Alan!

Keeping a wary eye on the office window, she made her way to her Camaro, not taking a deep breath until she'd reached the safety of the leather interior.

She winced when the motor began to purr, casting a nervous glance at the office as she eased the car toward the exit.

Stopping at the end of the drive to decide which way to turn, she remembered her gas card. Rummaging through the console, she closed her fingers around the hard plastic and blinked back tears of relief.

It was the first credit card she'd ever had and had been rarely used in recent years. Alan probably didn't even know it existed. She kept it in the car for emergencies. Her current situation certainly qualified as an emergency.

Now she didn't have to worry about getting a new motel room. Assuming the card was still valid, she could use it for gas and food, sleeping in her car on the way back to Detroit. Although the idea of sleeping in her car was personally repugnant and very likely dangerous, what other choice did she have?

There may be a perfectly logical reason for Alan the Rat deserting her. She'd decide if she wanted to hear it after she strangled him.

The card worked. With her tank full and loaded down with snacks from the gas station's convenience store, she set off down the highway toward the interstate, windshield wipers beating in time to the pouring rain.

She touched the stiff paper in her pocket and silently pledged to send a cashier's check for her motel bill as soon as she got back home.

2

The tree came out of nowhere, headed straight at her.

One minute, she'd been alternating scrubbing tears from her eyes with wiping the soggy tissue across the fogged front window. The next minute, the tree was barreling down on her.

She screamed and stomped the brake.

Tires locked on the slick pavement, forcing the car to hydroplane down the road.

Lightning jagged through the black sky, illuminating her car through the T-top. The rearview mirror reflected her panic seconds before car met tree with a bone rattling crunch.

Pain shot from her left elbow to her shoulder, taking her breath away and making her fingertips tingle.

The driver's door was smashed against the sturdy tree trunk, bent in almost to the point of reaching her hip. It took some doing, but she finally managed to wedge her hand far enough around to release her seat belt. Her door, however, was firmly stuck.

Trembling, she sat in stunned silence while the rain continued to pound the roof.

Heaving a disgusted sigh, she struggled out of her bucket seat and over the gear shift. Exhausted, she flopped onto the passenger seat to catch her breath while she peered out into the darkness and flipped open her cell phone. *No service.*

Where the hell was she, anyway? The car had spun so many times, she didn't know which way led out of town or which way led back.

"You are a woman of action," she reminded herself, reaching into the back seat for her briefcase and purse. "Sitting in the middle of God knows where, in the pouring rain, isn't going to help. You need to act."

There had to be a farm or house or something along this road. It was simply a matter of swallowing her pride, walking to the nearest place, and hoping they took pity on her.

Maybe she could even work off any money they loaned her to get her car fixed. Yes, of course. She was always hearing about how kind and generous country folk were. Now was their chance to prove it.

Shoring her resolve, she slipped her phone into the pocket of her suit jacket and opened the door. A wall of driving rain blasted her in the face with a million tiny, stinging, needle-like drops, nature's warning to stay in the car.

She'd never been one to heed warnings.

Gasping and coughing, she tumbled out onto the shiny pavement.

Rain immediately soaked her silk blouse, adhering it to her body like shrink wrap. She glanced down at her new suede pumps, knowing they would never be the same.

Numb, she leaned against the side of the car, then slid down to sit on the warm, wet road and assess the damage to her body. Except for her heart apparently trying to rip through her chest, she appeared to be okay.

She sniffed, emotion clogging her throat. To her horror, once again tears welled. What was her problem? She never cried. Despite her determination, tears filled her eyes, further blurring vision already obscured by the downpour. One tear, then another, trickled down her already soaked cheeks.

Reaching behind her, she shoved the door shut. No use in ruining the interior too. Dejected, she looked at the front tire, bent at an angle, while the wet ground rapidly soaked her derriere.

What a bitch of a day.

And where was Alan? Fiancés were supposed to cherish and protect, weren't they? Wasn't there some kind of rule about that? If not, there damn well should have been. But instead of protecting and cherishing, Alan the Rat Hunsinger appeared to have hung her out to dry. Stranded her, causing her to have to slink out of town like a common criminal.

Renewed humiliation washed over her at the idea of not even being able to pay her motel bill. She'd heard about the small town mentality. When the people heard about it, about the very real possibility that everything she'd told them had been a lie, it would not be pretty. Of course, it wasn't that she'd intentionally misled them. But the play of circumstances definitely cast her in a bad light.

Eyes closed, she sighed and rested her head against the cold side panel of her car. Rain sluiced through her hair to course down her face, tickle the sides of her nose, puddle on her lips.

What had Alan been thinking, to send her to such a godforsaken little town in the middle of nowhere and then desert her? Had she done something to bring it on? She hated rural life and anything to do with it.

She shuddered. The whole town was crawling with cowboys. Alan knew that, knew her aversion. Yet, here she was, another of Alan Hunsinger's victims.

Jaw clenched, she rolled to her knees.

A loud pop issued from her car. She looked back to see the air bag deflating over her steering wheel.

12 / P.J. Mellor

"Great. Now the air bag deploys." Her tears returned, threatening to choke her. With a sob, she leaned against the rear fender to slide slowly to the warm, wet pavement. Blindly, she reached to shut the door.

After an indeterminable time, she struggled to her feet again, straightening her sodden clothing. She picked up her briefcase and purse and hobbled down the road, her heels protesting every step.

Thoughts of Alan the Rat fueled her temper, put purpose to her steps. How dare he desert her? Hunsinger Properties' latest project's details were murky in her mind. No doubt about it, she'd let her relationship with Alan blind her to what was obviously a risky proposition at best. At worst, illegal.

She sighed and continued walking. The only thing that could make her miserable day worse would be the addition of a cowboy, she reflected as she trudged along the gravel shoulder.

At first she thought the rumble was distant thunder, but then she saw the lights approaching.

A truck appeared over the hill, barreling down the road, heading straight for her.

She dropped her briefcase and waved her arms, hoping the driver would pick her up.

Evidently, he didn't see her. The big truck went into a skid on the same curve she'd missed and came at her sideways.

Hopping back to avoid death, she was hit square in the face with a rooster tail plume of water from the oversized tires.

Stinging her face, it temporarily blinded her. Incensed, she blinked to regain her vision. Her nose burned. She tasted grit between her clenched teeth and staggered backward. Her foot connected with nothing as the truck slid past.

With a yelp of surprise, she fell off the edge of the road. She plunged downward, end over end, her clothing snagging on sharp branches and twigs that stung her face. Mud oozed between her skirt and thighs, wedging beneath her panties as she continued her slippery progress down the steep slope.

Scrabbling for anything to halt her progress, she grasped at everything along the way, her fingers scraping raw. One of her acrylic fingernails popped off, sending pain shooting up to her elbow.

She rolled, over sticks and rocks and assorted squishy things, to land with an unceremonious plop into an ice cold, fast moving creek or river of some kind.

With her luck, it was probably a sewer.

She sat, leaning back on her hands, and let the tears flow as the icy water raced around and over her.

Oh, yeah, the only thing that could possibly make my day worse would be the addition of a cowboy.

3

Samuel Davis Austin had heard all he wanted to hear about the big-city woman from Detroit. In all probability, she was most likely a crooked business woman at best. At worst, a thief. And if she was a thief, everyone needed to let the law take care of it.

But no, not the citizens of Slippery Rock. They'd called a town meeting and jawed about it until he thought he'd puke. And for some reason, they thought he would be able to do something about it. Anger surged again at the thought of their attitude. What was the woman's name? St. Claire. Right, Madison St. Claire. Well, whoever Madison St. Claire was, he wouldn't want to be in her shoes. The town was out for blood.

No wonder he preferred the ranch these days. Breeding horses was infinitely easier than dealing with people.

An abandoned car, wedged against a tree, snagged his attention. He searched the sides of the road for signs of the owner. A moment later, his truck went into a skid.

Letting loose a string of expletives to make a sailor blush, he straightened out of the spin. The anti-lock brakes engaged, the powerful engine protesting as he downshifted.

The truck came to a stop, its high beams illuminating a brief-case on the shoulder of the road.

No one would leave a perfectly good briefcase along the side of the road. He heaved a sigh and set the parking brake.

Stinging needles of rain beat him in the face, soaking his shirt and the front of his jeans. Grabbing his flashlight, he adjusted his Stetson to deflect the downpour and stomped to the side of the road to peer down into Harper's Creek.

The flashlight beam reflected off a patch of lighter color in the middle of the dark water. The patch moved. No doubt about it, someone was in the creek.

He cupped his hands around his mouth to be heard over the roar of the rain and creek water. "Hey! You all right?"

Madison looked up at the figure standing at the top of the cliff she'd toppled over. He was bathed in the light, water sluicing over his ridiculous hat.

Of course. Just what she needed to make her rotten day complete. A cowboy.

"No, I'm not all right!" she yelled back, struggling to stand. Her shoes were firmly stuck in the mud, so she plopped back down. "I fell down a mountain and now I'm stuck in the mud in some kind of river."

"It's not a mountain, it's a little bitty levee," he shouted back with what sounded suspiciously like laughter in his voice. "And that's a creek, not a river. Most of the year, there isn't even any water in it."

"Well, there's water in it now."

"Need some help?"

The man stood bathed in his high beams, hands on narrow hips, rain dripping from the brim of his stupid hat. What did he want, an engraved invitation?

"That would be nice, since it was you who nearly hit me."

His posture stiffened. "What are you talking about? What were you doing out here on foot, in this kind of weather, anyway?"

She counted to ten before yelling, "I like standing hip deep in freezing water in a torrential downpour! What the hell do you think I'm doing, communing with nature? Get me out of here!" *Moron.* She took a deep breath and tried to calm down. Despite being a—ick, ick, ick!—cowboy, he was in all likelihood her only chance of getting out of the mud. It wasn't his fault and she'd never been as irrational as she'd been lately. But then, she'd never been in a situation like this either.

"Excuse me?"

Obviously she'd touched a nerve with *Gomer*, judging by his posture and tone of voice.

"I'm sorry," she said, her throat hurting with the words. Calm. She had to try to remain calm in the face of rising hysteria. "I'm wet and I'm tired. I just want to get out of here. Now, are you going to help me or not?"

Maybe it wasn't exactly a calm thing to say, but she was about as calm as she was going to get. Her feet were not only stuck but were now numb from the cold water and muck. It was hard to be calm when all she wanted was to curl up and dry off and wait for the nightmare to end.

"Are you going to help me or not?" she asked again in case he hadn't heard.

"Not." He turned on the heel of what she assumed were boots.

"Wait!" He couldn't possibly be serious. Panic rose again, threatening to choke her.

He paused with his back to her a moment, then slowly turned.

"Look, I have a problem, okay?" She forced back tears of humiliation. It was hell having to ask yet another man for something. Especially a cowboy. "I really need some help here. My feet are stuck in the mud." Her vocal cords hurt from the effort to force out the words.

She threw her hands over her eyes as the powerful beam of his flashlight swung down on her again.

"Hang on," he called, "I'll get a rope."

A rope? Oh, he must have been planning to anchor it to the truck while he rappeled down to help. Good idea. That way, they wouldn't both become mired in the muck.

The cowboy returned, his well-honed body apparent in the way he moved when he swung the rope in a big arc. The grace of his movements mesmerized her.

Wet hemp stung her cheek.

"Ouch! You hit me in the face!"

"Sorry. Grab the rope and tie it around your waist, then I'll—"

"Wait! I'm not putting that around my body! Besides, it's wet and scratchy," she pointed out. It smelled too, but she was going to keep quiet about that part. No point in offending him.

"Look, lady, you're getting on my last nerve." He shifted, adjusting the brim of his annoying hat. "If you want my help, you have to help yourself."

"I don't know how," she whispered and drew a shaky breath when she realized how true it was. Where was the can-do attitude that had served her so well?

"I can't hear you. Well," he persisted, "what's it going to be? I'm not getting any drier out here."

Madison steeled herself and looked up with what she hoped was a pitiful pout on the off chance he could see her. In her experience, pouts always worked well with the macho types.

"Why can't you come down and get me? Please—" she tacked on as an afterthought. "It's really scary down here, all alone." The quiver she allowed in her voice at the end was a stroke of pure genius, even if she did feel like scum for trying to work on his sympathy. It was imperative that she remember her goal.

"I don't want to mess up my new boots." He shifted, rain plastering his white shirt to his broad shoulders and chest.

Great. So much for southern gentlemen.

"Oh, well, we wouldn't want that, would we?" she snarled. Was chivalry truly dead? "My brand new pair of six hundred dollar shoes is probably ruined! But I have no way of knowing, since they're stuck in the mud!"

"Ma'am, I don't give a rat's ass how much your fancy shoes cost. As far as I'm concerned, they're compost. Now, you have thirty seconds to do as I say. Tie the rope around your waist," he demanded.

She glared defiantly up at him.

"Fine." With a snap, he retrieved the rope. A long arm raised a few seconds later. A rope circle whooshed in the air through the rain a second before flying toward her. She ducked, but the smelly, heavy thing plopped around her head and landed on her shoulders with enough force to buckle her knees.

"Put it around your waist. Now." His harsh order cut through the downpour. His curse followed. "Okay, fine. You see this?" He waved the end of the rope and stalked out of the circle of light. A moment later, he returned. "I tied the rope to my brush guard. I'm going to get in the truck now and put it in reverse. If you don't want to be dragged up by your neck, I suggest you put the rope around your waist, hang on, and try to stay on your feet. I'll go slow, but if you fall, it's apt to be a bumpy ride."

Madison gaped at his retreating back. He couldn't possibly be serious. The engine roared.

It appeared he was.

She scrambled to pull the rope down around her waist seconds before being yanked unceremoniously from the muck. The mud gave a loud sucking sound when her feet pulled free, then swallowed her shoes.

Survival became her only thought as she held on to the taut rope with all her strength and stumbled up the incline.

Her big toe stubbed painfully on a boulder, and bits of sticks and gravel bit into her knees. The heavy downpour drowned out her pained yelp. Turning quickly to avoid being dragged facefirst through the brambles, her rear bumped and bounced over jagged rocks and razor-sharp bushes.

The rope stopped yanking abruptly, leaving her perched on the edge of the shoulder. She scrambled to remove the wet hemp biting into her armpits and tossed it aside. Several more acrylic nails popped off, setting off shards of pain in her fingertips.

She hissed in breath to prevent yowling her pain and thought of a few things she'd like to see pop off the cowboy.

Sam cursed his luck. Unless he was mistaken, and in his gut he knew he wasn't, he'd just pulled Madison St. Claire from the muddy water. If the town got wind of it, lynching might be revived.

But he couldn't find it in him to leave a lady stranded along the side of the road, up to her hips in the clay mud. He'd been raised better than that. He shifted into neutral and set the parking brake before jumping out to check on his damsel in distress.

He'd really intended to climb down to help her, but she'd made him so damned mad with her viper tongue. Through a haze of anger, dragging her up the hill had seemed like a brilliant idea. Now he just felt lower than a snake's armpits for doing it. He stalked to the front of the truck.

She lay half on, half off the shoulder, her chest heaving with exertion. Her flirty little skirt, shredded and wadded around shapely hips, revealed legs that made his eyes widen.

A quick assessment revealed very little damage to her body. Just minor scratches. She'd have some bruises for a day or two, but it couldn't be helped. He swallowed his guilt over the way he'd *helped* her, rationalizing it got the job done.

As he watched, the edge of the road sagged. She began to

slide, her dirty, long-fingered hands snatching for anything to prevent her fall.

He stepped forward to grab her shoulders just as her hands latched on to his ankles. Boot heels slid along wet pavement an instant before the eroded shoulder crumbled.

His curses echoed from the ravine, vying with the downpour's violence. A last minute grab netted the dangling rope that rewarded him by cutting into his palm. Their downward progression jerked to a halt.

Pain from their combined weight seared through his shoulder. Mud ground between his teeth. He spit out a hunk of weeds, then turned to look down at the woman. "Why the hell did you do that?" he shouted. "Of all the stupid—"

"What was I supposed to do?" she yelled back. "Just let myself fall back down the mountain?"

He grinned for the first time since leaving his ranch that morning. "I told you, this isn't a mountain, ma'am. It's only a little levee."

"Whatever." She heaved an exaggerated sigh and looked around. "Can you get us up?"

"Yeah." He grunted and pulled them up a millimeter.

"I don't want to be dragged by your truck again," she warned.

He winced. "No need. Can you reach up and grab my legs?"

"No problem. Your boots are practically in my face."

"See if you can climb up higher on my back."

She hesitated while rain echoed on the brim of his hat. "This is a joke, right?"

"No, ma'am. I can try to drag you up by my legs, but it would be a lot easier if you'd climb onto my back."

"Fine."

Her warm weight settled along his spine.

"Okay," he shouted, "now put your arms around my chest and hold on."

"Is this really necessary?"

"Yes, ma'am," he ground out, pulling with all his strength. They made slow progress, inching their way up the muddy slope. Cold mud slithered between his wadded jeans and the tops of his boots. A hell of a way to end a day.

Warmth from the hard body beneath hers seeped into Madison, bringing with it the urge to snuggle closer. She stiffened at the idiocy of that urge, reminded of the story of the gingerbread man riding the fox.

"It'd be easier going if you'd try to relax." The cowboy's strained voice echoed against her ear. "It's like carrying a wide load on my back."

"Wide load?" She would have hit him, if her hands weren't locked in a death grip around his hard chest.

"Forget it, okay? I don't know why weight is such an issue with you women. I didn't mean anything by it. Just relax, would you?"

You women? What the hell did that mean? She would have asked, but at that moment, he levered them onto the rocky shoulder and collapsed, pulling her around to rest on his chest.

The first thing she became aware of was the definite draft across her behind and the rain running between the juncture of her legs. Wrapped in the warmth of the cowboy's arms, it wasn't a totally unpleasant feeling. She allowed herself to rest on her warm human mattress for a moment, happy to be alive.

4

Sam felt the woman's body relax, her curves snuggled gently against the planes of his body. They fit together well. Firm breasts pressed against his chest with each breath. Warm softness nestled his sex.

Tightening between his legs told him his rest was over. He had to get her off him before he embarrassed them both.

What was he thinking, anyway, lying flat on his back beside the road in a rainstorm? He'd deserve it if he drowned.

He frowned at the way his body clearly wanted to stay in its present position. Stupid reaction. Just lust. Hormones. It was breeding season. He'd just been watching too much—it gave his body ideas his mind had no business dwelling on.

He rose, dragging her along with him. Lord, she was a mess. Dripping hair hung in matted strings to her shoulders. Black streaks ran from pale eyes down scratched cheeks, giving her the appearance of a sad Mardi Gras mask.

Her blouse, soaked with rain, clung to her generous curves like a second skin, its wetness making it all but invisible. By the light of the truck, her bra was also transparent, her nipples dark shadows that moved with each breath. His hands bracketed her narrow waist, shoved the skirt lower to cover the expanse of exposed leg, and then attempted to smooth the ripped fabric over her hips.

It didn't help. The sight of her pale flesh was burned in his mind. He drew a shivering breath and stepped back, breaking contact.

She looked up at him and blinked. "Don't you think we should be introduced before you start pawing me?"

He cleared his throat and decided to let the pawing remark slide. "I'm Sam Austin," he said, extending his hand.

"Madison St. Claire." Now that she wasn't screeching at him, her voice had a husky quality, caressing his insides like warm brandy. Tingles of awareness zinged up his arm from the spot where her small hand rested. She withdrew her hand, frowned a little, and absently rubbed her palm. "What do we do now?"

"Well, let's get you back to town and out of those wet clothes, for starters." He turned, stopped, and then looked back at her. "That your car wrapped around the tree yonder?"

She nodded, the muscles in her jaw working. He walked toward the disabled vehicle.

After a brief inspection, he re-joined her, wiping his hands on his jeans. "Looks like you have a broken tie rod," he said. He wondered if it would be enough to keep her from escaping before the mess in town was straightened out.

"What does that mean?"

"It means you can't drive it. It'll have to be towed. I can give you a lift." He waited a beat, then led her to the passenger door of his truck.

She stopped and faced him. "Wait! Where's my briefcase? I dropped it somewhere around here." She began walking toward the eroded edge of the road, oblivious to the possible danger.

He grabbed her elbow. "I have it here, in the truck. Now come on, you're soaked."

"But my purse—"

"—Is more than likely at the bottom of Harper's Creek. I'll come back after the rain stops and see if I can find it. How's that? Can we get out of the rain now?"

"I was leaving town." She avoided eye contact. "I mean, I don't need to go back to the motel. I've, um, checked out. I need to get back to Detroit—that's where I'm from—as soon as possible."

He nodded. He knew that. "Well, you're not going anywhere tonight." Nowhere he didn't know about, anyway. There was only one option, if he planned to keep an eye on her. "Why don't you come home with me? I have plenty of room. I'll come back tomorrow morning and get a better look at your car. We can decide what to do then. How does that sound?"

Madison blinked and bit back a less-than-gracious reply. How did going home with him sound? Like she was once again going to have to depend on a man for her well-being. Instead of replying, she nodded and allowed him to help her up into the cab. It smelled faintly of soft leather and something else she couldn't readily identify.

The cowboy rounded the truck and climbed in beside her.

Male. It smelled male.

5

Sam reached back and pulled out an old blanket. "You might want to wrap up in this. It's old, but pretty clean. At least it's dry."

"Thanks." Her quiet voice barely reached him. He watched her gather the worn blanket around her slumped shoulders. Somehow, he thought he preferred her spitting nails and yelling at him.

He shook off the notion of Madison St. Claire being anything other than an annoying nuisance and put the truck in gear.

The drive to the Rocking A was short. Sam's gaze kept drifting toward Madison with a will of its own. She sat huddled against the door, eyes staring blankly out the window.

What had he been thinking? He had no business taking this woman home. He had every reason to loathe her, just on principle. A big-city business woman, she'd blown into town spouting projected profits and stock option opportunities, hired people away from lifelong jobs with the temptation of easy money, and generally swindled the whole town.

Still, there was just something about Madison St. Claire that defied logic, causing his senses to sit up and take notice. Besides, it would be easier to keep an eye on her this way.

Driving past his sprawling ranch house, he continued to the back of the property where the old homestead nestled within a copse of life oak. A perfect hiding place.

Brilliant spring color exploded before his headlights. His grandmother's azaleas were in full bloom. He set the brake and turned to touch her shoulder, the dome light glaring when he opened his door.

"Madison? We're here."

She swallowed and turned wide eyes on him. His heart clenched. He was a dead man.

All his life, he'd been a sucker for big blue eyes. Madison St. Claire had to have the biggest, bluest eyes he'd ever seen.

"Where's here?" She sat straighter and peered through the windshield.

Okay, how much to tell her? The woman could not be trusted. He'd do well to remember that. Loathe to lie, he waited a beat. "Where I'm staying while I work here." Well, he *had* been staying in the old house while he spent so much time at the breeding barn, just over the hill. So it wasn't really a lie. "It's nothing fancy, but it's clean and dry." He walked around to help her down. "And I have plenty of food."

Her hand gripped his and the tingling started again. Maybe the rope had done more damage than he'd thought.

He pulled his hat lower against the sheets of rain pelting him with renewed vigor and scooped her up in his arms. "Here, let me just carry you before we both get any wetter than we already are." He loped to the small porch of the rock cottage and elbowed the door open.

Inside, he deposited her on the old couch and headed for the lamp on the table. The scrape of a match echoed within the snug room before a soft yellow glow illuminated the familiar surroundings. He'd had electricity installed years ago but preferred the old oil lamps.

He glanced around at the overstuffed chintz sofa and matching chair. Scarred but serviceable end tables and an equally scarred coffee table provided convenient places to set cups of coffee and the stacks of magazines and papers he planned to read sometime soon. It may not be fancy but it was comfortable and Madison could do worse for a free place to stay.

Madison watched Sam look around. Something about the situation just wasn't ringing true. Her well-honed instincts were seldom wrong.

She blinked and frowned. Scratch that. Her famous instincts were so far off the chart when it came to being duped by Alan the Rat, it was ridiculous. She flopped back against the surprisingly comfortable sofa and observed her host.

He was tall, several inches over six feet, if her estimation was right. Even streaked with mud, his once white shirt spanned an impressive set of shoulders and a wide chest. Mudcaked denim hugged lean hips and long legs. He'd pried his boots off on some contraption by the door. Pristine white socks looked incongruous next to the filth layering the rest of his clothes. She glanced down and grimaced. She looked worse.

He tossed his hat onto a coat rack by the door. The soft light reflected from the silky strands of his dark hair. Combed straight back from a boyishly good-looking, tanned face, it sported a dent where his hat had rested.

Dark eyes met her gaze. Intense, they seemed to penetrate. A brief smile creased his face, flashing straight, white teeth and killer dimples.

Heat blossomed in her cheeks. How ridiculous, to feel so, well, intimate, for lack of a better word, with a man she'd just met.

She stood, tugging self-consciously at the blanket. "I'm really exhausted and absolutely filthy. I appreciate your hospitality, but

I'm not up for conversation. If you don't mind, I'd like to take a shower and try to get some sleep."

"Sure. I should have thought of that." He shifted and looked toward what appeared to be the kitchen. "If you'd care to sit and rest a spell, the water should be hot in no time."

"Oh." She should have known a place this old wouldn't have a modern hot water heater. She sank back down on the sofa, thumbing the keypad of her cell phone. Still nothing. Maybe it had died in the creek when she'd lost her purse and shoes. She shook it, listening for the sound of water sloshing. "How long does that take?" Did she sound ungrateful? "And I guess I should ask how long will it hold out for my shower? I don't want to use up all the hot water before you take yours." There. That sounded like a thoughtful houseguest.

Sam watched the emotions parade across her mud-streaked face. A sly smile curled his lips. "Don't you worry your pretty little head about that, ma'am." He bit back a smile when, as expected, she bristled.

Of course, he was laying it on a bit thick, but he needed to shore up his resistance if he ever hoped to survive cohabitation with the female barracuda sitting on his grandmother's couch. He had to keep her out of sight until he could get to the bottom of the allegations. And he couldn't let feelings of pity interfere with his plan. The more outrageous his behavior, the better chance of her leaving him the hell alone.

"Fine," she said in a clipped voice, her lips pressed into a thin line. She stood and dropped the shiny cell phone on the couch before regally cloaking herself in the worn blanket, nose in the air. "If you'll just direct me to the bathroom?"

"My pleasure, ma'am." He gave a little bow and inclined his head toward the door at the back of the kitchen, tamping down his shame at what he was about to do. "It's right through that door. Go about twenty feet and turn right. You can't miss it."

"Twenty feet?"

He nodded.

Madison padded across the cold, cracked linoleum toward the door. "Must be a bigger place than it looks," she muttered. Grasping the tin knob, she opened the door and stepped through. Right into the cold needles of rain.

With a scream, she hopped back. Was there no limit to her humiliation? She plowed directly into the hard wall of Sam Austin's chest.

She looked up, way up, spitting strands of dripping hair from her mouth. It was difficult to see through the raindrops spiking her lashes, but the lunatic appeared to be grinning. "You sent me out the wrong door!"

"No, ma'am, I did not." His hick accent seemed even more pronounced to her irate ears.

Calm down, calm down, count to ten, her mind chanted, right before she shouted, "The hell you didn't!" She glared up at him. "It. Is. Not. Funny." Each word was punctuated by her index finger prodding a firm pectoral. "Look, cowboy, I'm in no mood for jokes. I'm sore. And wet. And muddy. I just want to take a shower and get some sleep so this miserable day can finally end." She took a deep breath. "Is that too much to ask?" She blinked back stupid tears that sprang out of nowhere.

He sobered instantly. "No," he answered, his voice quiet. "It's not." Warm hands on her shoulders propelled her toward the softly lit living room. "I'll heat the water now. I'll even start a fire to take the chill off."

She needed to keep her guard up. Unexpected feelings of dependence, like she'd just experienced at the mere touch of his hands, would not do. They would not do at all. Her mother had been dependent enough for both of them. She had no intention of following in her mother's footsteps.

Reality hit her when she processed what the cowboy had said. Her eyes narrowed. "There's no shower, is there?"

He shook his head, the glow from the damn lamp doing

wonderful things to his face. "No. But a nice hot bath would do just as well, wouldn't it?"

Her hands tangled in her mud-encrusted hair, lifting it up for closer inspection. "Do you have any idea how difficult it is to wash this much hair in a bathtub?"

He cleared his throat and looked away. If she didn't know better, she'd think the lout was actually embarrassed. But why would he be embarrassed? "No, I guess I don't."

Too tired to argue, her shoulders slumped. A small, bittersweet smile tugged at the corners of her mouth. Alan would be surprised at the idea of her being too tired to fight.

Emotion clogged her throat. No, Alan wouldn't give a damn, one way or the other.

"Fine." She blinked back tears. "Where is the bathroom?" When he started to point again, she held up her hand. "And let's not go there again. I'm too tired to play games."

Hardening his heart, he gazed coolly down at the disheveled woman. The top of her head barely reached his chin. His mouth went dry at the seemingly endless expanse of leg. For a short woman, she had the legs of a thoroughbred. Legs that could wrap around his hips and hold him tight.

Not that he was remotely interested.

"I reckon we don't have one." Technically, he wasn't lying. It had been the fruit house, used for food storage during winter months, and could not be accessed from inside the house.

"You don't have one?" The anguished look on her dirty face pricked his conscience.

He shook his head and shrugged, avoiding eye contact. "No, but there's a real nice tub hanging on the back of the house. I could bring it in for you and have it filled in no time." He pointed toward two metal buckets on a stove. "Won't take any time to heat the water."

"I'm sorry." The soft, husky voice was back, but it wasn't

fooling him. "I'm afraid I've lived down to the perceived Yankee reputation."

Damn straight. He knew the smile she turned on him was from the teeth out, as Gram would say. Probably worked on mush-for-brains Northerners.

She stepped back and turned up the most insincere smile he'd ever seen. "I should have said, thank you for your kind offer to heat the water. Please. That would be lovely."

Gagging would be too obvious, even for a would-be macho cowboy. Instead, he nodded, a carefully schooled lights-are-on-but-nobody's-home smile. Why did all the good looking ones have the warm, cuddly personalities of rattlesnakes?

An hour later, Madison sat up to her neck in deliciously warm water. Without rain pelting the tin roof, the cabin seemed incredibly quiet, restful and cozy. Her host was outside doing who knew what cowboys did in preparation for "bedding down."

Maybe he was stuck in the god-awful outhouse. Memory of her first trip sent a ripple of revulsion through her. How could people bear the stench? She'd held her breath and almost passed out before she gained fresh air again. If you could call any air on a ranch fresh.

She frowned, closed her eyes and sank farther down in the deep tin tub. A good, long soak was exactly what she needed right now. Time to regroup, gather her thoughts.

Plan revenge.

Sore muscles protested the tension the last thought generated. Maybe she'd worry about revenge tomorrow. After a good night's sleep . . .

Sam tossed his shower-damp hair in an attempt to get rid of the telltale moisture before opening the back door. Silence greeted him. Only the faint glow from the lamp by the front entry illuminated the old house. Was his guest in bed?

Barefoot, cautious steps took him to the end of the kitchen. Long hair hung over the edge of the tub, almost brushing the floor.

"Madison? You awake?"

Her eyes were closed, the curves that had tormented his cold shower cloaked in the dark, murky depths of the bathwater. Soap he used every day now smelled unbearably sexy. Erotic. Must be the pH of feminine skin.

His hand inched toward the fall of hair, finally brushing the wet strands. Liquid silk. His thumb lightly stroked hair as fine and soft as a newborn colt.

His traitorous gaze drifted to the forbidden treasures hidden beneath the water.

No doubt about it. He'd been without a woman for too long. Any woman would spur that kind of reaction.

Swallowing his juvenile lust, he turned just as the object of his speculation shifted, exposing the tip of one plump breast, drawing his attention like a beacon. Its dark tip puckered in the cooler air.

Sam groaned, stepping away from temptation, and fell over a chair he hadn't noticed in the darkness.

Jerked instantly awake, Madison frantically groped for the washcloth. Not big, it would at least give her some sense of modesty. Slapping the wet cloth to her bosom, she turned to find Sam on his knees, setting the kitchen chair she'd dragged over to hold her towel back on its legs, his head turned toward the doorway.

"What are you doing?" Her voice was a rusty squeak as she scurried to the other end of the oval tub, arms crossed over her chest. The accusation was in her voice, but she was really more interested in what held his attention by the door.

"Ah, um . . ." He swallowed audibly. "I just got back. When I didn't see you in the other room, I thought you'd turned in. I came in here to dump the tub. That's when I saw you. I didn't *see* you!" he rushed to assure her. "I mean that's when I realized you were still here. I mean, there." He jerked his head in her direction, still averting his eyes. "In the tub."

Oh, this was too much. His voice sounded suspiciously thick, as though possibly choking on embarrassment. She'd give a month's salary to know if he was blushing—

The smile slid from her face. She no longer had a salary. The impossibility of her situation gripped her throat, choking her voice. "It's okay. I shouldn't have stayed in the tub for so long anyway." Even knowing it was true , the admission caused a bitter taste in her mouth. Like it or not, she was dependent on the man before her for the time being. It was best to swallow her pride and play nice.

The cowboy lunged through the door, rattling furniture in his wake, only to reappear with the panties and bra she'd hung carefully over the fireplace clutched in one powerful fist. He shook them in her direction, still averting his eyes.

"Do you have any idea how flammable this stuff is? You trying to burn the place down?"

"They were wet, I thought—"

"You can *not* dry things by hanging them over flames."

"Well, mister know-it-all, how the hell was I supposed to get them dry? All my clothes are in the trunk of my car. I have to have something to wear."

The plank flooring vibrated as he stomped out of the room. Wrapping the big towel securely around her, Madison stepped from the tub and warily followed.

The living room was deserted. She inched toward the open door to the left of the stone fireplace. Through the doorway, the corner of a bed was discernable.

"Oh!" A hard chest hit her square in the face, knocking her back a step before hands, hot against the bare flesh of her shoulders, steadied her.

"Sorry. Didn't see you," he mumbled, then stooped by her feet. As he straightened, she felt the edge of her towel lift. Within nanoseconds, the damp terry was pulled away. Cool air seared her entire length.

She screamed and grabbed two throw pillows from the couch to belatedly protect her modesty. "What the hell do you think you're doing?" Vibrating with rage and another emotion she didn't care to examine, she glared at the cowboy. For some insane reason, she'd thought she was safe with him and could trust him. Had she misjudged him too?

He stood, eyes averted, madly waving the towel and a wad of some kind of fabric in her general direction.

"Shit! I'm sorry! I mean, I'm sorry for catching your towel. Well, I'm sorry for saying shit, too, but—damn! Woman, why don't you make some kind of sound or something to let an un-suspecting fool know you're coming? You likely scared ten years off me!"

"*I* scared *you*? What about me? You barge in like a bull in a china shop, then disappear. I'm the innocent party here—"

"Innocent? What makes you so innocent? I know—" He clamped his big mouth shut before his size thirteen boots could get stuck. Best not to tip his hand. Taking a deep breath, he instead said, "Look, I'm sorry, okay?"

He glanced through narrowed eyes. She stood beside the couch, one of Gram's pillows gripped in each fist, covering the very spots he'd die to get a good look at.

That is, if he was interested. Which he wasn't.

He extended his hand and shook the towel away from the shirt he'd grabbed from his drawer. "I thought maybe you'd need something to sleep in."

"I sleep in the . . ." She hesitated, white teeth worrying her lush lower lip. "Thank you, anyway, but no thanks."

Nude. She was going to say nude, he knew it. His gut tightened. The woman slept nude. Heaven help him.

"Well," he choked, then cleared his throat. "Why don't you sleep in my shirt tonight, okay? You were going to say you sleep in the nude, weren't you? Nude," he grumbled, praying his voice wouldn't crack. "What if the house burned down?"

She plucked the shirt from his numb hand, a smile hovering on her eminently kissable lips.

Kissable, that is, only if he wanted to. Which he did not.

"If the house burned down," she said with a smile, "I'd venture to guess I'd have other things to worry about than whether or not I was wearing a shirt." She backed toward the bedroom door.

His hand stopped the door before it closed. "Then you'll wear it?" What did he care? It wasn't as if he'd never seen a naked woman before. The heated image that thought germinated had him gnashing his teeth.

"Yes, fine, I'll wear it, okay?" Madison shifted and edged closer to the door jamb. Why was he staring at her, heated dark eyes devouring her one minute, then gazing with cold blankness the next?

He smiled down at her through the open door, teeth flashing white in the semi-darkness. "Thanks. Good night, Madison."

The door clicked shut.

She leaned against the solid barrier, swallowed and sighed. What was happening to her? She'd never had such a strong reaction to a man. The soft cotton of the T-shirt smelled faintly of him when she rubbed it against her cheek. "Good night, cowboy," she whispered.

6

Sam punched the lumpy pillow he'd found in the blanket chest and attempted to find a better position on the too-short couch.

Nude. Not in his house. At least, not alone. *No. Get rid of that thought.* Besides, she wasn't nude. She was wearing his shirt.

The same shirt he wore next to his skin was now against hers. Caressing the very nipples he could not get out of his mind.

He groaned into the pillow.

Flopping to his back, he shoved the blanket from his heated body. Maybe he shouldn't have built the fire back up, but he'd worried she would be cool in the bedroom, with the door shut. Alone.

If he turned just right, he could see through the firebox to the bed. Was she sleeping? Was she warm enough? He glanced down and snorted. He was warm enough for both of them.

The sight of her skin bathed in the lamplight had instantly voided the effects of his cold shower. It would have been so easy to shuck his jeans and climb into that old tin tub with her.

If he'd wanted to, which he didn't.

But the thought remained. Haunted him. Would she have welcomed him? Recalling her reaction to his clumsiness with her towel, probably not.

He yawned. Not that he'd have wanted her to, but . . .

Soft sobbing woke him. His eyes opened, ears straining to hear the cause of his wakefulness. There it was again. Heart wrenching sobs, unsuccessfully muffled by the pillow. His pillow.

Now what?

He resolutely turned to face the back of the sofa. A louder, more distinctive sob echoed within the quiet.

"Ah, hell!" He threw back the blanket and strode to the door. "Madison?" he called softly, easing the door open.

The lump beneath his covers quivered. A watery sniff sounded.

Before he could think of a reason he shouldn't be there, his hip softly bumped hers as he sat on the mattress beside her.

"Madison? You awake?"

"No," a pitiful voice, muffled by the covers, answered.

"You all right?"

She threw back the covers, nearly toppling him to the braided rug, and sat up straight to glare at him. "No, I'm not all right! I may never be all right again." A loud sniff was followed by what sounded suspiciously like a whimper.

"A-and I don't kn-know what to d-do!" Fresh tears overcame her. "I always know what to do," she finished pitifully.

He folded her to his bare chest, doing his damnedest not to notice how different his shirt felt when rubbed against feminine skin. "Shh, shh. Don't cry. It'll be okay."

Crying women always got to him. That was the only reason he felt the urge to hold her. The only reason his heart felt as though it might be breaking too.

Glistening eyes looked up at him. "I n-never cry."

His lips brushed her forehead. "I'm sure you don't, darlin'."

She sighed, sniffed and snuggled closer. "And don't call me *darlin'*."

"Wouldn't think of it." He began to ease from her, lowering her to the sheets.

She clutched him closer. "No! Stay. Please? Just for a while?"

He thought of all the reasons it wasn't a good idea. While he tried to come up with them, she snuggled down, drawing him with her.

Guess it wouldn't hurt to just lie here a while. He slid beneath the warmth of the covers and winced. He pulled her cell from beneath him and placed it on the nightstand, then lay as close to the edge of the mattress as possible. He could do this.

It would be an entirely different story if he were wildly attracted to her. But he wasn't.

He could ignore the trusting way she curled into him, the satin smoothness of her leg against his, the knowledge she wore nothing but skin under his old shirt. And he would, or die trying.

Warmth, fatigue and the sound of her breathing relaxed him. He'd just rest a spell and get up before dawn.

Smooth skin rubbed against his belly. A female moan ruffled the hair by his ear. His penis strained against the cotton of his boxers a heartbeat before her hand tugged them down to his knees.

Eyes closed, he grinned, enjoying the tactile pleasure of lips kissing their way across his chest and downward.

She took him deep into the warmth of her mouth, her tongue circling and sucking. His hips bucked while his hands sought the breasts that had filled his dreams.

Sam awoke to sunshine and the jolt of his bare butt meeting

the unrelenting surface of the braided rug beneath the four poster in his grandmother's old house.

That answered his first question of where he was. The next one—why he fell to the floor—was answered immediately by the fire breathing she-dragon glaring at him from the edge of the mattress.

Wild, fiery curls framed a face that looked considerably less than friendly. Blue sparks shot from her narrowed eyes. If looks could kill, he'd be dead.

"What the hell do you think you're doing?" The shriek was back.

"Evidently not sleeping," he muttered and crawled out of range to stand up and pull up his drawers. Did he get lucky while he was sleeping and not even know it? That'd be just his luck.

A pillow missile hit him square in the face.

"Get out of my room, you pervert!"

He caught the pillow and glared at her. "*Your* room? Pervert?" He advanced. It gave a small measure of satisfaction to see her clutch the covers to her heaving breasts and scramble toward the wall.

And that was the only context in which he'd noticed her breasts. Not how sexy they looked, how kissable the pebbled tips were, not even how he almost salivated with the desire to taste them through the thin barrier of the shirt. His shirt. Just that they heaved.

He experienced a flash of longing for the soft woman who had pressed against him so trustingly throughout the wee hours of the night. This morning, the dragon lady was back, in full scale.

"What were you doing in my bed? And, more importantly, what did you think gave you the right to fondle me"

"Fondle—?"

"Oh, don't play that game! When I woke up, not only were your hands all over me—under my shirt!—you'd pulled down your underwear and were trying to . . . to, well, have sex with me. Against my will! I—"

He gave a loud whistle, holding up his hand. "Now hold on a minute. First of all, I was here because you begged me to stay with you last night. Don't give me that wide-eyed look. It's true. And, for the record, if I was having sex with you, we would *both* have to be consenting. Which brings me to my third point. Thanks for the offer, but you're not my type."

He chuckled and ducked another pillow. "You're welcome to use any of the sweats in the bottom drawer." He nodded toward the old dresser. "Breakfast will be ready in about half an hour."

With that, he closed the door and reached for his jeans. Yep, it was turning out to be a fine day.

Madison placed her cell on the scarred table, slid onto a mismatched kitchen chair and stared at the artery-clogging spread before her.

Sam looked up from ladling gravy over his biscuit. "Expecting a call?"

She shook her head.

"Problem?" he asked.

She waved her hand over the table. "I can't eat this."

He swallowed a huge strip of bacon after only chewing a few times. "Why not?"

"Sam, there's enough food for a small army. My God, you cooked three kinds of meat!"

His eyes narrowed. "You never heard breakfast is the most important meal of the day?"

She watched him over the rim of the blue enamel mug. "I rarely eat breakfast. When—"

"Well," he said in a soft, intimate drawl that did strange things to her insides, "that explains a lot."

"What do you mean?" *Concentrate on his words,* her sensible side ordered, *not how hot he looks in daylight.*

"You have to be one of the orneriest women I've ever run across," he said, jerking her back to their conversation. "Maybe it's because you don't eat enough."

"Last night you said I was fat!"

"I never!"

"Oh, yes, you did." Pride stung, she looked down at the sludge the hick passed off as coffee. "I don't suppose you have a cappuccino or a nonfat latte?"

"Cappuccino is fattening," he shot back. He grinned, dimples winking in the morning sunlight filtering through the blue checked café curtains. "Ranchers work hard. We need a hearty breakfast to keep us going until dinner."

"You don't eat lunch?"

"Dinner is lunch," he explained.

"Then what's dinner?"

"I told you, lunch."

Was he deliberately being obtuse? "I mean what do you call the meal you eat last, usually in the evening?" *You hayseed.*

"Ah." He nodded. "Supper."

He shoveled a gigantic forkful of scrambled eggs into his mouth and attempted to smile. It caused his cheeks to puff out like a chipmunk. Not an attractive sight, yet it was difficult to look away. What was it about the man that drew her attention and made her categorize his features at the oddest times? She swallowed a gulp of bitter coffee. It was definitely best to maintain a distance. Safer.

She sighed. "I'll eat, okay? I'll have some toast, whole wheat, no butter, a little jam if you have it. I prefer strawberry."

"Why would any sane person want dry toast when there's

ham, bacon and sausage, eggs, biscuits and milk gravy?" He indicated a covered bowl. "There's even fresh cantaloupe."

She reached for the bowl. "Good, I'll have that."

"Fine. This isn't a restaurant, you know." He sopped up the rest of the gravy with the remaining biscuit, shoved it in his mouth and washed it down with a loud swig of coffee.

He took his dishes to the sink and said, "I have some work to do. I cooked breakfast, you can clean up." He tugged his hat in place.

She carefully kept her face expressionless. Whatever it took to keep a roof over her head and food in her stomach, she'd do it. For now.

She looked at her jagged nails. What she wouldn't give for a manicure and pedicure . . .

Halfway through the back door, he paused, shoved his hat up and stared back. "I was thinking about what you said last night, when you were crying—"

"What! I never cry."

He held up his hand. "I won't argue. What I meant to say was I know you're going to need money to repair your car and stuff. I need some help around here—"

"Sorry. I know absolutely nothing about ranches."

"Will you stop interrupting me, woman? What I was trying to say is I need help around the house. If you'll do the housework and tend the little vegetable garden out back, I'll pay you a fair wage. You do know how to do dishes, don't you?"

"Of course. City people eat off of plates too, you know."

He grinned, fueling a warm flush to wash over her. "I thought they might just eat their young," he drawled.

"Very funny." She stood and began gathering the rest of the plates.

"Can you prime a pump?" He pointed to the red metal thing at the end of the stainless steel sink.

How hard could it be? "Absolutely."

He nodded, pulling his brim low over his eyes, but made no move to leave. "Good. And you know how to operate the stove to heat the water?"

"Don't be ridiculous." She dropped the utensils in the sink with a clank.

"Okay." He shifted, seeming reluctant to leave her alone. Did he think she was going to steal the family jewels or something? Desolation washed over her. If he'd talked to anyone in town, probably so.

"I'll be fine, Sam. Don't worry. In fact," she said, placing the plates on the counter and turning to him. "I'm thinking about taking another bath after I finish cleaning up the kitchen. I'm still kind of sore."

He nodded. "I brought the tub back in after I dumped it. Just leave the water and I'll dump it when I come home." His head stuck back in through the open door. Warm lips brushed her cheek, morning stubble lightly scratching her skin. "Have a good morning, Maddie. Stay inside." He tapped the end of her nose. "And don't answer the door." With that, he was gone.

Clad in a pair of Sam's sweatpants, Madison leaned against the counter and frowned. Sam had no idea how useless his warning was since she had zero desire to broadcast her presence. Not yet, anyway. Her hand touched the spot his lips had warmed while she warned herself not to overreact. "Don't call me Maddie," she said to the closed door.

"C'mon, water," she pleaded. She peered up at the dry spout. "I know you're in there." Exactly how did one go about priming a pump? Painters primed walls. Did she need to coat it with something? While it was covered in bright red paint, it didn't seem to be a fresh coat. She seemed to remember a pump from a long-ago camp having a starter button of some sort. No buttons were apparent.

"You can do this, St. Claire," she mumbled, "it's not rocket science. You have an MBA. Surely you can figure out how a pump works." A nervous glance at the old plastic happy face clock nailed to the faded cabbage rose wallpaper made her palms sweat. She shouldn't have wasted so much time with her cell phone. Sam could be back at any time.

In the movies, they pumped and water came out. She'd pumped until her arms grew leaden. Nothing. Her pacing took her by the stove.

One bucket was half full. Her spirits brightened considerably. She'd just heat the water that was there and still have time to wash the dishes before Sam came back. She hoped. She confidently turned the knob.

A hissing sound filled the kitchen, along with the distinctive smell of gas. No flame.

This was ridiculous. What was wrong with the thing? Alan's stove was gas. All she'd ever done was turn the knob and presto! Flame. She leaned close to every burner, in the case a small, undetected flame existed. Nothing.

She coughed. Obviously the range was defective, she thought as she rummaged around for dishwashing liquid. She should probably tell Sam as soon as he came home. He'd want to get it fixed right away since he seemed to require immense quantities of cooked food.

She coughed again and staggered to the chair. Eyes streamed as another cough shook her chest. Her throat ached. Maybe she was getting sick.

Her head throbbed like tiny men with jackhammers had taken up residence. Suddenly exhausted, she slumped over on the table. She'd just close her eyes for a minute . . .

Sam whistled under his breath as he walked up the hill. Madison had filled his mind at odd moments all morning. It was a tad early to break for dinner, but he found himself between jobs and decided to eat earlier than usual.

It wasn't like he was anxious to see her or anything. He was hungry, that's all. Maybe a cold egg sandwich and a glass of milk. He frowned. How would he get the milk out of the refrigerator in the storage shed without Madison catching on about the electricity?

Man, what a jerk he was. What was his problem? Was he trying to punish her by making her do without modern conveniences? Maybe.

Outside the back door, he paused. And sniffed.

His booted foot pushed open the wooden door. Coughing, eyes streaming, he stumbled back, then took a deep breath and ran in.

Gas fumes filled the kitchen. Madison's still figure sat slumped over the kitchen table.

Eyes clenched against the fumes, he scooped her into his arms and staggered out the door.

Within seconds of being lowered to the grass, she began coughing. She struggled to sit up. Emotion tightened Sam's chest. He briefly closed his eyes, thanking God, before opening them to glare down at his guest.

"Are you okay?"

"I'm—" Cough. "Fine."

"You sure?" She nodded. He took another deep breath and ran back inside. Sure enough, every burner was on high. After remedying that, he threw open all the windows.

He returned to Madison, now propped on her elbows taking great gulps of air.

"I thought you said you know how to operate a gas stove," he said, flopping down next to her.

"I do. Obviously that one is defective. You really should have someone take a look at it, Sam. It could be dangerous."

He stopped scrubbing his face and peered through his fingers. "No kidding."

She nodded. "And while you're at it, you might want to have the pump checked out as well."

"What's wrong with the pump?"

"It doesn't work."

"Did you prime it?"

"Of course. Well, I tried."

He stood and walked to the back door. The fumes were almost gone. He stepped inside and looked at the pump, Madison close at his heels.

He picked up a jar, still filled with water. "What did you use?"

"Use?"

He shook his head. "City woman," he muttered. "Watch and learn, Maddie." He poured a thin ribbon of water from the jar into the top of the pump. With his other hand, he began pumping. After several sucking sounds, a trickle of water emerged.

Eyes wide, she turned her smiling face to his. "You made water!"

The urge to lean down and kiss her was overwhelming. That, combined with his relief that she hadn't asphyxiated herself, was the reason he acted on the urge.

Her mouth formed a small O when his lips claimed hers. Instead of smacking him, as he'd half expected, she melted against him, her softness forming to him like they'd been kissing all their lives.

He breathed in the soft, womanly smell of her, his tongue tasting the sweet interior of her mouth.

She gave a little whimper and hopped higher in his arms, her legs going around his hips.

His cock reacted, doing a little happy dance that its dry spell was apparently ending.

He slid his hands beneath the elastic waistband of his old sweatpants to cup the smooth cheeks of her bare bottom.

She whimpered and shimmied a little closer to the part of his anatomy leaping to attention.

He dipped his fingers into her wetness and moaned into her mouth.

She went wild, clawing at the snaps on his shirt, yanking it from his jeans.

He backed her up until she perched on the edge of the counter, then he stripped the sweatshirt from her.

Her breasts were perfect. Firm and full, the large peach-colored nipples puckering in the cooler air of the kitchen. Bending his knees, he drew a circle around one areola with the tip of his tongue before sucking the nipple deep into his mouth.

She arched, the soft pillow of flesh coming up around his nose, her scent surrounding him.

More. She needed more. Despite her words earlier that morning, she wanted this. Wanted him. All of him.

Rebound sex, a little voice in her head informed her, but she was in no mood to listen.

"I'm sorry," Sam said, inching away, the cooler air coming between them. "I just meant to kiss you, I—"

"Did you hear me tell you to stop?" She jerked him close again and ran her tongue around his mouth while her right hand slid down his chest to delve below the waistband of his jeans.

There it was. Just what she wanted, just what she needed. The tip of his erection bumped against her fingertips.

With a smile against his mouth, she slowly dragged her hand up and out to trace the evidence along his bulging fly before giving it a hard squeeze. When his penis twitched, she felt an answering wetness between her legs.

Her next thought shocked her, but she was tired of being cautious, tired of playing by the rules, tired of being used. It was time to turn the tables, even if only for a little while. Did she dare tell him what she really, truly wanted right now? Absolutely.

"When do you have to go back to work?" She smiled against the salty skin of his neck and kissed her way down to a hard male nipple, flicking it with the tip of her tongue.

"Anytime I want. What did you have in mind?" His hands were busy with her breasts, his lean hips grinding against her moist center.

"You, me, naked."

He nipped the tip of her breast and gave a bark of laughter. "Oh? And then what would we do, once we were naked?"

"You said you bred horses," she returned in a breathy whisper, her hand finding and stroking him, making him harder still. "You can't think of something we could do?"

"I can think of a few things," he said, his hand dipping into the sweats and playing with her wet folds. "I could do this, for instance." He fluttered his fingers, eliciting an eager wiggle. He plunged a finger deep within her. "Or this."

She gasped, spreading her legs wider, silently begging for more of the delicious sensations chasing through her. "Yes-s-s," she said, panting, "And I bet you could do more."

Another finger joined the first, rocking her world. She clasped her legs around his hips and rocked along with his movements, close, so close, to the release she sought.

He latched on to her nipple, sucking in time to the thrust of his fingers.

"More!" Panting and bucking against him, it was all she could do to force the word out.

His arm went around her, lifting her from the counter, his hand still inside the sweatpants, doing inflaming things to her as he carried her out of the room.

The soft fabric of the couch caressed her bare back while Sam did a fine job of caressing her front.

"Strip, cowboy," she whispered, lifting her hips for him to pull the now soggy sweats from her. Beyond modesty, she lay, naked, with her legs spread over the rolled arm of the sofa, and watched with unabashed enjoyment as Sam stripped off the shirt and threw it aside.

When he bent to kiss each of her knees while massaging her swollen labia as he began to trail kisses upward, it took all of her strength to stay on task. While she'd enjoy nothing more than a good tongue lashing from the hot cowboy before her, it was imperative she remain the one in control of the interlude.

She grasped his hair firmly in her hand and tugged until he looked her in the eye. "Not so fast, lover boy. You wanted me to tell you what I want. Remember? I want you naked." She looked pointedly at his jeans. "Strip. Take it all off. I want to see nothing but skin."

He grinned and reached for the top button of his fly. With

excruciating slowness, he released one button, paused, then released another button, not stopping until his erection bulged through the gaping opening in his white cotton boxers. He reached between her legs and petted her weeping sex.

She shifted, enjoying the feel of the work-roughened pads of his fingers against her sensitized, swollen flesh for a moment before saying, "Ah, that's wonderful, but not what I asked for. Drop 'em."

With a grin, he obliged, standing naked before her.

"Okay," she said, her gaze never leaving the impressive bit of equipment revealed for her pleasure, "now come closer so I can touch you."

He took a step and looked down. "Forgot to take off my boots."

"Do it!"

"I'd have to pull my pants back up to do that, do—"

"Okay. Stop. Plan B." She sat up and closed her hand around his hot, impossibly hard erection and gently pulled him toward her.

After kissing the tip, she traced around the head of his penis with the tip of her tongue, then gently blew on the moisture.

His hips bucked and she smiled.

"Let's play a game, cowboy." She massaged the droplet of moisture around the bulbous tip.

"What kind of game?" His voice was tight as he stepped a little closer.

Although it wasn't nearly as much fun as she'd envisioned, she tamped down her embarrassment and looked him in the eye. "It's called *fuck me if you can*. It's really lots of fun. We see how many positions we can get into, but the rule is you can only penetrate me once, then you have to find another position. After you enter me in that position, you have to pull out and I have to come up with another position. And so on until we both decide on a final position. Kind of like a sexual game of chicken." She tapped the head of his penis. "Are you up for it?"

"Who gets to choose first?"

"Me." She rose to her knees on the sofa, her behind facing him and wiggled her hips a couple of times. "Okay, cowboy, fuck me if you can."

He dropped to his knees on the cushions and, hot hands on her hips, entered her with a smooth, deep thrust.

She reached between her legs to caress his testicles, thinking she wouldn't mind if he stopped the game.

Instead, he slowly withdrew and stood up, leaving her feeling abandoned and vulnerable. That wasn't the point of starting the stupid game.

"I like this game," he said, positioning her over the back of the couch, her legs spread, feet tucked between the seat cushions. "My turn," he said with a grunt as he plunged into her eager flesh.

To her disappointment, he immediately withdrew. Breasts heavy, she dragged them along the fabric on the sofa back to help relieve some of her tension. It didn't help.

He held her at arms length when she started toward him. "Did you hear something?"

"Just heavy breathing." She grinned and pushed him to sit in the upholstered chair, then climbed to straddle his lap. "Now, where were we?" She positioned him at her opening and lowered onto him inch by inch, enjoying the warmth. "Here? Or maybe here?"

He returned her smile and arched his back, driving deep within her, then set her aside and stood. "My turn again and then I declare this game over."

He shuffled over to the couch.

She laughed. "Do you have any idea how ridiculous you look with your pants wadded around your ankles?"

"Yep." He plopped down to lay on his back and pulled her to sit backward, her legs spread on either side of his hips. He gave her bottom a playful swat.

Playfulness quickly gave way to very definite fondling. Madison didn't mind, so she stretched out on her stomach along his legs and enjoyed the feel of his fingers on her most intimate parts.

Games like they'd just enjoyed were totally foreign to her, but she'd discovered she liked them. A lot.

"Samuel Davis Austin!" a female voice shouted with enough force to rattle the windows. "What in tarnation is going on?"

8

Madison froze and looked back over her shoulder.

An old woman with snow-white hair glared at her over the back of the sofa. The woman's hair stuck out in spikes and blue daggers shot from behind her trifocal glasses.

Sam hurried to sit up, toppling Madison to the floor.

"Gram!" he said, his voice cracking as he tossed his discarded shirt toward Madison and yanked up his pants. "What a surprise!"

"No shit. I thought you'd be working, so I brought some stew and fresh bread for your supper. I'll just go put it on the table while your *friend* gets dressed."

Cheeks flaming, Madison struggled to get into Sam's shirt. "I'll wait in the bedroom until she leaves."

"Oh, no, you don't," he said, grabbing a fistful of shirt as she walked past him and dragging her back. "If I have to face my grandmother, so do you. Besides, she'll be nicer if there's company around." He gave an exaggerated shudder. "She can be a force to be reckoned with, I tell you."

"Sam, how can you say that about your grandmother?" She kept her voice barely above a whisper.

"Easy," he whispered back, "I love her, but I know her."

"I can hear you, hot stuff," his grandmother called from the kitchen. "Is your girlfriend decent? I'd like to meet her."

Despite Madison vehemently shaking her head, he grinned and called back, "Sure, come on and meet Maddie."

"The name is Madison," she hissed as the elder woman walked into the room.

His grandmother walked up to Madison and stuck out her hand. "Hi, Maddie, I'm Liza Davis, but you can call me Gram since you and my heathen grandson are getting hitched."

"What!" Sam and Madison shouted.

"Aw, I'm just yanking your chain." She grinned, revealing a row of small, perfect white teeth. "Although I wouldn't mind if you two hooked up. You'd probably give me beautiful great-grand babies."

"Gram!" Sam shot her a look it didn't take a psychic to understand. "Maddie is just staying with me for a while, until her car is fixed." He shifted his feet before meeting his grandmother's gaze. "I'd appreciate it if you'd keep her staying here to yourself for a while."

"No prob. Everybody I know to tell is dead, anyway." She paused by the front door and looked at them, head to toe and back. "I heard about some shyster Detroit business woman hightailing it out of town. That wouldn't be your friend, would it?"

"No, ma'am."

"Didn't think so." She stepped out on the porch and closed the door.

"Why did you lie to her?"

"Are you a shyster?"

"No! Of course not! But you knew she was talking about me and you denied it." She frowned and tried to work up some kind of attitude to prevent her from feeling sentimental about Sam lying to his grandmother. "Why did you do that?"

"Because it's the truth. You may or may not be a shyster, but you are here. That means you didn't leave town. So it wasn't a lie."

"Thanks. I think. Now what?"

He pulled her into his arms, rubbing his hardness against her. "Where were we?"

"About to make a big mistake?" She eased out of his embrace.

"You're probably right."

Although she'd said it, she found she was disappointed to hear him agree.

"Besides," he continued, "your game has made me hungry. I went out and picked up your suitcase this morning. It's out in my truck. Personally, I like the idea of you walking around in my sweats with no underwear, but I thought you might want to change into your own stuff after we eat. Then I need to go back to work. I have a stallion coming in this afternoon." He shook his head. "If I didn't need what he's got, I wouldn't fool with him. He's already hurt two of my prize mares."

"Then why are you allowing him to do it again?"

"I'm not. This time, he just gets to smell her, then he can make his deposit alone." At her look, he grinned. "It involves a big, padded collar and drum. Want to know more?"

"Um, no, thanks, I'm good." She had a vivid imagination.

After lunch, Sam left and Madison went into the bedroom to unpack her clothing. She'd hoped seeing her power suits would help rekindle her determination to rebuild her life.

At the motel, she'd sworn if she never went south of Ohio again, it would be too soon.

Her afternoon activities flashed through her mind, bringing a flush of remembered lust.

Damage control was obviously needed. She couldn't let her temporary insanity over a pair of killer dimples, long legs, lean hips and an absolutely lust inspiring butt keep her from doing what needed to be done.

She had to make sure the sort of insane attraction she'd experienced with Sam today never happened again.

Longing washed through her. She glanced at the red leather suit in her hand. What was happening to her? The idea of putting the expensive garment on practically had her breaking out in hives. Sure, most of her business clothes weren't actually her choices, but Alan always had good taste. Didn't he?

She narrowed her eyes and took a good look at the restrictive clothing of her life in Detroit. "Oh, no. I was a business whore." No, that couldn't be right.

She was just feeling on edge and out of sorts due to being confined in the small house with no amenities. That had to be it. Didn't it?

Irrational joy washed over her at the sound of Sam calling her name an hour later. Hiking up the baggy sweats, she had to restrain herself from running into his arms.

"Hey, sweet thing," he said with a laugh, lifting her from her feet for a hug. "Miss me?"

Had she missed him? She'd known him less than twenty-four hours. How could she know him enough to miss him? She glanced at her useless cell phone on the table, then back at Sam. Maybe what she had felt when he was away was just culture shock.

While she pondered the possibility, he pulled her sweatshirt over her head, filling his palms with her breasts.

Maybe the way he made her feel when he touched her was what she really missed. Maybe she would feel it with anyone who filled a sexual void.

Sam drew her attention when he released her breasts and

picked up her shirt. "I didn't mean to upset you. Here. Put this on to cover temptation." He grabbed her hand and pulled her into the living room, indicating she should sit on the chair while he paced to the end of the room and back.

"I had your car towed this afternoon. Skeeter said it may take a few weeks to get it fixed. Sorry. He's not only the best mechanic in town, he's the only one."

She nodded and tried to not watch the play of muscles beneath the worn denim as he walked. "Did he happen to give an estimate?"

"No. Won't know until he gets into it." He bent his knees to look her in the eye. "Is there someone you need to call?"

"Hmm?" She put down her cell, only just realizing she'd been trying to power it on. "Oh, no. There isn't anyone." Her throat ached with unshed tears. She didn't want, didn't need anyone's pity. But Sam deserved to know the truth. "You know who I am, what I was here for, so you probably also know, by now, I was leaving town without paying my motel bill."

"It crossed my mind."

She sighed and stared at the firebox for a few minutes. "My fiancé, rather my *ex*-fiancé, Alan the Rat Hunsinger, was the mastermind behind everything."

She leaned forward, eyes pleading for him to understand. "I had no idea what he was up to! I still don't. Not really. I just know the project has been scrapped, my corporate charges closed." She gave a short, ironic laugh. "When I checked before leaving the motel, I discovered he also closed my personal bank accounts, along with my charges, and had my home phone turned off. How's that for devotion?" She picked up her cell and put it back down. "I suspect my cell has been turned off too. Either that or it's ruined. Same difference."

She drew a shaky breath, blinking back tears. "I trusted him, Sam. I trusted him and he not only betrayed me, but he also left me holding the bag. I'm the one who will be blamed for all of this! I should have known better than to give him that much power. Whatever possessed me to put his name on my bank accounts? I even let him have a key to my apartment. What was I thinking?"

Sam bumped her hip with his, his arm pulling her to rest against his side as he settled next to her. "You were thinking you were going to marry him, to share the rest of your life with him. Of course, you would give him a key. I can even understand how you might put his name on your bank accounts." Sort of.

She nodded, her head rubbing against his shoulder. "I knew you'd understand." Another sniff and a sigh followed. "I don't know why, but I did," she murmured. She took a deep breath and continued in a small voice. "By the time I realized what happened, it was too late. Now no one at the corporate office will take my calls. Sam, all I had was a gas credit card. I had no choice but to take off. But I will pay back every cent I owe. And I'll do my damndest to get back the money people invested with Hunsinger Properties. I swear, I will!" Her voice cracked.

"Shh," he crooned, pulling her closer. "I know you will, darlin', I know."

"Don't call me darlin'," she said with a sigh.

His arms held her securely, seeping feelings of being safe and protected into her bones. She could stay like that forever.

His scent enveloped her, warm and tangy. Primal male.

Warm hands drew lazy circles on her shoulder. She purred and snuggled closer. On hand dipped beneath the baggy sweatshirt. Callused fingers felt incredibly right on the bare skin of her back, across her ribs, lightly tracing the underside of a suddenly heavy breast.

With each pass, sparks arced through her, shot down her abdomen and pooled in her pelvis. It really wasn't right. He was taking advantage of her perceived vulnerability and she shouldn't allow it.

She shifted, seeking a closer connection, loathe to leave the sheltering warmth that surrounded her. A few more minutes wouldn't hurt.

The heat of his lips blazed a trail of fire across her cheek, giving her time to resist, before settling firmly on her mouth. How could any living, breathing, woman resist? She groaned and opened her mouth for him, squirming on the worn upholstery. Velvet tongues danced, escalating her desire. White hot, her passion flared, sparks dancing along each nerve ending.

She climbed onto his lap, straddling his lean hips. It may be wrong, but right now it was the only game in town.

They both groaned when Sam's hands, now under the shirt, cupped her breasts. He shoved the fabric up, feasting his eyes and then his mouth on her.

Madison arched her back, amazed at the sexual energy zipping through her. She never wanted it to end.

Her hands shook when she gripped the front of his shirt and pulled. The snaps gave way in rapid-fire succession. Soon, the hot, smooth skin of his chest was beneath her questing hands. Her fingertips memorized each contour, all the shifting muscles. And there were a lot of muscles.

It went on forever and not nearly long enough.

When Sam finally dragged his lips from hers, her heart thundered, her lungs wheezing with the effort to regulate her breathing. Next to her ear, his breath came in hot pants against her skin. Big hands skimmed her from hip to neck and back down, leaving a trail of fire in their wake.

It was insane. They really should not be doing this. Or that.

She bit back a whimper when Sam set her aside and stood.

"Much as I'd love to continue this, I really do have to get back to work." He snapped his shirt and tucked it in. "Sure you don't want to come watch?"

She shook her head. "A horse masturbating isn't really high on my to-be-watched list."

He glanced at the clock on the rough hewn mantle. "That won't happen for another hour or two. I have another breeder coming out with his mare before that." He leaned to brush his lips across hers and whispered, "Quarter horses are beautiful animals. Put on some shoes and come with me."

"I don't have anything in my suitcase except heels." She glanced down at her more than casual attire.

"Gram's barn boots are outside the back door. They'll probably fit you."

Madison clopped along beside Sam, hurrying to keep up with his much longer stride, the knee-high rubber boots flopping on her feet with each hurried step.

Sam's hand was warm and reassuring in her own as he pulled her along toward a huge structure just over the hill from the cabin.

As soon as they crested the hill, the wind shifted, bringing with it an odor that stuck in the back of her throat. Unable to stop her automatic reaction, she gagged.

Sam laughed and put his arm around her, lifting her off her feet. "C'mon, city slicker, pick up the pace."

An older man Sam introduced as Bud, the ranch foreman, walked up, holding a big leather halter attached to two lengths of chain.

"Wilkins is already here. I was just going to get King," Bud said. "You want to do it?"

Sam nodded and took the apparatus as he walked into the barn, Madison trotting along behind him. He jingled the chains. Immediately a low, rumbling sound came from the one occupied stall on the right, about halfway through the cavernous building.

"Maddie," Sam said, stopping beside the stall door. "I want you to meet King Maker IV. Because we're family, he allows us to call him King." He reached over the gate and rubbed the nose of easily the most beautiful horse she had ever seen. Of course, she hadn't seen all that many horses.

Dark red-brown hair shined in the low light of the barn. The horse turned intelligent dark eyes toward her. A brilliant white streak, looking almost like a flame, went from the tip of his nose up the middle of his face to disappear in a delicate point between his ears.

King pawed the ground, setting off vibrations under Madison's feet.

Sam jingled the chains again, earning another deep, almost growl from the horse as it pranced within the confines of the stall.

Sam threw the bolt and led King out by the strap of leather surrounding his face.

Madison hopped back. She knew she was probably gaping, but now she knew where the phrase "hung like a horse" came from.

Sam followed the line of her vision and grinned. "Impressive, isn't he? Be glad you're not wearing perfume," he added with a wink.

She looked back at the horse then tore her gaze away from easily the biggest penis she'd ever seen. "How does he walk around with that thing?"

Sam turned and led the horse toward the wide, open door at the back of the barn, Madison following at a safe distance. "He doesn't. He's been bred enough that it's his natural reaction. When he hears the harness jingle, he gets excited and lets down 'cause he knows he's going to get lucky."

Bud and another man stood in the grassy area behind the barn, next to what Madison could only assume was King's hot date.

"Stand clear," Sam said as they approached the mare. "Once he gets her scent, he loses his mind. You don't want to be in his way."

She'd scarcely found a spot by the far side of the barn when King let out what could only be interpreted as the horse equivalent of a roar and mounted the mare. No foreplay. Poor King had even less moves than Alan. Shocking in its violence, the mating was over almost as fast as it began. King may be hung, but he didn't have much staying power, from what she could tell. The stallion stepped away and backed up. Sam let up on his hold on the leather strapping. Immediately, the mare's owner began walking her around the area as Bud walked up to take the reins for King. Sam patted the horse's neck and stepped back.

"Hose him down and give him a cigarette, Bud."

"You encourage your horse to smoke?" she asked in disbelief when Bud led the now docile horse away. How did he hold the cigarette?

Sam laughed and hugged her to his side as they walked back through the barn. "Relax, it's an expression. You sure you don't want to stay around?"

"No, thanks. I've been traumatized enough for one day. I think I'm going to get going on weeding the garden." She smiled up at him. "May as well start earning my money."

"Good idea. But take it easy. You're not used to Texas heat." He kissed her forehead. "I'll try to get back in time to help a little."

She decided to ignore the little pat on the butt he gave her.

9

Madison wiped her forehead with the sleeve of the sweat-drenched sweatshirt and sat back on the ground, wiggling her toes in the borrowed rubber boots. She glared at the neat rows of vegetables. Weeding was not fun. And weeds looked remarkably like vegetables. She'd discovered that when she'd pulled up a radish. Chagrined, she'd replanted it but who knew if it would survive. She was a radish killer.

Throwing her weight behind a particularly stubborn clump of weeds, she ignored the shadow that fell across the garden.

With one final tug, the weed released its hold on the dirt. Madison fell back on the ground. Sitting up, spitting dirt out of her mouth and wiping it from her eyes, she looked at the prize in her hands. The root was long and kind of . . . orange?

"That's a carrot, you know," a deep voice said from somewhere above her.

It didn't sound like Sam, but she was still surprised to see a stranger. "I just figured that out, but thanks," she said, standing up and wiping her hands on her pants.

The man was tall, but shorter than Sam, and had the wiry

build of someone who worked hard for a living. Dressed in jeans and dusty dark leather chaps, his boots had definitely seen better days. A sweat-stained chambray shirt, ripped off at the shoulders, completed the ensemble. He grinned, his teeth flashing in his shoe leather face, and tossed aside his cigarette.

He took a step toward her.

She took a step back. There was something about the man that told her he could not be trusted. Of course, judging by her past experience, what did she know?

"Hank Riley," he said, extending his hand. "I work here on the Rocking A. I don't remember seeing you around. I know I'd remember you."

She stared at his hand for a beat, then wiped her hands on her pants and shrugged. "My hands are dirty. You don't want to shake, trust me."

"Need some help?" Again he stepped toward her and again she stepped back, the tiny hairs on her neck rising.

"She's got help, Riley," Sam's voice boomed from behind her as he strode toward the garden. "Get back to work."

"I was just introducing myself to your *lady friend.*" Riley's posture stiffened.

It may have been her imagination, but she could have sworn Sam's shoulders grew as he squared off with the ranch hand.

The testosterone level in the air definitely rose.

"She's more than my lady friend. Much more. Stay away from her."

"Sure thing, boss." He tipped his hat at Madison and ambled toward the barn.

Sam grasped her shoulders and swung her around to look in her eyes. "Are you okay? Did he do anything?"

She wrenched away. "You mean before or after he had his wicked way with me under the cabbage leaves?" Who was Sam to act all territorial?

"Damn it, Maddie, I'm not kidding. I don't trust Riley. Didn't like him when Bud hired him, but since my opinion wasn't asked for, I didn't want to go against Bud's decision. But if he touched you or—"

"Relax, Sam, I'm fine. And don't call me Maddie." She toed off the steamy boots and wiggled her toes in the little patch of grass by the back door. "I can take care of myself."

His hand on her arm stopped her from opening the back door. "You don't have to. Not while you're here. Let me help," he urged in a quiet voice.

"You already are, Sam. You're paying me to take care of the house. All I need, right now, is money to repair my car."

"So you can go back to Detroit?"

"Of course. I'm going back to Detroit! There's nothing for me here, except maybe a jail sentence." She pushed open the door and stepped into the kitchen, her stomach already growling at the thought of eating Sam's grandmother's stew.

"I meant to tell you," he said, placing his hat on the rack by the door, "While I was getting your car towed, I made a couple of calls. Hired a lawyer. Just in case you need one," he hurried to assure her.

She hung her head. "I don't even want to contemplate that possibility."

"People are going to want answers, Maddie. And since you're the only one around who had anything to do with the project, they'll most likely want them from you." He held up his hands when she looked up. "I'm just sayin'."

He put his arms around her and pulled her close. "How about I pump and heat some water so we can share a bath after supper?"

Madison watched Sam move around the kitchen, reheating their dinner. She was in way over her head. A cowboy. Hadn't she learned anything from her mother's mistakes? Sam was unlike anyone she'd ever dealt with and it was imperative she not make any wrong moves that could cause a possible future setback. Or worse, a broken heart.

Even though she didn't believe in love at first sight, there was something about the cowboy moving effortlessly around the kitchen that inspired more than lust.

After they ate, she would take a bath. Alone.

10

Water sloshed over the end of the tub with each thrust of Sam's hips. Knees locked around his waist, Madison gasped for air while watching his greedy mouth on her breast.

No doubt about it, the cowboy's body was a lethal weapon. And he certainly knew how to use it to its full potential.

Pleasure shimmered through her, radiating outward. She'd experienced more orgasms with Sam than in her entire previously non-existent sex life. What she'd been missing was mind boggling.

Sam chose that moment to lick his way up her chest to her mouth. "Stay with me, darlin'," he urged in a throaty whisper.

She forced a laugh. "I have to stay with you, I don't have anywhere else to go." Settling more securely astride him, she said, "And don't call me darlin'."

"I wasn't talking about where you slept." His hand snaked between them to find and massage her engorged nub.

Her third climax of the night roared through her. Back arched, she sucked in gulps of air and tried to not drown in sensation. Immediately boneless, she slumped against his shoulder and waited for her heart rate to recover from warp speed.

"That's what I meant," he said against her ear. "Now you're with me."

Instead of protesting his macho declaration, she snuggled closer. Speech required too much effort.

Sam's chuckle echoed in her ear. "C'mon, sweetheart, let's get you dried off and tucked into bed."

She allowed him to lift her from the tub and dry her off with considerable more diligence than required. Had her last orgasm not robbed her of brain cells as well as the ability to move on her own, she would have protested.

In a sensual lethargy, she allowed him to dress her in another of his T-shirts. Even his heated kisses as he did so, on her breasts, stomach and between her legs, could not rally much more than a contented sigh. She really shouldn't allow him to manhandle her.

Summoning her strength, she raised her head from his shoulder after they were in bed. "Don't call me sweetheart," was all she could manage to whisper.

"Rise and shine, lazy bones!" Sam's cheerful voice boomed as he swatted her behind. "We're burning daylight!"

Madison rolled over and threw her arm over her eyes to block the relentless sunshine streaming in the window. "Go away."

"Now, Maddie, don't be like that. Up! We've got things to do, people to see."

The bed dipped with the weight of her suitcase when he tossed it to barely miss her feet. Obviously he did not intend to go away.

She yawned and stretched, ignoring the way Sam's gaze followed her movements. "What things and what people?"

"First off, I'm taking you to breakfast, then we're going shopping. I looked through your stuff before you woke up.

Good Lord Almighty, woman, don't you own any casual clothes?"

Blinking, she let the remark about going through her possessions slide when she realized he was right. When was the last time, other than sleeping, that she had not worn a suit? She had no idea. Somehow, during her association with Alan, she'd lost the real Madison St. Claire. Assuming she'd ever truly existed. "No, I guess I don't."

"Well." He rubbed his hands together and tugged her from the warm softness of the mattress. "Today is your lucky day. Not only are you going to eat a breakfast to put meat on your bones, you're going to get a whole new wardrobe, one suitable for life on a ranch."

"Sam, I appreciate it, really I do, but I can't afford to buy new clothes."

"Maddie, I've seen your work clothes. Somehow I don't see you wearing them to weed the vegetable garden or feed the chickens."

She straightened. "Chickens? You didn't say anything about chickens."

He raised his hand as he walked out of the room. "Fifteen minutes, Maddie. Be ready to go in fifteen minutes," he repeated as he closed the door.

"Don't call me Maddie!" she shouted, only to hear his bark of laughter. In reality, she didn't really mind it, but it was a reminder she needed to keep her guard up.

The strand of pearls with matching studs in her ears gave her just the right touch, she thought, examining her reflection in the cheval mirror at the foot of the old bed. The off-white raw silk suit with matching camisole enhanced her coloring and was the most conservative of her wardrobe. A frown creased her face. Chalk up another mistake of her normally sane judgment.

Alan had insisted all the flashy, short, tight clothes were a business asset. She should have trusted her instincts and not been so eager to please.

She glanced at her bare left hand. If only she hadn't let him talk her into leaving her engagement ring at home, she could have sold it and at least paid her motel bill and passage back to Detroit.

Setting thoughts of her ex-fiancé from her mind, she stepped into the matching raw silk covered pumps and walked out to meet Sam.

He had shaved, donned a shirt and combed his hair, but looked uncomfortable when he stood as she stepped into the room. She bit back a smile at his old fashioned courtesy.

His eyes swept over her, doing funny things to her heart rate.

He cleared his throat. "You're not gonna wear that, are you?"

Stopping in her tracks, she gaped at him. Obviously she could do nothing right anymore. "Why wouldn't I?"

Madison's fists were on her hips, stretching the silky thing she had on underneath her suit coat until he could see plumb through it to the dark nipples underneath. The woman wasn't wearing a bra.

He forked his fingers through his hair and huffed out a breath. "Well, for one thing, it's kind of dressed up for the place we're going."

She took a deep breath, her nipples straining against the thin fabric. "We've already established I need more casual clothes."

"Don't look at me like that. I'm not the enemy." He drew her stiff form into his arms. "I think you look real pretty. Hell, I guess I'm jealous."

"Jealous?"

He nodded, then leaned his forehead to touch hers. "I don't want other men looking at you."

"I seriously doubt that will be a problem."

"You're not wearing a bra, Maddie," he said, easing the jacket from her shoulders. "I can see plumb through this." He tweaked her nipples, enjoying her little gasp of surprise. "I love your nipples, darlin', and I'm territorial. I don't want anyone else looking at them." He bent to run his tongue over them through the thin fabric. "Or tasting them." He bent his knees and drew one puckered tip into his mouth, thoroughly wetting the blouse.

"Sam," she said in a shaky voice, "Now my blouse is all wet."

He grinned. "Just your blouse?" He ran his hand up under her skirt to the telltale moisture between her legs and tsked. "We need to get you out of these wet things." She nodded, a slightly dazed look on her face, as he led her back into the bedroom. "Then we'll find something else for you to wear."

He closed the door and savored the sight of her standing by the bed, her nipples wet and erect through the silky top. He popped the top button on his fly and glanced at the clock. They had plenty of time to release a little pressure and still get to the café before it stopped serving breakfast.

"Let's play my game today, Maddie," he said, advancing on her.

Her eyes widened, instantly alert. "Game?"

He nodded and placed her hands on the cannonball post of the bed. "You might call it a fantasy of mine. Hold on and don't move unless I tell you to."

The sound of her skirt zipper echoed in the quiet when he slid the tab down. After shoving the skirt to her feet, he dropped his jeans and boxers and rubbed his aching shaft against the satiny soft cheeks exposed for his pleasure by a pink satin thong.

She moaned while he massaged her, tweaking her nipples through the wet blouse.

"Raise your arms, sweetheart," he whispered in her ear.

After he'd dragged her blouse up and off, he paused and admired for a moment the picture she made, standing in her high heels and thong, before dragging the scrap of silk down and off.

He nudged her legs apart, bending her at the waist, her hands still clutching the bedpost. Rubbing his tip up and down in her moisture, he smiled when she purred and did a little shimmy, arching her sweet little ass higher, urging him.

He reached around to cup her breasts, holding on while he plunged into her welcoming wet heat.

Withdrawing until she whimpered, he paused, then plunged into her again. And again.

She made some wild little movements, but he was so lost in the moment, in his passion, he couldn't have stopped if his life had depended on it.

Her back stiffened, the muscles in her butt pulling on him, dragging him deeper, while deep within his cock was milked by a velvet clamping.

Madison's second choice wasn't much better for his concentration. Bright red, the high-necked leather jacket fit her lush figure like a second skin and the matching skirt barely covered the necessities. And Maddie had great necessities.

He gripped the truck steering wheel and concentrated on the road.

"Sam, did you see the guy by the gate?" Her voice broke through his thoughts, forcing him to switch mental gears.

"Hmm?"

"Didn't you see him? The guy on the horse?" She shivered and added, "He looked so, I don't know, sinister."

"Probably Riley. The guy you met." He turned on his signal and turned onto the highway. "I know what you mean. The guy gives me the creeps. He never seems to do much but hang around and watch everyone else work. I'm gonna have to talk to Bud about him."

After a few minutes, he said, "We're heading into Greenleaf. It's bigger than Slippery Rock and they have a nice café there. There's a western outlet just on the outskirts. We can pick up some work clothes for you." He grinned and winked. "Along with some sensible shoes."

Maddie needed work clothes for more than just work. If she kept wearing the sexy things she had in her suitcase, the only thing he'd accomplish would be wearing out his pecker.

And she would be leaving as soon as she could. He'd do well to remember that and not get attached.

"Here we are." Sam pulled into a parking place in front of a plate glass window that read CORA'S CAFÉ—BEST FOOD AND SLOWEST SERVICE IN TEXAS.

Two hours later, they exited the café.

"I may throw up," she said, as Sam helped her into the truck.

"You'd never know it, the way you were shoveling in the chicken fried steak back there."

"How kind of you to point that out. I was hungry. I only had a few bites of stew last night. Unlike someone else I know, who ate enough to feed a third world country."

"Let's get you some decent clothes." He pulled out of the space and headed south on the town square.

"Sam? I want you to know I appreciate all you've done for me and I'm keeping track of every cent. When I get this mess straightened out, I'll pay you back."

"Did I ask you to? I don't need your money, Maddie." He wasn't cut out to be a spy. The guilt was eating him alive. Now she was grateful. He didn't want her gratitude.

"It wouldn't be my money, you macho jerk, it would be a repayment of the money you loaned me." She crossed her arms and said, "And don't call me Maddie."

"I didn't loan you a damn dime—"

"The hell you didn't!" She took a deep breath, chanting low.

"Now what are you doing?" He was itching for a fight, for some reason. Maybe it was guilt. But Madison St. Claire could push his buttons faster than any other human being, just sitting there in her little red number, humming.

"Finding my center of tranquility, not that it's any of your business." Her head fell back on the seat. "Oh, great! See that? Now I've lost it."

"Darlin', I have no idea what you're talking about—"

"And stop calling me darlin'!"

He signaled and made a sharp left into a deserted strip center off the highway.

"What are you doing?" she asked, scooting toward the door.

He flipped the childproof lock to prevent her escape, then grabbed her, dragging her across the seat until they were hip to hip.

"Helping you find your tranquility."

11

Madison rested her head against Sam's shoulder while she tried to regulate her breathing.

Sam's sweat-slicked chest heaved against her own, skin against skin.

She noted her suit coat draped over the steering wheel. Her skirt was wadded around her hips. Sam absently petted her left buttock. While she'd love to stay in exactly her present position, she had to keep in mind her plan. A plan that did not include humping the gorgeous cowboy beneath her at any and every opportunity.

Funny. She'd always thought her mother weak willed in her infatuation with cowboys. Maybe it was the way they moved their hips.

She watched Sam stretch to remove her panties from the rearview mirror.

"You might need these." He grinned, twirling the red silk around his index finger. "Although I think they looked mighty fine right where they were." He winked. "I'll just take them off you again."

She climbed from his lap with as much dignity as possible, given the situation. "Don't try it." Grabbing the panties, she fell back onto the passenger seat and squirmed to get them on and up her legs. Her broken fingernail snagged on the panties. "Could we stop somewhere to get some nail polish remover on our way home? I need to soak this junk off."

Sam chuckled and started the car. "Sure. But right now, let's go get you some real clothes."

The way things were going, maybe she should look for a chastity belt. Slumped against the window, she watched several telephone poles go by before a thought struck her.

"Do you have a phone?"

"On me? Or at the cabin?" Sam glanced in his mirror, then turned into the parking lot of a huge western wear outlet.

"At the cabin. I know there's not WiFi, but I have my laptop and if I could hook up to a phone line, I could possibly go on-line to see if I could find out what Alan was up to and maybe even figure out a way to get out of this mess." When he kept his eyes on the lot, searching for a parking place, she added, "I may even be able to find a way to get everyone's money back."

He pulled into a space, got out and walked to her door. As he helped her down, he said, "Sorry, no phone in the cabin."

Sam clamped his jaw shut when Madison's shoulders slumped in defeat. He'd told the truth. There was no phone line in the cabin. But not only was there a phone at the big house, it even had WiFi. The cell phone in his pocket felt like a hot branding iron. Swallowing his guilt, he led her into the store.

Sam's grandmother cooked as much food as Sam did. Madison scanned the laden table in the cabin's kitchen and tried to think optimistic thoughts. Had these people never heard of cholesterol?

"Welcome home!" Liza placed a smacking kiss on Sam's, then Madison's, cheek. "Bud told me you'd been out most of the day getting Maddie some work clothes, so I thought I'd bring supper over. Set yourself down and dig in." She walked to the back door. "I just need to get the Jell-o mold I brought."

She reappeared, carrying a metal mold Madison swore she'd seen in banquet halls. How did they eat all that and still move around?

The cholesterol count for the meal alone had to be off the charts. Madison scooped some green beans onto her plate. A small piece of chicken, hopefully a breast, small dollop of mashed potatoes and a slice of tomato completed her meal.

"Is there a problem with your food?" Sam's grandmother looked anxious.

"Ah, no. There's just so much . . . I don't know where to start."

"Well, honey, let me help you." Liza ladled huge mountains of food onto Madison's plate, then covered everything in a thick layer of aromatic gravy.

Madison salivated. The chicken fried steak they'd had in town had to be one of the most deliciously satisfying meals she'd ever eaten. She speared a green bean and popped it in her mouth. Covered in gravy, it tasted heavenly. She closed her eyes, trying not to groan.

She listened to Sam and his grandmother talk about various people who apparently lived nearby, their voices blending to a blur while she enjoyed her meal.

"Apple or peach pie, Maddie?" Liza stood over her, a pie in each hand.

Madison blinked down at her empty plate. Had she eaten all that? "Um . . ."

"I have plenty. I'll just give you a sample of both."

Madison made a silent vow to work exercise into her to-do list. After all, it would be rude to refuse a piece of homemade pie.

* * *

With a shriek that only hinted at the horror she felt, Madison jumped to her feet from where she'd been weeding the last row in the garden.

Sam was at her side before she filled her lungs for her next scream.

"What is it?" He held her securely in place when she'd love nothing more than to climb up into the safety of his arms.

"A snake! It slithered over my hand." She pointed a shaky finger in the general direction of the slimy monster and shuddered. "There! Under that last plant!"

Sam kneeled to peer under the gently swaying green carrot tops. He held up a wiggling, fat, brown string. "Maddie, darlin', it's not a snake. It's just a little ole earth worm. See?"

"Keep it away from me! Yuck!" Another shudder ran through her.

Sam tossed the worm back into the garden and wiped his hands on his jeans. "I think you've had enough excitement for one morning." He leaned down to kiss the tip of her nose. "Why don't you go on in and wash up? Sandwich fixings are in the cooler. Bread's in the breadbox. Gram brought a new loaf this morning while you were chasing the barn cats. Make me two sandwiches. I'll be in directly."

"I'll make the sandwiches next," she grumbled, watching where she stepped. "I promised your grandmother I'd feed the chickens."

Sam stopped. "Have you ever done it before?"

Madison shrugged. "No, but how hard can it be? Don't look at me like that! It's not as complicated as the pump. She showed me where the feed was. You just fill the bucket and throw the seeds until they're gone. Really, Sam, it's not rocket science."

"But—"

"Don't worry, I won't mess it up." She wiped her hands on her thighs and headed toward the shed to get the feed. Her colleagues in Detroit would laugh themselves silly if they saw her feeding chickens and weeding.

The thought gave her pause.

They'd probably laughed their asses off anyway, when she was left holding the bag for Alan. They probably thought she had it coming for sleeping with the boss's son.

Screams had Sam running back toward the house. Amid the terrified shrieks, chickens squawked.

He rounded the corner of the chicken house and skidded to a halt.

Madison stood in the middle of a bunch of crazed chickens, one arm held protectively over her face, her hand holding the tin pail aloft while the other hand flung great handfuls of feed in the general direction of the irate fowl.

"Help!" she yelled over the strident chicken screams. "Sam! Help me!"

He strode into the pen, shoving the insistent chickens aside with the toe of his boot until he reached Madison. He pulled the pail handle from her death grip and threw the feed into the far corner of the pen. The chickens immediately followed their dinner.

"Sam!" She jumped into his arms, wrapping her legs around his hips, her arms all but cutting off his air supply. "Thank you! They were attacking me. I could've died," she said against his neck.

He did his best not to laugh. He really did. But it was a losing battle.

She leaned back in his arms to glare at him. "It's not funny, Sam Austin! They had their beady little red eyes trained on me. And they bite! It was horrible! Who'd have thought chickens could be so vicious?"

He let her slide to stand before him. "Maddie, they're chickens. Chickens don't bite, they peck. Besides, you're bigger than they are."

"They ganged up on me," she protested.

"Naw, they just saw the feed bucket and wanted to eat."

"Well, no one told me they had no manners." She sniffed and frowned at the chickens, who were now frantically pecking the dirt. "Can't you train them or something?"

"I don't know." Sam scratched his head, pretending to consider the possibility. "Never heard of a chicken trainer." He bit back another laugh when she swatted his arm and stalked back toward the house.

"Maddie! Did you collect the eggs?" It was the wrong time of day, but she wouldn't know that. He couldn't resist baiting her.

She stopped until he caught up with her. "How do you do that?"

He whispered the delicate details in her ear.

She paled.

"You're kidding, right?"

"I heard some interestin' talk about your Maddie while I was in town." Bud swung his saddle onto the fence and reached for the reins while gentling the old horse.

Sam stepped up into his stirrup and shot a hard look at the new hand who looked for all the world like he was eavesdropping.

Riley turned and walked away.

Sam settled into his saddle and looked down at his foreman. "That so? What did you hear?"

"You know danged well what I heard. But I trust your judgment. I know you wouldn't have brought her here if there was any question of her honesty. What I don't understand is how you two hooked up in such a short time." Bud removed his hat and scratched his head. "Last time I mentioned the Hunsinger

Properties deal and the slick city woman involved, you acted as though you had no idea who I was talking about."

"So?" He wasn't ready to explain his relationship with Maddie to anyone. If what they had could even be called a relationship.

"I know you're a grown man and entitled to run your own life." One worn boot scuffed the dirt. "Aw, hell, I told Liza I wasn't any good at this type of thing." His blue eyes pierced Sam. "Neither of us understand how you two, I mean, with her reputation and all, how you two ever got together."

Sam nodded. "Nothin' to tell, Bud. Now, if you don't mind, I need to check on those pasture fences before it gets dark." There it was, the guilt over deceiving not only Maddie but everyone he knew. If only he could have done it any other way . . .

"Son?"

Sam stopped and looked back at the man who'd been like a second father to him.

"We just don't want to see you get hurt," Bud said.

Sam adjusted his hat. "I know what I'm doing." It was just the explaining of it that was tying him in knots. He knew what he was doing, all right, just not why. All he knew was he felt a burning desire to keep Madison St. Claire by his side and would do anything, fight anyone, to make sure it happened.

What had started out as a simple plan to keep her around until she could be found guilty or innocent had rapidly evolved into something much more complicated. He'd think about the whys and wherefores later.

Right now, he had a fence to tend. Physical labor always helped him think better.

He closed the pasture gate and let King take off at a full gallop. Maybe the wind in his face would help him sort things out.

Hank Riley leaned negligently against the big oak not far

from the gate. The sullen expression on his harsh features shifted, stretching the jagged scar that ran from temple to chin along his left cheek, when Sam reined King to a stop before him.

"Riley." Sam inclined his head. The ranch hand responded by touching the brim of his hat. "Not enough work to keep you busy?"

Riley pushed away from the tree. He sauntered to a stop, hands on hips, next to Sam's horse.

"Plenty to do, boss man, plenty to do. I was just takin' a break."

Madison chose that moment to step onto the front porch, the clack of the screen door drawing their attention. Unaware of her audience, she vigorously shook the throw rugs, the action jiggling her breasts beneath the T-shirt knotted at her midriff.

Any other time, Sam would have paused to appreciate the view. But the look on Riley's face made Sam's blood boil in a different way. Never prone to violence, he wanted to pound Riley until his eyes swelled shut.

"Get back to work, Riley," he growled, tugging his hat low. "Second thought, saddle up and come with me. We've got fences to mend."

He watched Riley leisurely saddle his horse. The idea of working alongside the surly man was not appealing, but the idea of Riley being anywhere near Maddie was less appealing.

"Sam-uel!" A singsong female voice called from the front of the cabin. "Sam?"

Madison's head clunked on the top of the oven. The voice was obviously in the house. Didn't people knock in Texas?

"Sam? Are you decent? I just—oh!" A curvy redhead stopped short at the kitchen door. Her far set, heavily made-up green eyes widened, then narrowed as they raked Madison from her hastily done ponytail to her bare feet. "Who are *you?*"

Madison dropped the sponge and scraper she'd been using to clean the oven into the bucket, wiped her hands on a dishtowel and stood. Although she stretched to her full height, the other woman still towered an easy six inches above her. Achingly aware of the contrast she made with her jean short coveralls and tank top compared to the tall, model-thin woman before her, dressed to the nines in pale green silk, she schooled her features into her coolest business woman persona.

"I could ask you the same question." She extended her hand. "I'm Madison."

The redhead's eyes became slits, color high in her cheeks.

Madison let her hand drop to her side.

The other woman's shoulders slumped. "It's true, then," she said, sinking to a kitchen chair. "When I heard Samuel was shacked up with a woman out here, I was so sure everyone was mistaken." Tears shimmered in her eyes.

Madison almost felt sorry for her. Almost. Uneasiness tugged at her. Did the whole town know where she was? Worse, did everyone think she and Sam were *shacking up?* Of course, they technically were, but she'd hoped no one would know.

"Why wasn't I told?" the tearful woman asked.

"Excuse me. I don't understand. Why should you be?" Madison pulled out another chair and sat. "Who are you?"

"Rachel Turnbull." The look she shot Madison was pure venom. "Samuel's intended."

Sam took the steps in one long stride. He was sure it was Rachel Turnbull's 4Runner he'd seen tearing out of the drive. Rachel could twist and turn even the most innocent things into damning evidence. Damage control was a given.

"Maddie?" He ran to the kitchen and looked out the back

door. The freshly weeded and watered vegetable garden was empty. Even the kittens seemed to be missing.

From within the cabin, a drawer slammed. Following the sound, he stopped at the bedroom door.

Madison threw handfuls of lingerie into her smaller suitcase. Beside it, on the bed, her garment bag was already stuffed with her suits.

"What are you doing?" He strode across the room, fighting down panic, and grabbed her arm.

She jerked away. Suspiciously bright blue eyes flashed at him. "What does it look like I'm doing? I'm getting the hell out of town—like I tried to do before you ran me down."

"You can't leave! Not now, anyway." Not like this. "Things are still up in the air in town. You need to lay low until they calm down. Then there are your car repairs. I thought we agreed—"

"Yeah, well, I thought we agreed too—I thought we had an understanding—until I met you fiancé!"

"My what?" He gripped her shoulders, forcing her to face him. "Maddie, darlin', I swear to you, I've never been engaged. I'm telling you the truth."

Her shoulders sagged and she sat on the edge of the bed. "But she seemed so convincing."

"Red hair? Tall?"

She nodded.

He sat next to her, his arm holding her securely to his side. "I'm sure she did. Rachel Turnbull is a pain in the ass. That girl's had a thing for me since we were kids. But I swear, it was always one-sided."

"You don't have to convince me, Sam. It's not like we're involved or anything." She shrugged. "I guess I just sort of freaked."

"Maddie, you're closer to me than any woman has been in a very long time." He tilted her chin, making her look at him.

"Don't you know me at all? I'd never do the things I've done with you if there was anyone else in the picture."

She looked at him, then slowly nodded. "Yes, I guess I do know that. You're not the type."

"Damn straight." He grinned and slipped the straps of her coveralls down her shoulders. He traced her breasts through the tank top and said in a husky voice, "Now let's get to the good part."

"The good part?"

"Yeah," he said, stripping the coveralls down her legs and laying her back on the bed, "the part where we kiss and make up . . . and stuff."

12

Sam laid the journal he'd been reading on the end table and scowled at Madison's curvaceous backside. Encased in heart-trippingly brief running shorts, it afforded him a spectacular view as she bent from the waist.

"Maddie, I told you, people in the country don't jog."

"I know." She regarded him upside down from between her legs while she petted and kissed one of the barn cats she'd adopted. "But I'm people in the country and I *do* jog."

"And cats don't belong in the house," he grumbled.

She smiled and returned to an upright position, then began twisting, torturing him with glimpses of her cleavage. He'd always considered himself a leg man, but Maddie's endowments had him drooling like his dad's bluetick hound.

"Besides," she continued, oblivious to his torture. "I bet between you and your grandmother shoving food at me, I've taken in more calories in the last week than in a whole month at home."

"Any luck getting your laptop up and running? Maybe you should try again." Maybe the change in topics would distract her from her intended jog. He'd had no success with her computer, but that didn't mean she would fail as well. He needed access to her files if he hoped to help prove her innocence. At least fiddling with the computer would keep her home with him.

"No, I have a feeling it's ruined. Must've taken in too much water."

"Stay here, Maddie. With me." He could get that skimpy top off her in a flash, given the opportunity.

"I can't, and don't call me Maddie." Her smile told him she didn't really mind his nickname anymore. "I need this exercise. At the rate I'm going, I won't be able to fit back into my clothes when I go back to work."

Sam sat up straighter. "Go back to work? You're planning to work for that SOB when you go back?" He clucked and shook his head. "And here I thought you were smart."

"I am smart." She placed both hands over her head, gripped her elbows and stretched slowly from side to side. The brief thing covering her breasts practically groaned with the strain. So did Sam. "And because I'm smart, I plan to march right into my old office and find out exactly what Alan the Rat is up to. Then I'll nail his balls to the wall."

Sam winced at the mental picture for a second, glad he wasn't Alan the Rat. He snapped out of it when she kissed the head of the white fur-ball, grabbed her cell and headed toward the door. "Wait! Why are you taking your cell? Does it work now?"

"No." She glanced down at her hand where her thumb caressed the keypad. "Maybe I'm hoping it will magically connect." She tossed it on the side table and headed for the door.

"Maddie," he called. All he'd need was for her to go past the bunkhouse and give the hands an eye full. "There are wild animals out there." Not counting his employees. "And snakes! Big, poison ones." One look at her face told him that was his trump card.

"Snakes?" she asked in a tiny voice.

Damn. He hadn't meant to scare her. "Well, they're actually pretty far from the housing area," he said, backpedaling. "And they're more scared of you than you are of them—"

"Don't count on it!" She looked hesitant. "Why don't you come with me?"

"I get enough exercise."

"Well, if I don't do something fast, I'll end up looking more like one of your cows." She turned and ran through the door and down the drive before he could get his boots back on and follow.

Dread tiptoed up his spine. Vague feelings of impending danger washed over him. Feelings like that were rarely wrong.

He stood on the porch, trying to figure out which way she went.

"Trouble in paradise?" Hank Riley struck a match to light the thin cigar clamped between teeth that gleamed in the shadows.

His words prodded Sam like a hot poker.

"That's none of your concern, Riley. And what are you doing? You have no reason to be up here."

Hank chuckled, his deep voice sounding sinister. "Pretty thing like that, I'd think you could come up with all sorts of ways for her to work off extra energy." He sauntered away. "I know I sure as hell could."

"Stay away from her." Sam's words hissed from between clenched teeth.

The hand laughed and kept walking.

Sam stood on the porch, heart pounding, fists balled, before he took off after Riley.

"Hey!" He caught Riley's shoulder with his fist, spinning him away from the bunk house door. "I meant what I said!"

Tobacco-stained teeth flashed in the feeble porch light. "Seems to me, if you can't satisfy your woman, maybe she should find herself a real man."

Boots scraping against the wood heralded the appearance of several ranchhands.

Through a haze of anger, Sam slammed Riley against the rough siding. Several sets of hands tried to pull him back, but his frustration and anger gave him the strength of ten men.

His men scrambled to restrain him, the roar of blood in his ears making their voices distant. His face close to the other man, Sam growled, "Leave Maddie alone."

Shocked silence followed. The grip on his arms relaxed and Sam stepped back, his anger still simmering below the surface. It was not like him, but he couldn't think rationally when it came to Madison St. Claire.

Bud's face gradually came into focus. He released Sam's arm, his hand hovering close enough for Sam to feel its reassuring heat. Bud's voice sounded abnormally loud in the ensuing silence.

"What are you men looking at? Go on, get out of here! You too, Riley. Move it!" His heavy hand landed on Sam's shoulder. "I think you probably have better things to do, too."

Sam walked back to the house, giving himself time to cool off. He listened to the night sounds, straining to hear footfalls on gravel but heard only his own labored breathing and heartbeat, along with the crickets and distant sounds of livestock.

Unable to stand it another minute, he stomped to the barn and saddled his horse. King balked at the bridle, obviously not thrilled with the thought of leaving his comfortable stall. After what seemed like hours, they finally exited the barn.

How far could one small woman get on foot? He sent up a prayer that he'd been right about snakes being afraid.

13

Madison's heart pounded, only partially from exertion. Snakes. Sam said there were snakes. And wild animals. How wild and what kind? Her eyes scanned the darkness. Why had she insisted on going out in the dead of night? She would never have considered jogging at night in Michigan.

Face it, it's only because Sam said no.

Tiny hairs prickled on the back of her neck. Was she lost?

She turned and ran in the direction she thought was toward the house. Soon, she heard steps running close behind her. Several steps. What if it was a pack of something? Did they have coyotes or wild dogs in this part of Texas? It had to be something at least that big. And several of them.

Heart in her throat, she ducked behind a massive tree and hid, trying to quiet her breathing.

"Whoa, King, whoa." Sam patted the lathered neck and looked around. Where the hell could she be? He'd covered every reasonable direction. Maybe that was the problem. What was reasonable to him might not be to Madison.

Defeated, he turned the quarter horse toward home. They hadn't taken more than two steps when a woman's scream pierced the darkness and Sam's heart. Strangled with fear, he dug his heels into King's ribs and prayed.

Madison stared up at the malevolent cowboy who held her tightly against his chest, and screamed again. The first scream was because he'd startled her when she'd turned from her hiding place after the horseback rider had passed. The second one was from pure fear. She put her heart in it, feeling the tendons tighten with the effort all the way down to her feet, and prayed somehow Sam would hear her.

"Jesus, Mary and Joseph, lady, I think I'm deaf in one ear now." He placed a smoky smelling hand over her mouth, cupping it just enough to avoid her teeth. "Be quiet. I'm not gonna hurt you." His foul breath fanned her face moments before he nuzzled her neck, his stubble biting painfully into her tender flesh. Arms of steel banded her, restricting movement. "Relax, beauty, the beast is still at the castle. We have plenty of time to—oomph!"

Her knee connected with his upper thigh, scant inches from the intended target. His arm relaxed just enough for her to break free and scream again.

Ba-bump, ba-bump. Her attacker's words were drowned out by her frantic heartbeat. One callused hand dove beneath her sports bra as he ripped it from her body, fingernails dragging painfully across her nipple.

Fabric scraped the skin over her ribs when the sturdy garment gave way. Revulsion mingled with terror in her throat, right before the man began to levitate.

With a roar, Sam picked Hank Riley up bodily and threw him against the tree. Seeing the shredded fabric of Maddie's top in Hank's fist brought a fresh haze of anger.

Sam yanked the fallen man up by his collar and shook him

like the snake he was. Sam's fist connected to Riley's right eye with a satisfying echo. Still holding on to the jerk's shirt, Sam punched the bloodied cowboy again before throwing him to the ground.

"Get out!" Sam yelled. "When I get back to the bunkhouse, I want to find you gone. You can come back tomorrow morning and collect your pay from Bud, just stay out of my sight." He shoved the man with a well-placed boot on his behind. "Now go, before I decide you need another lesson on how to treat a lady."

Hank stood and spat a bloody stream, then wiped his mouth with the back of a dirty hand. "Seems to me, if you was half the ladies man you think you are, your little piece of city ass wouldn't be off gallivantin' around the countryside half nekked."

Sam growled and lunged. Madison's hand closed over his arm.

"Sam, please," her voice, quiet against his back, stopped his momentum. "Let him go."

"You lucked out, Riley." He leaned closer to the beaten man. "This time."

As soon a Sam released him, Riley ran and disappeared into the darkness.

Sam bent to retrieve her top, slapping it against his thigh to get some of the dirt out. He watched her, standing with her arms crossed protectively over her breasts, her eyes as big as a scared rabbit.

Hell, he wasn't cut out to handle this kind of emotion. He'd never felt true murderous rage before. Hadn't thought himself capable. Until tonight. Until he'd seen Maddie being pawed by that no account Hank Riley.

"You okay?" He walked toward her, keeping his eyes focused on her face, her wide horror-filled eyes. Any place but her bare chest.

Revulsion ran through him. He was no better than Riley, lusting after a terrified woman.

"Thank you," she whispered. "I don't know what I'd have done if you hadn't shown up."

He forced a laugh. "You'd have been fine. Heck, I was actually protecting Riley. He didn't know what he did, crossing you."

He removed his shirt and draped it around her shoulders. A shudder ran through her, moving the fragile bones beneath his palms. There it was again. That pity thing. Just when he thought he had a handle on his emotions where Madison St. Claire was concerned, something would happen to drag him right back.

"Let's go home and get you cleaned up." His hand guided her toward the waiting horse.

She stiffened. "He's a lot bigger up close." She gave a nervous laugh that ended in an unsuccessfully swallowed sob.

"Oh, Maddie." He folded her trembling body close. They gently swayed. "I'm so sorry you had to go through this, darlin'."

Teary eyes looked up at him. A trembling smile curved her lips. "No, I'm sorry, Sam. You were right. I had no business going out in the dark alone." Choked up, she licked her lips.

By light of the full moon, Sam followed the movement and swallowed a groan. She hadn't even told him not to call her darlin'.

14

Madison rolled to her side in the weak morning light and watched Sam sleep. Although they'd had plenty of sex, it was the first time he'd spent the night, all night, in bed with her.

She'd just been so needy after her run-in with that creepy ranch hand. And Sam had been so wonderful. Not only had he saved her, but afterward, he'd tenderly bathed her, then carried her to bed.

Although she'd practically begged him, they had not made love. At the time, she'd thought it sweet. Now she wondered if possibly the thrill of sex with her had worn off for him . . . while for her, the desire had only become stronger.

And now he lay sprawled beside her, in all his naked cowboy splendor. At least his top half was naked, not to mention splendid. She peeked beneath the sheet. Yes, naked. Totally naked. Totally splendid. She flopped back against the pillow and stared at the ceiling.

Now what? If it wasn't love, it was just sex. She'd never woken up with a naked man before. Was there some sort of protocol? The few times she and Alan had had sex, he'd gotten up and gone home shortly afterward. Or she had. But with Sam it was different.

Sleeping with Sam Austin was bad enough. But now she felt all warm and squishy when she looked at him. She couldn't help the sappy grin on her face.

Getting involved physically with Sam had not been one of her more carefully thought out moves. That was exactly the problem. She hadn't thought at all. Couldn't think, with him taking up all the space, just breathing.

So her current quandary was all his fault. She'd obviously inherited her mother's propensity for cowboys. She hadn't had half a chance from the beginning. Still, if he weren't such a big, sexy package of a man, maybe none of this would have happened. She, after all, couldn't be responsible for her actions when her brain was deprived of oxygen. And who could fight heredity? There was a very real possibility she was genetically predisposed to cowboys. That didn't necessarily mean she loved him.

Sam rolled toward her, one arm flopping possessively across her equally bare middle to gather her close. Warm lips pressed to her temple, morning stubble prickling her skin. "Mornin' darlin'." His lips hovered over hers. "Stop whatever you're thinking and kiss me."

She forced herself to pull away and sit up, clutching the covers around her. Kissing him in her current emotional state would lead to sex. Truthfully, kissing Sam in any state of mind, in her case anyway, led to sex.

Sam heaved a sigh and sat up, raking his hands through his hair. "Maddie, whatever is going through that mind of yours, just stop. I can see by the look on your face it isn't something I want to hear." He stood and stepped into his pants, pulling the denim up but not bothering to button the fly. "I'll go make coffee and see if Gram left us anything for breakfast. You're probably just hungry. You know how you get when your stomach is empty."

Sam shuffled into the kitchen. Today would be the day he told Maggie the truth. She'd been punished enough. What was the point in forcing her to continue using the outhouse and trying to read by oil lamps? He'd have the refrigerator reinstalled as soon as possible too. Dang, he should never have let it go on so long. How would he explain?

His cell vibrated against his hip. With a glance toward the bedroom, he pulled it out and squinted at the number as he stepped out on the back steps to answer.

"Hey, Matt. I'm fine. Do you have any news for me?" He listened for a while. "No, I never was able to get her computer on. Does it really matter? Okay, I'll be there in a little while."

How the hell was he going to slip away with Maddie's computer without her noticing?

Luck was with him. He'd just turned on the burner under the coffee pot when he noticed the laptop lying on the kitchen table where Maddie had been fooling with it the night before.

"Maddie," he called, "I have to go out for a little while. Coffee is about ready. I'll be back in time to have breakfast with you."

"Okay," she called back.

He'd tell her everything as soon as he got back, he vowed as he slid the laptop onto the seat of his truck, hopped in and started the engine.

After carefully making the bed, Madison took her time getting dressed in her last pair of clean jeans. Gram had offered to do their laundry, but she'd ask Sam to take her to a laundromat. There had to be one somewhere. Maybe even as close as the bunk house.

Thoughts of the bunk house reminded her of her altercation

with Hank Riley. She certainly hoped he was long gone by now.

After pouring a cup of coffee, she glanced at the table. Odd. She could have sworn she'd left her laptop there last night.

A look around the living room and bedroom failed to produce the missing computer.

Maybe Sam had taken it to see if it could be repaired. Smiling, she sank back in the kitchen chair, the little white kitten she'd named Snowball on her lap. Of course, that's probably what Sam did. What a great guy. No wonder she loved him.

Her heart lurched. Love. Did she love Sam? She certainly liked him and lusted for him . . . but love? Where was the panic, the queasy feeling in the pit of her stomach, that thought usually brought?

"Wow," she whispered. "Maybe I really am in love."

Maybe she'd surprise Sam and make breakfast. She had mastered the stove burners. She was a satisfactory cook. All she had to do was find the icebox where the food was stored.

"Let's make breakfast, Snowball." Humming, she set the cat on the back steps and looked at the three out buildings, trying to remember which one she'd seen Sam use. She'd check the storage shed first.

The old wooden door creaked open and Madison sent up a silent prayer there were no spiders or snakes before stepping inside.

What she saw made her gasp.

Marble tile shone beneath her bare feet. She gaped at the huge sparkling bathroom complete with an oversized whirlpool tub and separate shower stall.

Madison forced herself to breathe, to swallow around the lump in her throat. Her cheeks burned with humiliation. Tears blurred her vision.

Old hinges creaked. The door blew shut, but not before she saw a light switch. Feeling her way to the wall, she flipped the room into blazing brightness. She walked over and sat on the closed toilet seat. Tears she'd held at bay fought their way out in great wracking sobs.

A lie. Her whole life was nothing but a stinking lie. First Alan, now Sam. Sam didn't love her. How could he? He didn't even trust her enough to tell her the truth about the damn plumbing and electricity.

He'd allowed her to continue to gag during her trips to the outhouse and strain her eyes in the feeble light of the kerosene lamps. If he'd lied to her about those things, what else was he lying about?

She had to leave. Sam's spare keys to the farm vehicles were on the hook in the kitchen. He could retrieve whichever one she took at the airport. She would find a way to contact him with the money for her car and have it shipped. It was Saturday. Matt, the lawyer Sam hired, had said the case against her should be dropped by Monday.

She'd hoped to stay with Sam forever, she realized, but it didn't matter now. Nothing mattered.

15

Sam hummed as he let himself into the kitchen. Matt said the information locked in Maddie's laptop was the information needed to clear the remaining charges against her.

Hearing her rustling around in the bedroom, he picked up the pace. He had a burning desire to hold her and make love to her. But first, he needed to tell her the truth about everything.

"Maddie!"

She stood bent over her open suitcase. He looked at the other open suitcase, half filled with her business clothes, then at her red-rimmed eyes. "Maddie?" He reached out to her, but she backed away.

He dropped his hands.

She squared her shoulders and bit down on her lip. "I'm packing."

"Why?"

"Have you forgotten my career is in shambles?" She gave a watery laugh. "I may still be facing charges in Michigan."

"All the more reason to stay right here."

She shook her head. Her voice became a husky whisper. "I appreciate all you've done for me, Sam. But I can't stay where I'm not trusted. It's time to go home."

"Not trusted? I trust you. Damn it, you are home! This is your home, with me."

"No! No, it's not! If you really trusted me, you wouldn't have done the things you did like let me believe there was no electricity or, or indoor plumbing." Her eyes filled with tears, making him feel lower than he already did. "Sam, you know how awful the outhouse was and yet you still let me use it, day after day, gagging and hating every second of it. You *knew* it and you said nothing. Nothing!"

She grabbed a tissue from the dresser and wiped her nose. "If you trusted me, you'd never have put me through that."

"I can explain. I admit, I wanted to take you down a peg, at first. Then, things changed and I didn't know how to tell you. I was planning to tell you when I came home today."

"Gee, thanks." She threw a handful of lingerie into her suitcase. "When were you going to tell me you *own* the Rocking A? It doesn't matter. Despite everything, I appreciate all you've done. Thanks."

"Thanks? That's it? Thanks, Sam?" His voice rose with each step he took until he had her backed against the bed. "What about us?"

"Sam, you know as well as I do that there is no us." At his growl, she hurried on. "Oh, I know it was great while we were together. I guess we just got sort of caught up in it all. But, Sam, you said it yourself, I'm not your type."

"Maybe I changed my mind." He would not beg.

"We're from different worlds. I'm big city, career oriented." *Or at least I used to be.* "And you're, you're a . . ."

"Cowboy? Go ahead, say it. You made it clear, right from the start, what you thought about cowboys. About me."

"No! Never about you. Well, okay, maybe at first. But not now."

He jerked from her touch and stepped away.

"I just would like to know what in the hell is your problem with cowboys!"

She stiffened and backed him toward the door. "They're over-sexed, egotistical, shiftless, no good—need I go on? And my mother could never resist a damn one of them!" She nodded. "That's right. I watched an endless parade of them pass through her bedroom door whenever the rodeo was in town. Do you wonder, now, why I despise the very thought of them?" Tears streamed down her face. Her voice raw with emotion, she gripped his arm.

"But you're not like them. I realized that as soon as I met you." She clutched his arm. "I did! I just was too stubborn to admit it. But now it's time for me to leave. Please, Sam, just let me go."

"Are you going back to him?" The door to his heart slammed. Loving Maddie hurt too much.

"Who? Alan? Are you crazy? Why would I do that?"

"Because you're leaving me."

"Obviously you don't have a very high opinion of me, Sam, if you think I can hop from one man's bed into another."

"That's what you did when you left him."

His cold words stung. Why did he have to be so calm and hateful?

After she struggled with the zipper for a few moments he closed her suitcases for her.

"How were you planning to leave? Your car isn't ready." A muscle ticked in his jaw.

"I thought I'd borrow one of your trucks and you could pick it up at the airport." *Tell me to stay. Tell me you're sorry and you love me and you want me to stay.*

"I'll have Bud come round and pick you up. He can take you to the airport." He tipped his hat. "Good-bye, Madison St. Claire."

The door clicked shut behind him. Madison stood, eyes closed, tears silently coursing down her face. Every cell in her body screamed in agony. Had anyone ever died of a broken heart?

16

Sam growled his frustration and attempted to cinch his saddle again.

"Easy boy, it's just an innocent piece of leather." Bud's weathered hands reached past him to finish the job.

Sam jerked and stepped back, eyes narrowed.

"Why don't you go after her, son? It's been months. Seems to me, you're hurting as much today as when Maddie first left. Maybe she's having the same feelings."

"Don't count on it."

Sam swung up into his saddle and picked up the reins.

"Think about it," Bud urged.

Sam nodded and nudged King.

His personal life was a disaster. His work was suffering. So far, the others had picked up the slack, but he knew it couldn't go on forever. Maybe Bud had a point.

His loneliness was a gnawing thing, eating at him every hour of the day. And the nights were worse.

Even the kittens missed Maddie. Unable to stand staying in the cabin, he'd taken them all up to the main house with him, where they slept snuggled up around his body every night. All except Snowball. Maddie's favorite. Try as he might, the kitten was nowhere to be found.

He turned the horse toward home, no closer to a decision.

He slowed as he rode past the homestead. Of course, it was only his imagination, but the old house looked empty. Sad. Deserted.

Just like him.

Tying King to the post, he walked up on the porch. Memories of Maddie meeting him with kisses made his eyes burn. He toed off his boots and walked into the dimness.

Damn it! They should have had a lifetime of memories, not just a meager handful of days.

Slow steps took him to the bedroom. Their bedroom. His sock-clad foot touched something, just under the bed. He bent and retrieved a mud-encrusted torn piece of fabric. Her skirt. It was the sexy little skirt she'd had on the night they met.

He clutched it to his heart as he curled up on the bed.

Darkness greeted him when he opened his eyes. A rustling sound alerted him.

"Maddie?"

"No, you fool, it's me." Gram's soft tone belied the sting of her words. "You done wallering in your pity now?"

He sat up, shoving the skirt behind him, and wiped his eyes. "Yes, ma'am."

"Well, now what you gonna do?" She came closer and climbed up next to him, taking him in her scented arms, stroking his hair as she'd done so many years ago. "I'd offer to rock you, but you'd break my bony old legs."

He gave a watery chuckle. "I appreciate the offer, anyway, Gram."

Her hand stopped him from getting up. "Go to her, boy. You belong together. It's plain as day. What you two had was rare and precious. Pure magic." She drew a breath and whacked him lightly on the back. "You know she called, yet you never called her. Swallow your pride and go after what you want. Bring Maddie home."

"She made it clear, Detroit is her home." He glumly got to his feet. "Mine is here."

"Seems to me, home is anywhere your heart is. Right now, I'd say it's in Detroit. Go. We got along right fine before you came along. Believe it or not, we can probably muddle through without you. Besides, you've been about as much good as tits on a bull since Maddie left. Go to her, Sammy, go."

"You're right. Why couldn't I live with Maddie in Detroit? I have a degree that's just gathering dust. I bet I could find work there."

"Of course you can, jackass. Now get, before I get all mushy."

Sam kissed her weathered cheek and opened the front door.

Madison kicked off her heels and padded to crank up the air.

It had been four months, two weeks and three days since she'd left the Rocking A. In all that time, not one phone call or letter from Sam. Not counting the laptop he mailed to her. You'd think she could take a hint.

Knocking vibrated her condo door. She squinted through the peephole and sighed. Alan. Again.

Without unlatching the chain, she opened the door and said, "Go away, Alan." An expensive loafer-clad foot stopped her from closing the door.

"We have to talk. How can we work things out if you won't even talk to me? Why is your cell off?"

"Work things out! Ha! There is nothing to work out, professionally or personally. Maybe I turned my cell off because there's no one I care to talk to anymore."

"Now, Madison—"

"Don't you "now Madison" me! If you're serious about

wanting to make things right with me, pay me back all the money you stole from me. Then go to Slippery Rock, Texas, and tell them you were the ratfink who squeezed them dry! I hope they hang you!" She shoved the door, but his foot remained.

"I have a business proposition for you."

"I wouldn't do business with you again if you were literally the last person on earth."

"So are we off to the boonies to live happily ever after? Now that I'm out of a job, at least temporarily, I was thinking about subletting your condo—"

"In your dreams, Hunsinger!"

"I happen to know the association forbids pets." He looked down at Snowball as she sauntered to the door and stopped to give a big kitty stretch and yawn.

"Are you threatening me?"

"I know money is tight until you find another job—"

"It wouldn't be if you'd pay me what I'm owed."

"Yes, well, the court ordered Father to repay all the people in Texas who lost money, most of which he has already done, and you ASAP. In fact, the money is probably being transferred, even as we speak."

"Thanks."

He stopped her from closing the door.

"I do appreciate what a good sport you've been about all this. The old Madison would've been out for blood." His smile was wan. "You've really changed."

"Too bad I can't say the same about you." Madison closed the door.

She glanced at the phone. She would not call. Bad enough she'd called Gram, just to hear her voice before hanging up. The second time, the old woman had cussed her out before Madison spoke up. Gram had urged her to come "home."

There was really nothing to keep her in Michigan. Until living in Texas, she'd never noticed how dreary her building was or how rude the drivers. And it rained an awful lot. Now she was ready for Texas sunshine and blue skies.

But would Sam want her back?

Snowball climbed up on her lap and she buried her face in the downy soft fur. "I miss him so much," she whispered, choking back tears.

Sam stood outside the door marked St. Claire and vibrated with rage. He'd seen the slick looking guy in the suit leave. It hadn't taken Maddie long to find his replacement.

Well, that was just too damn bad.

Forget knocking.

One fierce kick of his size thirteen boots made history of the wimpy northern door.

Madison screamed and jumped up, clutching the kitten he'd searched high and low for.

"Sam? What are you doing here?"

He kicked the sagging door shut and stumbled into the apartment to scoop her into his trembling arms. All his vows to not beg flew out the window.

"Maddie, darlin', I've missed you so much. Please, don't send me away. I can't make it without you. I tried. Hell, I about drove everyone nuts." His strangled chuckle tore at the lining of his throat. "I don't care where we live. Anywhere is home, as long as I can share it with you. I can find a job here, if that's what you want—"

"What about the Rocking A?" She still looked stunned.

"Bud and the others can run it. All I care about is you." His voice softened. "I love you, Maddie. I want to spend the rest of my life with you."

These were all good things. Why was she still so afraid? Because Sam had let her walk out of his life without a backward glance, an inner voice told her. It had been four months, two weeks and six days of sheer hell. Without so much as a phone call.

He was thinner than she remembered, older somehow, sadder. The separation must have been hard on him too. He grinned at her, flashing killer dimples and white teeth.

And still gorgeous, she thought. What does he see in me?

"I missed you," he said. "I'm sorry I didn't tell you about the bathroom and electricity. Can you forgive me?"

"You must not have missed me too much." She wanted it to work as much as he seemed to, but the fact that he'd taken so long nagged at her. "You didn't call or try to contact me at all."

"You didn't call me either." He stepped closer; her back touched the wet bar. "I'm crazy about you, Maddie." His sweet breath warmed her ear. His finger brushed her nipple, which puckered traitorously through her silk shirt. "Crazy for you." He continued in that sexy drawl that always turned her blood to molasses. "Crazy for this. For us. Together."

Madison concentrated on moving the air in and out of her lungs.

"Maddie?"

She looked up into fathomless dark eyes, hot with desire.

"I think if you don't put me out of my misery and kiss me, and do it now, I'll surely die."

He pulled her against the hard chest she'd ached for, dreamed about, for the last four months, two weeks and six days.

Hot, firm lips covered hers. They swallowed her words. If she could have formed a coherent thought, they would have robbed her of that too.

The Samuel Austin bone-melting, guaranteed to satisfy, mind-liquefying kiss was still in definite working order. And it worked thoroughly, devastatingly well.

A whimper escaped Madison's throat as she leaned into Sam, drinking in the sweetness of his kiss, of his embrace, like the dying-of-thirst woman she was.

Her shaking hands skimmed the taut, hot skin of his back, stroked the silky smoothness of his hair, spanned the width of his shoulders. Then she gripped his shoulders and pushed him away.

"Wait a minute, Sam." She locked her elbows when he would have stepped forward. "Why did it take so long to come to this conclusion?"

"I had some things going on."

"For four months, two weeks and six days?"

Sam winced. "That long?"

Tears blurred her vision. The inside of her nose burned.

"Ah, darlin', don't cry."

"I was miserable without you," she managed to choke out.

"Oh, baby, I'm sorry. I knew it was wrong to let you walk out. I'd have come straight away. I wanted to, but . . . I guess it was that macho thing you're always going on about."

"Then what took so long?"

"Well, I said I realized it, didn't say I was willing to do anything. At first." He raked a hand through his hair. "But as soon as I admitted I couldn't go on without you I decided to come bring you back." He pulled her into his arms. "I love you, Maddie."

He wanted her back. He loved her. Air lodged in her throat. A great weight pressed on her chest. A heart attack. She was having a heart attack. This could not be happening.

"Oh, Sam." Fresh tears filled her eyes as she touched his beloved face. Through her tears, his grin flashed white.

"Oh, Maddie," he teased, then hugged her fiercely. "Let's go home."

BREEDING SEASON

VONNA HARPER

1

Loud bawls from the twenty-two heifers inside the corral she was repairing stopped Wendi Rennert in mid hammer blow. Looking up, she saw they were all staring at a spot behind her. Lifting the hammer over her head, she whirled.

A bull!

Lumbering toward the welcoming heifers!

She might have spent the last ten years away from the family ranch, but she knew enough not to stand between pure testosterone bent on doing what nature had intended and cows either in heat or nearing said condition. Backpedaling, because no way was she going to turn her back on a near ton of libido, she took note of the massive chest, broad, straight spine, solid legs, and long, swaying penis. Behind the penis, heavy, thick testicles rocked in time with the bull's movement.

"Go! Get the hell out of here! Where did you come from, damn you! These aren't your heifers, they aren't!"

If the mostly chestnut-colored beast heard her, he gave no indication. Instead, he remained zeroed in on the wooden fencing she'd been working on. Cursing herself for having taken down every railing between the anchoring four-by-fours in this one section, she bent and snagged a dirt clod.

"Damn you! You have no right." She chucked it at the bull's head.

The clod struck a short horn and disintegrated. The bull didn't slow. And as he plowed through the opening she'd inadvertently supplied for him, she noted the brand on his right flank. A lazy, looping W.

W? That was the Wagner family brand but her *neighbors* didn't keep bulls, at least they hadn't back when she'd called rural Harney County, Oregon home. They'd either had them brought in or relied on artificial insemination. Of course they might have changed their practices while she'd been gone.

The beast was now in the middle of the herd, bouncing up and down as he snorted and bellowed. Just like a man! Show him some females, particularly fertile females, and he loses what few brain cells he has. Fighting the urge to fling the hammer between his legs where hopefully it'd do the most damage, she reached for the cell phone in her front jeans pocket. She'd actually started to work her way through her address book before she remembered she hadn't had a need to call the Wagners, or more precisely, Mike Wagner, for years.

Her heifers had no dignity, no modesty. The maiden cows were nervously prancing about, but several who'd figured out what bulls were good for had already turned their backs to him, their tails lifted. So much for wondering whether they were in heat.

"Damn it! You *ladies* are suppose to go the AI route. I've already paid for the semen."

Throwing back his head, the bull bellowed. Then he hurtled his heavily muscled body forward, rising onto his hind legs at the same time. His front legs landed on the back of the nearest cow; a moment later his rear end rolled forward. From where she was, Wendi couldn't see the actual mating, but it was happening, damn it!

So what was she suppose to do? Trying to stop a couple of dumb stupid animals in midfuck made sense only if she had a death wish. From the looks of the interloper, he was in prime condition, not worn down from earlier servicing. So he'd come here hot and horny, had he? Unless someone hauled him out of her corral, he'd stay put for as long as he could stand—or more precisely, mount.

The two were still going at it, oblivious to their attentive audience, when she put one and one together. She had to go into the farmhouse where she'd grown up, look up the Wagner's phone number, and tell whomever answered that they'd better come collect Stud Studly.

She was halfway to the house when movement to the south caught her attention. Because the Wagner ranch was west of her family's, she didn't make a connection until she realized someone on horseback was coming her way. The horse was cantering, the rider barely moving in time with the easy gait. Lifting her arm to block the sun, she studied a sight that easily took her back in time. According to her parents, she'd started riding before she could walk. She'd loved everything about her childhood: the ties to the land, empty vistas, the scent of earth and cattle, sleepless nights spent helping with calving, harvesting hay, hot summers and icy winters.

But then she'd grown up and left.

She knew that figure. More than that, her body knew the feel of his hands on her, his lips on hers, his cock powering into her then virginal pussy.

Mike Wagner.

Even with the cattle bawling, she kept her gaze locked on the tall, rangy man astride the roan. She couldn't tell whether Mike had gotten any taller since she'd last seen him shortly after she'd graduated from high school, but his shoulders were definitely broader. He sat upright, his muscled arms close to his body and the reins easy in his fingers. No doubt about it, he'd added muscle to his legs as witness by the hard knots beneath his faded jeans. And now that he was pulling to a stop a few feet away, she noted the faintest of lines at the corners of his chocolate eyes, his skin so deeply tanned the color seemed permanent. Under his well-worn cowboy hat, midnight hair sought freedom. Remembering how she'd once run her forefinger over his narrow nose and broad chin, she wondered whether they would feel the same as they had back when she was discovering the difference between the sexes.

What about his cock? Would her cunt remember its contours?

"Wendi," Mike said. "Wendi—what's your last name now?"

His looking down at her made her feel small, something that didn't often happen to a woman who'd topped out at five-foot ten. "I took back my maiden name after my divorce," she said.

"Did you."

"Yeah. Ah, I didn't expect to see you. My folks told me that your folks said you'd moved to Tennessee." *And that you'd gotten married.*

"I had. But I'm back."

I'm. no mention of a wife.

She'd been so incredibly naïve the night they'd walked into the family barn and into each other's arms. She'd been shaking, so she'd been unable to unbutton his shirt, but he hadn't been in much better shape. For a girl who'd grown up watching everything from chickens to pigs procreate, she'd had no inkling that sex could be so scary, so unnerving, so everything.

"Wait," she blurted. "Now I understand why you're here. That's your bull."

"Fred."

"What?"

"I named him Fred, couldn't think of anything else at the moment. He got loose while we were unloading him and two other bulls over at the Thurston spread." Mike shook his head. "Looks like I got here a little late."

His comment and yet another bellow from the still-plowing Fred broke her free from the power lurking in Mike's eyes. "You could say that. Mike, we're not keeping most of those heifers, so even if I'd wanted him here, I'm not after high mating loads. I saw his testicles. He's huge. Get him out of here."

"Not while he's busy. One thing I've learned in the past couple of years, don't ever try to interrupt a bull when he's humping."

All right, she could buy that. Given Fred's single-mindedness, he'd probably stomp the living crap out of anyone who tried to get in the way of his favorite activity.

"Then as soon as he's done." She glanced at the Mike's saddle. "You didn't bring rope? I guess I could loan you—"

"Wait a minute." To her consternation, Mike looked amused. "You're not suggesting I try to lasso him and drag him away are you?"

"Of course I am." Staring up at him was making her neck ache. Not only that, she didn't exactly feel in control of the situation because no matter how much she tried, she couldn't forget what had taken place in her parents' barn when they were teenagers. "Last winter my dad ordered enough sperm to settle every heifer we have. They're hardly going to stand for AI with Fred around. Hell, excited as they are, I don't know how I can get them into the holding chutes."

"You?"

"Yes, me."

To both her relief and unease, Mike swung out of the saddle and landed not nearly far enough away. Of course his heeled boots in contrast to her tennis shoes contributed to the height difference; she didn't feel anywhere near almost six feet tall. He held out a calloused hand. After shifting her hammer to her left hand, she gripped his fingers. Something that reminded her of the first time she'd touched an electric fence zinged through her.

"It's been a long time," he said.

"Yes, it has." *Too long and not long enough.* "You're looking good."

"I'm looking how many years older than the last time we saw each other."

He was still holding her hand, and although she should have wiped sweat off her palm before offering it to him, she couldn't bring herself to break the contact. *Good* didn't come close to describing him. There was a settled quality to his features that hadn't been there before. Not only did he seem quieter and more at peace with his body, but what had once been teenage energy had rolled into adult confidence. Back when they were in high school, he'd talked about all the things he wanted to do with his life beyond this sparsely populated part of the state: career decisions to be made, and a restlessness that mirrored hers. If he was still restless, she didn't sense it. Quite the opposite, he seemed comfortable in his skin.

Skin that was making hers sing.

"It's really been that long, hasn't it," she muttered, finally drawing her hand free. A loud, rolling snort followed by a thud turned her attention toward the corral. Fred was back on all four legs now. He seemed to have forgotten his mate and was pawing the ground, head up and eyes bright as he scanned the herd. "What is he, tireless?"

"Pretty much. That's why I bought him. What brought you back here, Wendi?"

That's right, say my name in that deep and sexy voice of yours. "What? My folks—did you hear, my mother had a stroke. She's much better now, but it shook the whole family. They're trying to decide whether to keep the ranch or sell it."

"What about your brothers? Don't they want—"

"You know my brothers. Neither of them ever wanted to hang their futures on ranching. Jerry and his wife moved to California last year. Jeff's about to become a father for the third time; they were already in southern California, which is one of the reasons Jerry moved there."

"Where are your folks? I'd like to see them."

"On their way to Ontario. I don't expect them back for a couple of weeks."

Mike frowned, and maybe she was imagining it, but it seemed as if he was leaning toward her, curling himself around her as if protecting or sheltering her, something she didn't need—any more. "So you're here alone?"

"Except for the Marshal boys. They come after school every day and on weekends to help out."

"Hmm."

"Don't," she snapped, suddenly angry, or was that defensive? "If you're thinking my family has bailed on me, leaving me to—" She pointed at Fred, who was trying to get his nose under another heifer's tail. "—to take care of everything, I can handle it. I'm the one who insisted my folks go on the first real vacation of their lives."

He nodded and yet his eyes still seemed to be saying she was here alone. Either that or she wanted him to be thinking about that. She should be asking what he'd been doing with himself beyond what his parents had told hers and they'd passed on, why he was back in Harney County and whether he was married or single. Instead, she studied the heifer Fred had obviously set his sights on.

What was it like to be on the receiving end of so much attention? To have the only stud for miles around chasing after her would be a heady experience all right. True, there was a little matter of where else he'd already deposited his sperm today, but the heifer didn't seem to care, as witness by the way she was tossing her head and repeatedly shoving her rear end in Fred's direction.

Heat lived between the two animals, plain and simple. Uncomplicated lust. Granted, it would be one way lust if the heifer wasn't in heat, but animal instinct was all about mating when the time was ripe.

Mating.

Sex.

Fucking.

2

"What are you doing?" she demanded of Mike when he picked up the hammer and scooped a handful of nails from the bucket on the ground.

"Fixing the fence." He hoisted a two-by-four into place. "You don't want your cattle running all over the county."

"But you're closing your bull in. Look, this isn't his harem."

"Why not?" Bracing an end of the board against a post, he started nailing. "Grab that other end, will you? Keep it level."

Despite her urge to warn him not to order her around, she complied, and in a matter of minutes the previous opening no longer existed. Dropping the hammer, he walked over to where he'd ground tied his horse and started patting the mare's neck. "Fred's going to be here awhile."

Reluctantly dragging her gaze off the man whose body had been made for physical labor, she studied the action on the other side of the fence. Fred was at it again, snorting and wheezing as he powered his penis into heifer number two. A ranching childhood had taught her certain fundamentals, not that this particular one was any great mystery. "Great libido on him. I take it that's why you bought him. He's a producer."

"And he reminds me of myself."

That stopped her. "I'm not sure how I should respond."

"You don't have to." With one hand in his mare's mane, he turned his attention fully on her. "I'll say it. I was so horny at eighteen that it's a wonder I was able to accomplish anything."

"I know the feeling," she blurted. Then, shocked by her admission, she clamped her hand over her mouth.

His head tilted a little to the side, he drew her hand away. Still holding it, he shook his head. "We need to talk about *it*, don't we? After all, it looks as if we've both come back. We're going to be seeing each other."

I want that. It scares me how much I do. "We certainly will be for as long as Fred insists on laying claim to my cows. Ah, what you said about having been horny back then, I was so hung up on what was going on inside my mind and body that I didn't give any thought to what it was like for you."

"Really? I couldn't keep my hands off you. That was pretty self-explanatory, wasn't it?"

"I'm sure it would have been if I was thinking straight, if I'd known more about the opposite sex."

"One of life's great mysteries And all that time I thought you were the one who knew what was going on."

"Not me. Hardly." As he'd done after they'd shaken hands, he was still holding on to her fingers. And she was still responding.

"In other words, we were both out of control."

They could be talking about a million other things, catching up on what they'd been doing since they last saw each other, her learning whether there was a woman in Mike's life, maybe spelling out why she was divorced. Instead, they'd jumped into the middle of what had taken place between them during the end of his senior year.

"Yes," she belatedly said. "I guess we were out of control. Hormones and all that."

"Immaturity."

Too close to telling him she didn't feel a minute older than she had when he'd taken her virginity, she clenched her teeth. "It's funny. Living as close to each other as we did and going to the same school, you'd think we'd have been sick and tired of each other."

Smiling a little, he held her hand up where he could study it. She'd stopped wearing her wedding ring over a year ago and no pale line remained to remind her of it; maybe that's what he was looking at. "I think," he said, "we each took a look at the other kids and decided the pickings were pretty slim. We picked each other by default."

"Point taken. There were what, four boys in your high school graduating class?"

"And a total of twenty girls between the freshmen and senior years."

"Pretty pathetic. Where in the list of those twenty girls did I rank?"

"Pretty high from the get go as I recall, especially once you started developing curves."

If she wanted to play it safe, she'd counter with a joke to the effect that she'd taken off after him because not only was he a lofty senior to her junior status but he also had wheels, specifically, a pickup that ran, albeit with most of its paint gone and a cracked windshield. But she was suddenly nearly as scared as she'd been the first time she'd let him touch her breasts.

His body was speaking to hers again.

And with Fred and her heifer doing their thing a short distance away, how could she think of anything except sex?

Not that she'd jump Mike's bones, of course.

"It's funny how it happened, isn't it," she mused. "Our getting roped into showing some younger kids how to square dance and . . ." Thinking back to the first time she'd touched Mike closed her off from the present. Her body remembered his hand on her back and then twirling in tight circles under his arm while he lightly held on to her fingers, getting dizzy and briefly resting against his chest. Even as she'd laughed off her awkwardness, she'd longed to remain pressed against him. Instead of pushing her away, he'd wrapped his arms around her while apologizing for seeing how many times she could spin. She'd looked up at him and he'd looked down at her. And his hardening cock had pushed at her belly.

She'd felt as if she'd grabbed hold of a lightning rod in the middle of a storm.

"I got a hard-on smack in the middle of that dance demonstration," he said. "Hell, it was practically a way of life in those days. I was so embarrassed."

"I didn't know what to do," she admitted, although truth be told, even as she'd backed away from him, thoughts of cupping her hands around his erection had muddled her thinking. "Then I got worried that the little ones would see."

"Is that why you leaned into me again?"

"Yes." *Part of the reason anyway.*

"I thought you were teasing me."

For some reason the comment made her think about her hand, and she pulled it free. "I didn't know how to play those games. I still don't. One thing about being a ranch kid, not much time for hanging out."

"Do you ever wish it had been different?"

"No, not at all. I loved living here, cow pies and all. What about you?"

She'd posed her comment in an attempt to switch off at least a little of the electricity humming between them, but maybe he didn't get her attempt to lighten the mood. Either that or he had no intention of dodging a potentially dangerous moment. "You were always the kid next door," he said thoughtfully, "or

I should say the kid living in the ranch a mile down the road. Then one day I looked at you and you'd grown breasts and had hips."

And you had a man's cock. "I take that as a compliment."

"Do." Shaking his head, he planted his hands on her shoulders. "I was about to say you're a beautiful woman, but that sounds as if I don't care about anything but physical looks."

"The physical is important."

"Yes, but it isn't everything."

He was looking down at her again, his intensity making her feel as if he'd stripped off her clothes. Suddenly she wanted to be naked before him, stretched out on her back with her legs spread and her arms reaching for him. Fred and the heifer were both bawling now with the rest of the herd occasionally chiming in. Her parents were out of the country and the teenage boys who helped out wouldn't be here for hours. Mike had come alone.

They were adults, consenting adults.

"What?" he said, the deep tone breaking into her thoughts. "You're looking—I don't know what to call it, preoccupied."

No matter that it was the most insane thing she'd done since she couldn't remember when, she wrapped her arms around his waist. When she slid closer, her legs went between his. "I'd heard you'd gotten married."

"I did, but I'm not anymore."

Like me. "What about a girlfriend, fiancé?"

"I don't play that game, Wendi. I'm either attached or I'm not."

And he was unattached, just like her.

Two eligible people with a three-hundred acre ranch to themselves and cattle mating a few feet away. She hadn't trembled around a man for a long time, but she was shaking now. Shaking and incredibly alive, energy running through her nerve endings and her pussy heating and nipples growing hard. Belatedly she remembered that she hadn't bothered with a bra. *What are we going to do*, she wanted to ask him. *Where is this headed?*

"Are you going to tell me to leave?" he asked.

"Do you want me to?"

"No—although maybe I should be saying yes. It's been a long time, so long."

Since he'd last had sex or since he'd last seen her? "Yes, it has," she said. "I, ah, do you want to go sit down somewhere relatively cooler? Talk?"

The way his mouth twitched made her wish she could take the last word back. No, I'm not interested in talking, his expression said.

Well, neither was she!

Insane and impulsive and immature as it was, she longed to climb all over him, to erase the years and for them to become teens again. Teens caught in the middle of the terrible and wonderful need that had spread her naked legs back when she'd barely known what she was doing.

"What are you thinking?" he asked.

She still had her arms around his waist, and his hands continued to rest on her shoulders. "That—that I haven't forgotten."

"What?"

Say it. Get it out in the open. "What having sex with you was like."

By his expression, she guessed he hadn't expected her to be so honest. "You didn't think I'd say that?" she asked.

"No, I didn't."

"What about you? Have you forgotten?"

Pulling her against him, he folded his arms around her. When he spoke, his breath heated the top of her head. "I thought I had. Life—life has taken us in different directions. We were so naïve back then, so stupid in a lot of ways."

"I was a virgin."

For a moment he did and said nothing. Then he pushed her back so he could look into her eyes. "I know. I didn't when we went into your folks' barn. Hell, I wasn't thinking about anything except . . ."

"Getting into my jeans?"

"Something like that. Plus praying I wouldn't mess it up because the whole sex thing was pretty new to me too. There'd just been one—let's just say a *mature* woman gave me my initial lesson."

When he glanced to his right, she knew he was looking at the barn where she'd had sex for the first time—with him. She smelled hay and grain, sweat and sex's unique scent. Felt his cock pushing through her hymen. Remembered digging her nails into his shoulder blades because the penetration had hurt. Heard his muttered surprise and apology followed by a quick and hard thrust that left her feeling as if she'd been skewered. Confusion because she hadn't known how long it would be before he'd finish whatever it was he was going to do while inside her.

"Why didn't you tell me it was going to be your first time?" he asked.

At seventeen she would have lowered her head so he couldn't see how embarrassed she was, but not only did the question no longer throw her for a loop, but she also wanted to be honest to this man from her past.

This man who'd become part of her present, at least for today.

"I'm not sure." Somehow she'd pulled his shirt out of his waistband and her fingers now rested on bare skin. "Part of it— you were about to graduate and go off into the world. I found that intimidating. You were free, ready to start this great adventure called adulthood while I still had a year of study and tests ahead of me. You were mature while I—"

He laughed. "You thought I was mature? I was scared to death I'd come before I got your jeans off."

Once again it occurred to her that they should be tackling safe subjects instead of jumping into the middle of *the fuck*. But the truth was, she didn't want to talk about anything else.

Or do anything else.

"You were?" she finally thought to ask. "The way you suggested that since my family had gone to the fairgrounds for that 4-H competition we should check out the bed in the barn—you seemed so confident. So in charge."

"So horny, more like it." He laughed again. The sound made her ask herself how long it had been since she'd heard a man's laughter or been in a man's arms.

And her body needed these moments.

"Is that why you didn't say no?" he asked. "Because I intimidated you?"

"No, not really," she reassured him as her fingertips recorded his heat. The flesh around his waist was soft but beneath she found the strength she craved. The life she needed. "I wasn't intimidated. Not really."

"What, then?"

Loaded question and yet one she had no intention of avoiding. "My hormones were raging just as much as yours. I couldn't think straight. Hell, I'm not sure I was thinking at all."

"And now we are?" Perhaps punctuating his question, he ran his hands down her arms and from there to the small of her back. He pressed the heel of a hand against her spine, forcing her to arch her pelvis toward him.

"Thinking?" she all but babbled. "You're asking if I know where this is heading?"

"Something like that."

A loud, harsh bellow shook the air. Taking the sound as proof that Fred's sperm was now inside yet another heifer, she shook her head. Then, because standing with her legs feeling like cooked spaghetti was taking all her strength, she leaned her head against Mike's chest. His cock, his hard and pressing cock, touched her through the layers of fabric. More than touched.

"That bed in the barn is still there," she said.

"Are you saying what I think you are? Because if you're not—"

"Don't ask questions, Mike, please."

3

His family, too, had incorporated a small sleeping area into their barn, and Mike understood that the bed in the end stall here served as a place for people to rest while keeping an eye on ill or laboring livestock. He'd spent his share of nights catnapping on the mattress at home while waiting for a calf or foal to be born. From the looks of the Rennert *bedroom*, it hadn't been used for awhile, but at least there were sheets and a blanket. He couldn't say whether there'd been any straw on the floor the night he'd buried his hot and aching cock into Wendi's equally hot and incredibly soft pussy but now some had drifted into the small space.

Pussy? At eighteen he might have used the word around his male classmates but he'd never so much as contemplate uttering it at home or around a girl. Times had changed. He'd changed.

Wendi might be only three or four inches shorter than him, but she carried no extra weight, which made her seem fragile. If she'd gained some padding since he'd last seen her, if her long, pale hair wasn't caught in a single braid that rained down her back, if her lashes weren't so thick and her blue eyes so filled with depth, maybe they wouldn't be back in here.

But she was and they were.

His cock throbbed. Hell, it felt as if it might explode if either of them touched it! Granted, he hadn't had sex in awhile, but it hadn't been this hard and insistent for years.

Maybe since the first time he'd dumped his load in her.

She'd been walking a little ahead of him, and if he'd been going by her steady if slow strides, he would have believed she wasn't the slightest bit off balance—if she hadn't blurted what she had, her eyes hot and glistening.

Her? he mentally corrected. Like he wasn't eager and unnerved and a kid all over again.

"Do you want to talk about your marriage?" he asked as they rested their arms on the railing that defined the sleeping area.

"No. Do you want to talk about yours?"

Amber had been and still was the most intelligent woman he'd ever known. Where he'd concentrated on finding ways to support himself that also fed his need to remain in touch with the earth, she'd been challenged by education for education's sake. She could think rings around him, but when he'd asked what she thought or felt or wanted or even loved, she'd been at a loss. Amber hated being out of her element, and eventually she'd come to hate him, in part because he kept her off balance and because they'd discovered a fundamental difference in their thinking.

"No," he said. "I don't want to talk about her." *Or anything.*

"I thought I saw you once," she said softly, her arms not tight around her middle. "I'd flown to New York for a business meeting—I was working for an electronics firm and my boss couldn't make the trip. During a break, I went for a walk. There were thousands of people hurrying along. All I could think about was how much I wanted to leave and how could anyone stand being shoved up against people all the time. I was waiting for a light to change—not everyone was—when I thought I spotted you waiting to come from the other direction. I could hardly wait to grab you in the middle of the crosswalk and ask if you wanted to run out of there with me."

"I've never been to New York."

"Once was enough for me."

"That's why you're back, then," he said, "because you don't like crowds?"

Her lips parted, softened. She still clutched her middle. "I'm still trying to figure out what brought me here, but you're right. I don't do crowds."

"Me either. I think growing up surrounded by space and quiet became something I need to feel complete. It just took several years and some unwise decisions to figure it out."

"I understand," she whispered. "Believe me, I do."

It occurred to him that they were talking to be talking. Maybe he should ask her to spell out what she expected and wanted from him, but hadn't she had sex with him the first time because she'd thought he was mature, in charge? He wasn't, but he did know one thing. He was turned on. Hungry. Wanting her.

Wondering if she still felt the same way, he slowly unbuttoned his shirt. Her eyes locked on his every move. When he was done, he reached for her blouse and pulled the hem free. She covered his hands with hers, not trying to stop him, just there, sending her warmth into him.

Meeting her gaze despite the effort it took, he tackled the bottom button, the backs of his fingers brushing her jeans as he worked. The next button brought him to soft, warm, bare flesh just above her waist. His throat threatened to close down; his mind roared. If she asked why he stopped with just those two buttons before running his finger pads over her ribs, he wasn't sure he could come up with an explanation. Maybe something about needing the touch of skin against skin.

Maybe desperately trying to teach himself patience.

Relinquishing her hold on his hands, she turned her attention to what lay under his shirt. Women had touched him there, of course, more than he could recall but not nearly as many as wanted to. He wasn't a boastful man, and he'd only briefly gone after sex for the sake of sex following his divorce, but he understood that he represented something that turned women on.

Cowboy. He was born and bred a cowboy. Women were drawn to that. Throwing in broad shoulders, a flat belly, narrow hips, and a wardrobe that consisted almost entirely of jeans pretty much completed the stereotypical picture. But much as he'd first been surprised by and then enjoyed the attention, he wasn't a poster child for a possibly dying lifestyle. He was who and what he was, and if a woman couldn't take the whole package, which included hearing the land sing, he wasn't interested.

Closing down his thoughts, he set about tackling the third button. For some reason it refused to immediately give up its hold, causing him to shake his head. She chuckled. "What?" he asked.

"Your look—like you're pissed because my blouse is putting up a fight."

"I don't care about your blouse. All that matters is that you're not telling me to stop. You aren't, are you?"

"No." Her eyes burned with a dark light that roared through him. "Maybe I should be. Hell, maybe I should be yelling that this is insanity."

"Are you going to?"

"No." She sighed and didn't quite close her mouth. "No, I'm not."

"All right." The two words took a great deal of effort. "I

needed to hear that because I want, hell, you know what I want. If there are any brakes today, they'll have to come from you."

"I understand," she said, her eyes darkening even more.

By putting his mind to it, he managed to free the rest of her buttons, but although the next step was obvious, he hesitated. She wasn't wearing a bra, which meant the moment he pulled the blouse away, he'd be seeing what women considered personal and private and were seldom far from a man's thoughts—this man anyway.

And the moment he exposed her, he might be lost.

Past hearing the word *stop* if she uttered it.

It was being in the barn where a virgin had trusted her body to him years ago, that and the sexual energy Fred and the heifers were giving off. And having been nearly celibate for the past few months. And other things he didn't comprehend.

Shaking off the question of what those incomprehensible things might be, he skimmed his fingers over her breasts without first letting them out of hiding. Her shiver and quick intake of breath might have shifted the control to him if he wasn't already doing all he could do to keep from throwing her onto the bed.

Damn but she'd gotten to him!

Light filtered into the barn, but at the moment her features were in shadow, either that or he'd lost the ability to send what his eyes were taking in to his brain.

Why now? Why did his body feel as if it consisted of a giant, demanding cock?

Trapped in a red haze, he yanked her blouse down to her elbows. Before she could shake off the garment, he spun her around and cinched his arm around her waist, holding her tight against him. The blouse now served as a crude restraint, forcing her arms at her sides. Holding her in place and past caring that his cock ground into her back, he ran his fingers over her breasts. With the first touch, she froze. With the second, she threw back her head and panted.

"Oh god, god," she muttered.

The barn was timeless and impersonal. Her parents had built it without consulting a blueprint or bothering with a building permit. Nearly square, it had been designed to accommodate eight spacious stalls as well as the open area in the middle. No animals were being housed in it at present. No one could see what was taking place inside the weathered walls.

Her breasts matched her body's lean and athletic frame, and as he trailed his nails over their contours, he wondered at nature's gift. They fit in his palm. More than that, they stole what remained civilized in him and turned him into a two-legged breeding bull. Her breasts might have been designed in part to give her pleasure, but he was more than gaining his own enjoyment from them. He could possess her via the command in his fingers, control her reactions, push her past restraint or hold her on the brink.

Or he could if his blood wasn't pounding in his temples.

Reality slipped away. In his mind he became a cowpoke just off the range after weeks of driving cattle. He'd gone into the local saloon and ordered a whiskey, which he'd inhaled while taking in the soiled doves who were giving him the eye. One thing about whores, even though he'd have to pay for their services, they were up for whatever he wanted. They might even teach him a few tricks. They'd call him handsome and say nothing about the stink from weeks on horseback. They were who they were, breasts and hips and available cunts.

Not thinking, he shifted his hold so his restraining arm pressed against Wendi's exposed breasts. The hand that had been exploring her breasts now went to her mons, grinding through denim. When she spread her legs, he leaped at the unspoken invitation. Having to reach around her prevented him from plundering as deep as he wanted to, that and the barrier her jeans provided, but he could stroke and press, rub and scratch.

"Hmm. Hmm." Throwing back her head again, she nevertheless managed to press her buttocks against him. "Oh shit, yes."

The seventeen-year-old Wendi had been scared and unsure of her body and probably even more afraid of what he intended to do to it. Although she'd been turned on, she'd also fought the sensations he'd had a hand in creating. In contrast, the woman she'd become accepted her body for what it was—sexual.

Desperate for the kiss of skin against skin again, he spun her around again, instantly grabbing for the jeans' fastening. She started to shake off her blouse. "No," he ordered. "Stay like that."

"But I can't use my arms."

"That's what I want."

Cocking her head to the side, she licked her lips. He had no doubt that lust swam deep in her eyes. Studying her reaction as best he could, he freed her waistband and then undid the zipper. Taking it slow despite his body's insistence on getting to the main act, he worked the denim down her hips, stopping with the fabric bunched over her knees. Her panties were satin and brief enough that her navel was exposed. The contrast between fragile cloth and tough-as-leather jeans fed the animal in him.

Grabbing her upper arms, he spun her once again, this time pulling her off balance so she had to anchor herself against his chest. Fabric prevented her from widening her stance more than a few inches, but it was enough to allow his hand entrance. With one arm back over her breasts and flattening them, he closed his eyes and skimmed his fingers over warm, moist skin that was softer than the finest fabric.

Her cunt lips were built along the same spare lines as the rest of her body, making it easy for him to reach what lay between them. His forefinger dipped into her core. Once there, he concentrated on increasing the invasion, slow but steady, take charge and yet gentle.

He struggled to ignore his screaming need.

She moaned and muttered something he didn't hear, ground the back of her head against his shoulder, rolled her hips one way and then the other. Even with the blouse restraint, she managed to rake her nails over the sides of his thighs. The deeper he plunged into her, the more insistent her clawing became.

"Shit, shit, shit," she chanted. "Can't take—I can't take—"

"Yes you can." Turning his head, he nipped the side of her neck. "You're going to take it. No getting loose. Mine now, mine."

4

Mine. Mine.

Whether Mike was serious or joking didn't matter to Wendi. For someone who'd recently declared she craved space around her, she loved being held tight against this man. Even more, she loved his hand between her legs and his finger in her pussy. Her breasts ached, not from the pressure caused by his arm but because they were swollen, stretching her skin. Her nipples prodded his forearm in near duplication of what his cock was doing to her backside.

Thinking to remind him of his condition, she pushed her buttocks back. Although his finger lost some of its hold in her, enough remained buried in her dripping hole to grip her attention. She couldn't use her arms. True, it wouldn't take much to free them, but she could pretend. Her legs, too, were restrained, leading to thoughts of how she was going to spread them once they were on the bed.

If he took her on the bed.

Mouth sagging open, she gave up trying to pull her world into focus. Sex with her husband had been polite and civilized, safe, and yet, she'd told herself, satisfying. He'd never gripped her the way Mike now gripped, had not once zeroed in on her core without first caressing and kissing elsewhere until her muscles loosened and she'd signaled her readiness.

In contrast, Mike had taken her much as Fred had done with her heifers.

And like the heifers, she gave as good as she got. She had to!

"Ah," she sighed as she straightened. Granted, doing so meant his cock no longer impatiently prodded her, but his fore-finger had already regained lost ground. Telling herself she'd done what she had so she wouldn't risk injuring his manhood, she slipped into a space ruled by nerves and veins. Wanting.

Her legs fighting their restraints, she rolled from side to side, careful not to move her hips any more than necessary. His fin-ger still controlled her, that single work-hardened digit stroking inner tissue that wept liquid heat. Just when she thought she'd come from his manipulation, he pulled out, wrenching a cry from her.

"Hush," he ordered. "No begging."

"I need—"

"I know." He touched his drenched finger to her lips. "Taste yourself. Tell me what you're thinking."

Opening her mouth, she sucked him in. She couldn't put a word to what her sex juice tasted like, but that wasn't what he'd asked her. Gathering what she could of her thoughts, she waited until he drew his finger away. "I'm in heat," she blurted. "Just like that, a touch from you and I'm in heat!"

"I know."

Before she could ask how he'd become so knowledgeable about her body, he set her upright and walked around her so they stood face to face. Although she felt slightly foolish with her clothes half off, the inner fire remained too high to be ignored.

"I love seeing you like this." His mouth in a straight line, he cupped the underside of her right breast. "Mine."

"I'm not," she countered because that was what modern women said. "I don't belong—"

"Right now you do. Just as you control me."

How lubricious that was, how absurd. After all, the only thing she'd accomplished had been to pull his shirt out of the waistband. Well, damn it, that could and should and would be changed!

Rolling her shoulders back, she clasped her hands behind her. The blouse slipped to her wrists, yet she drew out the moment of freedom. Mike was the town marshal, she some criminal he'd just arrested, maybe a horse thief. But instead of hauling her over to a tree for a necktie party, he'd thrown her into the one jail cell in town. He'd spend the rest of the day and the night watching while she paced and pleaded and promised.

Finally she'd make him an offer neither of them could refuse.

Sighing, she let the blouse drift to the hay littered floor. Then, although she lost her footing and came within a whisper of falling, she took a mincing step toward Mike and wrapped her arms around his neck. She felt like a fool with her legs tethered by her own clothing, and yet there was something incredibly erotic about not being able to get away.

From having her heated sex trapped between her legs.

"We were so circumspect the first time," she said because she didn't know how to deal with silence. If he looked down and she stood on her toes, they could kiss. Kiss. "I didn't know what to do about your clothes."

"That's why we fucked with my pants around my ankles?"

Having him crouched over her with his untanned ass sticking up in the air while he pumped into her hadn't been funny back when they were teenagers, but she could laugh now. Or maybe the truth was, she was too deep in need for anything else to penetrate. "I couldn't make myself take them off. What if I made a mess of it, what if you thought I was being too bold?"

"But you were bold."

She had been, actually. Not during foreplay when her nerves kept short-circuiting and she hadn't known what if anything to say and couldn't think where to put her hands. The pain when he first entered her had come between everything else she felt, but she'd ridden it out. When the last wave of discomfort receded, she'd tunneled every bit of her being into exploring the sensations coming from her pussy.

Hot. Hungry. Demanding.

With her fingers looped through his waistband to ensure her balance, she set about getting his shirt off his wide shoulders. Instead of helping, he stood looking at a spot behind her with what might or might not be an amused expression. Gathering the shirt up in her hand, she threw it as far as she could.

"I didn't know what to think," he said in a husky tone she didn't recognize.

"About what?"

"The way you acted that first time. I was trying to work up whatever wherewithal I'd need to withdraw so I wouldn't hurt you any more than I had when you started scratching and biting me."

"I don't remember that." *Or do I?*

"I carried the scratches for a week."

"Did you tell anyone how you got them?"

"I never told anyone what we did; did you?"

She shook her head. She'd wanted to. She'd wanted to shout out what she'd learned about that thing called sex, but the act had been between her and Mike. Their private moments.

This was another private moment, altered by the years that had passed and yet essentially the same.

Maybe too much the same.

It wasn't cold in the barn, but it was cooler than it had been outside. Still, Mike's body had retained the heat she'd sensed when she'd first gotten close to him. She caught no whiff of cologne or aftershave, nothing artificial. He'd been sweating today, no surprise if he'd been trying to wrestle a determined bull around, but her nostrils were well-accustomed to that scent. It spoke of physical labor and a man unafraid of diving into whatever needed to be done.

How many men had she worked and talked with in recent years who smelled as if they'd just stepped out of the shower—and passed through a men's fragrance department on their way to wherever they'd left their clothes? Suddenly all those aromas were foreign. Only his remained true to the way she'd spent her first eighteen years of life.

That's why she was so hungry. Because Mike was fundamental, elemental.

"Take off your jeans," she ordered.

The corners of his mouth lifted. "What about my boots?"

"You know what I'm saying! I need you naked."

"Then you should be the same."

Being handed responsibility for her own stripping was almost more than she could contemplate, almost more than she could put her fractured mind to. Besides, no way could she gracefully pull it off. Still, until she had, their bodies couldn't join.

By holding on to the railing that defined the sleeping area and taking small steps, she made her way to the mattress. Collapsing on it, she fell backward but then sat up so she could untie her shoes. To her consternation, Make was watching. "Don't laugh. Whatever you do, don't laugh."

"I'm not."

No, he wasn't, and because he'd turned so that more of the muted light reached his features, she easily read his expression. Intense and anticipating. Needing one thing in life.

Mike Wagner wanted to have sex with her again. Just as she needed to fuck him.

Removing her shoes, socks, jeans, and panties had never been this hard. Of course having his attention on her even as he complied with her order factored in, heavily. Fortunately, she'd completed the complex task by the time he stepped out of his shorts.

His cock was everything. The beginning and ending of her existence. Large, larger than she remembered. Harsh in its redness, taut and ready.

Her mouth dried, only to flood. A moment later her fingers tingled and her breasts were so hard they ached. She didn't trust herself to stand. Neither could she keep her hands from straying between her legs. Eyes still steady on him, she stroked herself. A moaning sigh escaped; even after it ended, she couldn't think how to close her mouth.

He seemed frozen in time, an unwrapped present, not yet hers to take and yet freely given. Because he'd managed to divest himself of his clothing while still standing, he towered over her. A quick snapshot of Fred bearing down on a heifer weighing half what the bull did added to the fantasy of Mike taking her. He'd stride over to where she sat on the side of the bed. Planting his hands on her shoulders, he'd shove her back. Then he'd force her legs apart and power himself into the opening he'd exposed. She'd start to reach for him only to lose strength. Only when he slid his hands under her buttocks would she remember where the core of her strength lurked so she could wrap her legs around him and seal his body to hers.

Missionary style. The same as that first night.

Once more her mouth dried, forcing her to swallow several times. A distant bellow drifted into her consciousness. "Fred," she said.

"Fred," he repeated.

"How does he—"

"I don't know."

No more conversation, nothing left to be said. A cowboy standing over her while her body both melted and grew strong. She'd wanted this! Not just raw fucking with a readily offered cock but this one, only this one. Those chocolate eyes, the too-long hair, calloused fingers and work-carved legs slightly bowed from years on horseback.

Leaning back, she let the mattress support her. But although she wanted nothing more than to open her sex to him, she was her conservative parents' daughter, so she only extended her arms. And waited.

"What?" she forced.

"I didn't bring protection."

For several seconds the words didn't penetrate, but then although she tried to fight them off, they did. "We didn't use anything the first time."

"I know." His fingers fisting, he shook his head. "I'd been so damn anxious wondering whether *it* was going to happen that I'd forgotten."

"And it never entered my mind."

"We dodged a bullet."

"Yes," she agree. "We did. But it's different now."

"How?"

Had he moved a muscle since bringing up protection? If he had, she didn't remember. "I just had my period. I'm not fertile."

"That's not the only—"

"I know. Mike, I swear, I don't sleep around." *Wanted to but didn't.*

His slow nod let her know he believed her. "I had myself tested a couple of months ago," he said. "For a few months right after my divorce I, well, I'm not proud of the way I acted. But I was clean."

"And since then?"

"The few times I used a rubber."

"Then." She swallowed. "We can."

5

As he stepped into the small space she'd always called the bedroom, Mike smiled faintly. "Do your folks still sleep out here sometimes?"

"I don't know. I'd imagine so. I—I there was so much to talk about and do so they could go on their trip. Does it bother you that they might have used—"

"No. Does it you?"

Maybe it should have, but she was too far gone to care about anything but wrapping her naked body around Mike's. Leaning forward, she touched her fingers to his hips. His expression unreadable, he studied what she was doing before closing his hands around her wrists and lifting her arms over her head. She willed herself to relax.

"It's a double bed," he said unnecessarily.

"At least it isn't a single."

Still holding her arms high, he stepped closer. As he did, she widened her stance so his legs were now between hers with her knees touching the outsides of his calves and his cock nearly at eye level because the box spring and mattress had been put directly on the ground.

Watching her, he drew her arms back until she had no choice but to fall onto the worn coverlet. Although he released her, she remained where she was. Barely able to see him, she contented herself with pressing her knees against him until he took a backward step. Not alarmed but not content either, she scooted around a little. After lifting her legs and placing them on the bed, he dropped to his knees, with his chest so close she had no choice but to run her fingers over it.

She'd intended the gesture to be gentle, reassuring maybe, an emotional reaching out, but there was too much life in him and too much hunger in her. Surging up, she tried to clamp her arms around his neck, but he again claimed her wrists, this time pressing her hands against her middle.

Leaning low so their faces were only inches apart, he studied her. One second after another pulsed past, the energy gathering in her core. "What?" she demanded. "What are you looking at?"

"You."

"Why?"

"I'm trying to reconcile past to present. What was it we both agreed right after I graduated, that we were going to leave this nothing place and see the world? We did and yet we're both back. Why?"

"You want to talk about this now?"

"No." He shook his head. "But afterward."

Afterward. Once more she tried to sit up, and although he continued to keep her hands at her waist, he dipped his head so their mouths met. They'd done considerable necking before that first time, much of it in the cab of his old pickup with the steering wheel and gear shifts in the way so she knew just how much to tilt her head so their noses wouldn't get in the way.

And she understood the vital balance between pressure and the slightest touch, just the right amount of contact.

Those were the fundamentals. What was impossible to direct or explain or control were the hot thrills colliding inside her.

When her neck protested, forcing her back down again, he came with her, blanketing her nude body with his, trapping their hands between them, sealing their lips together. She had no gentleness in her, no need for whispered exploration. She needed hardness, and more, heat, power, strength and energy.

By moving her head and opening her mouth, she snagged his lower lip between her teeth. Sucking on it made both of them shudder. He lowered even more weight onto her. And when she ignored his unspoken warning and continued to nibble, he wrenched one hand free only to run it between her legs, pressing upward.

"All right!" she gasped, relinquishing her hold. "I didn't—I wasn't going to hurt you."

"I know." His gaze so intense she felt she was being burned by it, he flicked her clit with his thumbnail.

"Not fair!" she blurted, squirming.

Instead of taking pity on her too-quick-to-respond sex, he stroked and stroked and stroked. "I'm not interested in fair," he said.

"So—I—see." Oh shit, shit.

"What's wrong, Wendi? Having trouble concentrating, are you?"

Concentrate? What was that? Her world consisted of his hand between her legs and his weight on her and his breath in her hair.

He kissed her again. And again. Quick and hard. Each time she struggled to match his energy, but his fingers were on the move and her legs refused to close. Only when he sat back up did she manage the wherewithal to pull her arms free. That done, she scratched his chest, leaving fine white lines.

"Damn you," he gasped.

"Me?" She rolled her hips from one side to the other. "What about you? You're the one who—"

Ah, yes! His middle finger went deep and strong into her, his palm now cupping her cunt lips.

"What were you going to say?" he taunted. "Lose your train of thought again?"

"Not fa—" she started to say only to have the words ooze out of her. Her eyes closed, and her arms fell to her sides. Breathing took every bit of strength she possessed as his finger made a slow circuit of her pussy. She reveled in the wet and warm gliding sensation, and although she didn't quite trust everything to him, she couldn't begin to contemplate anything beyond this moment and these hot shudders.

"You're wet. And soft. So soft."

He wanted her to say something? To think?

He kept at and after her, not teasing so much as taking her higher and higher. This was no simple making out, no juvenile necking, hardly foreplay even. It bothered her that she was unable to take him on the same journey, but regret came only fleetingly. She was readiness, wild wanting, burning lungs and melting cunt.

And then he was gone. Her body untouched.

Feeling the bottom of the mattress sag, she opened her eyes to find that he was climbing onto the foot of the bed. Desperate to accommodate him, she bent her knees. To her great disappointment, he didn't accept her unspoken invitation. Rolling her legs outward, she picked up where he'd left off while he positioned himself so his thighs and her feet touched. Was he watching her masturbate? Would he want her to bring herself to—

Something gripped her ankles and distracted her just enough

that her fingers stilled. Scooting closer, he lifted her legs into the air. When he released her ankles, her feet fell forward until they rested on his shoulders. His thighs were against her buttocks, flesh sealing to flesh.

"Mike."

"What?"

Releasing herself, she raked her slick hands through her hair. "I don't know."

"You're beautiful. Sexy, so sexy."

She'd tell him the same thing if she could put the words together but her right hand had found his thigh and was already stroking it. Just beneath the surface waited hard-hewn muscle.

And his cock rested on her mons.

Lifting her buttocks off the mattress brought him in alignment with her core, but the next move had to be his.

His.

Them. Fucking. Getting it on.

"You're ready?" he asked. "Tell me, damn it because I don't know if I can—"

"I'm ready! I need you. In me."

There. Him. The tip touching her opening and then sliding easily in. Closing her eyes again, she patted his thigh while he filled her. Her pussy was expanding, her tissues giving way to accommodate him, inner muscles clenching at him. Hearing herself begin to pant, she tried pulling on her hair to distract her from the liquid fire now flooding her veins and muscles, but the flood wouldn't stop or be ignored.

It came. Continued. Grew. Consumed.

"Oh god, oh god, oh god," she hissed.

"There!" He shoved, and she might have slid over the blanket if not for his hold on her calves.

She felt helpless, a vessel for his sperm, her arms nearly stripped of all strength. Sweat pooled on her throat and in her armpits. Slick heat sealed her buttocks to his thighs so that each time he plowed into her, she rode not just the thrust but the retreat as well. In an act that took no conscious decision on her part, she pressed her thighs together, increasing the friction between them. His grunts accelerated as did her panting breaths.

Vaguely aware that his fingers were pressing into her calves and shins, she alternated between raking one hand through her hair and scratching his thigh. No matter how many times she tried to warn herself not to exert too much pressure, the quickening deep inside her pussy made restraint impossible.

She'd reached that point. The place of no return. Memories of clinging to the back of a galloping horse fed her imagination. The wind was tearing at her, the scenery racing by as her horse's hooves pounded the ground. Its head was low, neck straining, ears flattened, mane whipping, muscled legs pumping.

Not just the horse. Her too. Body low against the laboring back, fingers gripping reins, legs clamping tight to sweating sides. Racing with the wind. Leaving gravity, letting go of sanity, springing free, becoming beyond human, beyond control!

"Yes, yes!" she screamed as something rolled and thundered deep inside. "Yes!" Clenching Mike inside her with every bit of strength she possessed, she hooked her hands behind his legs and pulled him even closer. "Yes! Oh god, yes!"

So quick. So hard.

Well, damn it, Mike chided himself, what did you expect? Go without sex for as long as you have and you're bound to have worked up a hell of a load.

But it was more than that.

Stretched limp as cut hay next to Wendi, he slid his fingers over her small, round breasts. Loss of control hadn't been an issue in years, and he'd believed that closing in on his thirties meant he'd stepped into that space called maturity, but fucking Wendi had made a lie of that thinking, hadn't it?

So much for seducing the lady with sweet nothings, whatever the hell those were. So much for impressing her with his control and staying power, his ability to slowly bring her to the point of no return. He'd jumped her bones, plain and simple. Boinked her. Speared.

"Do you want me to apologize?" he asked.

"For?"

"Coming like an eighteen year old."

"You did, didn't you," she said and rolled her head toward him. Strands of pale hair had come loose from her braid, and now stuck to her reddened cheeks. Her throat glistened and sweat rested between her breasts. Her eyes had a glazed look he suspected he'd find in his own.

"I'm sorry."

"No." She slapped his chest, or at least he guessed that that was what her intention had been. Unfortunately, or fortunately, there was no strength behind the gesture. "Don't apologize. I was—I wanted it as much as you did."

Hearing that broke through his letheragy, and although he still wanted to fall asleep, the need was less overwhelming than it had been a minute before. It struck him as funny that although he'd always prided himself on taking care of his livestock before tending to his own needs, he now felt as if he'd been ridden hard and put away wet. Knowing she'd understand, he told her.

"Remember," she said, "the rainstorms we'd get in early spring? How the sky would turn purple and the wind would rip through the grasses? The cattle and horses would spook. It—it kind of felt like that just now. Overpowering energy and need."

"Maybe because neither of us have had sex in awhile."

"Maybe."

Although she didn't sound convinced, he lacked the ability to ask why. Yes, he remembered those prairie storms when the electricity went out and the earth shook with the thunder, but he and the rest of his family had always been outside trying to keep the livestock from panicking. He'd never understood why rain and thunder and lightning short-circuited horses' and cows' brains when a storm made him feel rawly alive.

That's why he couldn't sleep. Because fucking Wendi Rennert had brought him back to life.

And now that he'd tasted that life, he craved even more.

6

A prickle of awareness slipped into Wendi's mind. Sensing the prickle signaled something serious, she tried to ignore it. Her body craved, demanded, really, to remain in this drifting place. Floating was warm and mindless, a space protected from not just the outside world but thought itself.

She and Mike hadn't had sex, they'd fucked. Hard and fast and intense. Rutting.

That's what she couldn't run from and was keeping her from falling asleep, wasn't it? Instead of moving past her teenage crush on the boy a full year older than herself, she was back where she'd been ten years ago. Maybe the only difference was that she was no longer naïve but was now a woman who understood her body's carnal needs and had learned how to incorporate them into a civilized existence. At least she had until she'd spotted Mike riding toward her.

She'd jumped into bed with him within minutes of that meeting.

And that was terrifying.

"What got you into the cattle breeding business?" she asked, belatedly trying to bridge the gap of the ten years they'd spent apart living separate lives. She was on her side on the too-narrow bed, her arm draped over Mike, who lay on his back. "Supplying bulls and sperm is so specialized."

"Yeah, it is. And I'm still learning something new all the time. Hopefully I won't keep making the same mistakes."

"Mike, you know ranching. I can't believe you'd screw up."

He smiled, the gesture bringing his features to life. His bone structure was more defined than it had been at eighteen. Mature. Adult. "Hard to fathom, isn't it. Seriously, it happens because the more sophisticated cattle raising becomes, the more vital it is to supply a quality product."

"That's what you do, then? You either provide frozen quality sperm or a variety of bulls for your customers to choose from?"

"Basically. Are you sure you want to talk about this?" His lids drooped.

You look so damn sexy that way. "It's what you do, part of what you've become. So yes, I'm interested."

"I'd rather talk about you."

Something soft and warm seeped into her. Thanks to their gymnastics of several minutes ago she'd been pretty much numb from the neck down when she'd posed her initial question, but his words, to say nothing of holding on to a naked man, were hard to ignore, not that she was trying. "I'll take that as a compliment, but I'm serious. How did you get into this specialty?" *And why did you come back here instead of running your business from wherever you were?*

"Evolution." He scooted onto his side—which gave her a few scant more inches of space—and placed his chest, belly, hips, and limp cock within easy reach. "I was managing a thoroughbred ranch, focusing on the breeding process, learning on the job."

"Horses? There's no money in hay burners."

"That's what our folks told us, isn't it, that cattle will always be money crops, while horses are expensive hobbies."

That had been true up to a point. Granted, ranch folk needed sturdy horses to help manage the cattle, but the majority of horse owners had them because they loved them. "Thorough-breds." She mulled over the word. "What do you know about race horses?"

"More than you do, now." He draped his arm over her hip and rested his hand on her buttocks in a move meant to help her maintain her balance. Unfortunately—and maybe deliberately on his part—the touch wasn't something she could ignore. Not that she wanted to. "After I'd gotten my degree—I'd majored in animal husbandry with a business minor—the corporation I'd been working for part time made me the offer I thought I wanted."

Thought? Hoping the opportunity to ask him what he meant would surface, she asked about the corporation.

"It's one that specializes in horses." His features darkened. "Horseflesh is a commodity to people like those who hired me. Racing is big money, competitive as hell and about as stable as gambling, a huge ego boost for those at the top of the heap."

"You didn't like your job?"

He didn't hurry his response, and despite the distraction of his close-as-hell body, she concentrated on his expression. "I liked what I did. My major responsibility was the management, welfare, health, and training of the horses. I also worked with foals, conditioning them and getting them used to being handled. These were the cream of the crop, no knock-kneed work nags like we grew up riding, but the kind of horseflesh that takes your breath away. Sleek and muscled, high strung with legs made for speed—you would have fallen in love with them same as I did."

Of course she would. Just thinking about thoroughbred fillies and colts discovering their world and what their bodies were capable of took her back to the few times she'd seen racing stock. Those animals were indeed different, athletes in the purest sense. Beautiful. Sometimes awe-inspiring. High maintenance.

"But they couldn't all be winners," she said. "That's what you're saying, isn't it?"

"Yeah. Those who didn't measure up were sold for whatever the corporation could get for them. But because they were naturally high strung, too many of their new owners didn't know how to handle them."

The conversation was deep and getting deeper, delving into places she didn't want to go in the aftermath of making love and yet necessary if she was going to get to know the man whose sperm was still in her. "How—how long did you work there?"

"Longer than I should have. More than a year after Amber and I separated."

"Amber?"

"My wife, ex-wife."

There it was, one of the details she needed to learn about him, maybe the most important one. "Did she work for the same corporation?"

"No. The corporation—they owned a hundred acre complex—had started branching out into other horse breeds that appeal to the moneyed set. Because Amber competed on the jumping circuit, she came out to see what they were doing. That's how we met."

"Oh."

"Jumping isn't full time for her; she'd never try to make a career out of it. She's an attorney. But she's competitive and believes that jumping competitions help her hone her skills in the courthouse. Also, she finds working with horses more satisfying than with people because horses listen."

A moment ago, she'd resented Amber's place in Mike's life,

but now she found herself liking the woman. Why, then, hadn't they been able to make a go of it? Much as she wanted to know, she didn't want Amber, or her ex, in the double bed with them today. Maybe tomorrow, if there was going to be a tomorrow for her and Mike.

"Okay," she drew out the word. "So you were working with horses. I don't understand how you wound up switching to bulls."

Mike rolled onto his back again, taking her with him so she now lay half on top of him. Instead of trying to keep her head up so she could study his expression, she rested her cheek on his chest and listened to his heartbeat. She hadn't done this for so long, had forgotten how intimate the embrace could be.

Intimate and intimidating. Frightening, even.

"I'd gotten more and more involved with the breeding process, from both the standpoint of stallions and mares," he said. "The people I worked for had always been wealthy. They didn't experience what our families accepted as part of life, the lack of security, good times and bad. I started thinking that I should be able to incorporate what I was learning about horse breeding into something that wouldn't be undermined by a recession."

"Like cattle?"

"Like cattle. There was some unused acreage they agreed to let me use. It wasn't enough for a lot of heifers, which in part pointed me toward bulls. I was able to parlay some connections into buying a couple of yearlings. Because most bulls mature between eighteen and twenty-four months, those two didn't have value for the better part of a year. I hit the jackpot the first time, a jackpot that gave me the nest egg I needed."

"What do you mean by jackpot?"

"The average mating load for a productive bull is thirty to forty cows over a three-month period. Both of my bulls settled nearly fifty cows apiece in a little over two months."

"Oh, wow! That's wonderful."

Instead of agreeing, he sighed. "I would have been more ex-cited if I wasn't just coming out of the other side of my divorce. That plus my dissatisfaction with the corporation's materialism was costing me too much sleep."

Her sense of vulnerability had faded while he was talking, but it now slammed back into her. She didn't want to risk see-ing any deeper into Mike's personal life than she already had. Not this afternoon, with the aftermath of sex still loosening her muscles. "So that's when you moved back to Oregon?" she asked, hoping the question was a neutral one.

"Yeah."

Was he aware that he was patting her buttocks and that his fingers were venturing closer and closer to her crack? Making her restless.

"Hauling those bulls across the country couldn't have been easy. The few bulls my folks had were more trouble than they were worth. Hard to force animals that size to do anything they don't want to," she said.

"Those are used to being transported—by then I had four bulls—so that wasn't a major factor in—hell, I don't know why this is so hard to say."

"What?" His self-searching tone grabbed her. "Mike, we've known each other our entire lives. I'm an old friend."

"Friend?" He pressed the heel of his hand into the small of her back.

"Yes, friend," she insisted. "Who did I run to the morning I found that pinto foal I'd helped deliver dead? You. Because I knew you'd understand how much I hurt. That's the kind of relation-ship we had." *Had.*

"I haven't forgotten that. Did you know, when I was hold-ing you and you were crying, you weren't the only one."

"I wasn't thinking about anything except how much I hurt."

"Of course you weren't. All right. I'd committed to work-ing for the corporation for five years but only made it for four.

BREEDING SEASON / 159

When I tendered my resignation, I decided to be honest. I told them it didn't set right with me that they saw their horses as merchandise. They told me I was wrong, that they loved their winners."

"Their winners." She would have said more except that Mike was now lightly massaging the spot he'd just pressed and she felt the contact all the way to her womb.

"Yeah. That's what I threw at them. To breed horses simply so they'd have the cream of the crop, to discard those that didn't live up to their standards—part of me wanted to stay and try to change the system."

"You're only one man." *Man.* "What could you have done?"

"That's what Amber said, that she picks her battles—she's a county prosecutor—instead of going after everyone who runs afoul of the law."

"She has a point."

"I know she does. But it bothered me that she wouldn't listen to me. Her philosophy is, if you can't change the system, accept it. She works with people but lacks a certain empathy. Brilliant but emotionally distant. She says, that way things don't get to her."

There it was, a clue into what had gone wrong between Mike and Amber. But in the middle of trying to decide what to say to get him to elaborate, she remembered she didn't want a serious conversation, or maybe any conversation.

"Maybe I should heed her advice," she said, again looking for a light tone. "That way I could tell the student loan people I'd decided I wasn't interested in repaying my debt."

"Hmm. What would you do with your money?"

Thank you for the ridiculous question, she silently told him. Yes, she assured herself. He wasn't interested in baring any more of his soul than he had. "Buy all those cast-off race horses and put them on a ten-thousand acre spread."

"You've got a hell of a student loan."

"It feels like it. I had a few grants and scholarships but college is so damn expensive."

"Tell me about it."

"Was it worth it for you? I mean, do you think you could have accomplished what you have without getting a degree?"

"Why do you ask?"

"Mike, I didn't know what I wanted to do when I started," she admitted. "In a large part I went because I figured that was the way to get out there and experience the world."

"Did you graduate?"

"No." Their bodies had been in contact for so long that her skin felt as if it had stuck to his, and yet she didn't want to move. In fact, she couldn't remember when she'd felt more content. And yet the potential for something beyond contentment hovered around the edges, a potential she wasn't sure she dared explore. "I made it into my junior year before . . ."

"Before what?"

Damn. Trapped by my past. "A man. I let him get between me and my education."

"Your husband?"

"Ex. Yes." There. Both their failed relationships laid on the line. Only, how to move beyond that before things got too serious? "I convinced myself that building a life with Seth was more important than going after that degree I still couldn't zero in on."

"Do you regret your decision? Maybe you can go back."

"I've thought about it." She lifted her head and looked at him. Then she lowered her head to his chest and once more picked up the rhythm of his breathing and heartbeat. "But I want to ranch. I know how to ranch."

"You're back for good, then?"

The barn was slightly stuffy, and she should be outside on this beautiful summer day so she could study the horizon and smell smells as old as her memory. "I hope so."

He didn't respond, and although he went back to massaging her back and buttocks, she wondered what her admission meant to him. Did he care? Oh yes, he'd surely like the idea of having a willing bed partner around; what man wouldn't? But maybe that's all he wanted or needed from her. Maybe, like her, divorce had made him gun shy.

That's what they would become? Fuck partners feeding off each other whenever the hormones started yelling?

Why not? It was safe. Unencumbered.

Outside, Fred let go with another hard bellow. She couldn't say whether that meant he'd speared yet another heifer or was letting *his* herd know who was in charge. "It's so simple for animals," she mused. "None of those emotional hang-ups we humans allow to complicate things."

He pushed himself into a sitting position. Startled by the unexpected move, she started to do the same, only to have him take hold of her shoulders and push her back down. He sat sideways with the leg closest to her tucked under him and the other hanging off the side of the bed. Staring at a point someplace behind her, he rested a hand in the space between her breasts. Much as she wanted him to claim her breasts, she loved the idea of him looming over her, perhaps planning his next move.

But if he was preparing to tell her that he was going to leave—

Why should that bother her? After all, hadn't she just spent the last few minutes telling herself she didn't want anything more than sex and he'd already given her that?

7

"Have you stayed in contact with Seth?" he asked.

"What?" Out of all the things he could have said, that was the last she expected, or wanted.

"You heard me," he pressed.

"Yeah, I did. What I don't understand is why you're asking."

Perhaps whatever he'd been staring at no longer interested him, because he speared her with a gaze that challenged her to ignore it. "Maybe I don't have a right. Hell, I'm not sure I want the answer." The hand between her breasts twitched. "Amber used to accuse me of hiding behind the strong, silent cowboy image, but, if I did, it was because I didn't want to argue, which was one of her strengths. Now I'm asking you the kinds of questions she sometimes threw at me."

"Mike?" Taking hold of his wrist, she moved his hand to her right breast, silently asking him to capture it. "I don't want to talk about her."

"You don't—all right, neither do I."

"Hopefully you understand why I backed away when you asked about Seth. Can't this just be about you and me?"

Watching her with an intensity she found disconcerting, he lightly ran his fingertips over her breast. The slow, sensuous circles forced her to grind her bottom into the mattress, and she couldn't think how to slow her breathing. "What is there between us?" he asked. "Other than jumping each other's bones."

Damn him for thinking he had the right to prod her for honesty! "Isn't that enough? Oh, and the little matter of how much reimbursement I'm going to ask for if all my cows wind up carrying Fred's offspring. Don't forget, my family has already paid through the nose for the sperm to get the job done. I doubt that the AI service will agree to a refund at this late date. After all, I'm sure the sperm has been harvested and frozen."

"It has. According to my record, that sperm comes from my bulls."

Her mouth dropped open. Even the unrelenting impact of his fingers wasn't enough to distract her. "Oh," she finally and less than brilliantly came up with. "Why didn't you say so before?"

"Maybe I wanted to wait until I had you at a disadvantage." With that, he lowered his head and ran his tongue over her nipple.

Shit, shit, shit! By digging her fingers into the blanket, she managed to keep her hands off him, but it was so damnably hard. Her vision blurred. Her nipple had been on alert before he started tonguing her; now it was turning into a throbbing mass of nerves. Even harder to control, moisture was pooling inside her, and she had no choice but to grind her thighs together.

"Stop it," she whimpered.

He lifted his head a few inches but remained so close that his warm, moist breath instantly coated her *beleaguered* breast. "You don't really mean that."

"I—do."

"Then prove it." He became a blur; a heartbeat later, he raked his teeth over her left breast. "Get off this bed. Get dressed and go back to mending fence."

Fence. What fence?

"You'd like that, wouldn't you?" she managed. "To know you've won—"

"This isn't about winning or losing, Wendi, and you know it." When he straightened, she couldn't decide whether to be grateful or give in to instinct and beg him to go back to what he'd been doing. Maybe, if his hand wasn't at this moment settling over her belly, she could have found her answer. Expecting him to press the heel of his hand against her as he'd done with the base of her spine, she clenched her teeth and started silently counting to distract herself. Instead, the touch remained light. He wasn't, she finally concluded, trying to possess her so much as communicate wordlessly. As for why he'd chosen a decidedly carnal communication—

"When I realized Fred was heading for your folks' place and took off after him, it was like going back in time. 'What if she's here,' I wondered. 'And if she is, what is she like?' "

"Like? In what way?"

"You know." His hand inched lower.

Playing me. He's playing me. "No, I don't. Spell it out for me."

If he caught the accusatory tone, he gave no sign. Instead, his mouth remained too damnably close and kissable for her sanity, and he continued his slow but steady assault on her mons. Once he'd conquered that part of her—

"Hell," he said, "heading for this spread put me in a time warp. I kept thinking about back when I could hardly wait to see you."

"Of course you did. You knew I'd spread my legs for you."

"What's wrong?"

"Nothing." *Concentrate. Don't let his touch distract you.*

"You're lying."

Despite the words hovering between them, she didn't immediately reply. How could she, with the touch she'd tried to warn herself against taking her into the past he'd spread open between them? Only, she wasn't just being bombarded by ten-year-old memories, because a few minutes ago they'd built upon that past. "Not lying," she managed. Despite herself, her control over her legs slipped, causing the distance between them to increase. No way could she tell herself she didn't want him here. "It—it scares me that just a few minutes after setting our eyes on each other we were tearing at each other's clothes. What are we, no more civilized than Fred and the heifers? We're no longer impulsive kids; we're suppose to be adults."

Although he nodded, he didn't halt his invasion of her body or senses. With his arm now supporting his upper body, he had no trouble keeping his mouth within inches of her breast while working his free hand ever closer to her core. The anticipation caused her to tremble.

"I'm not scaring you," he said, his breath again moistening her breasts. "I know it isn't that."

"You think you know everything about me."

"I didn't say that. Don't put words into my mouth."

"Then what?" she snapped. Damn it, why were her eyes closing and why hadn't her thigh muscles heeded her order to close her legs and keep them that way?

"Sorry but I don't get why you're trying to pick a fight."

Because if I don't I'm a goner. "It doesn't bother you that we're all over each other the moment we're back together?" she repeated. By amassing every bit of strength left in her, she managed to close her fingers around his wrist, but she didn't try to pull him off her. Soon, yes soon. Right after—after what?

"It wasn't right away. First we talked."

"Big deal. For a few minutes."

"Wendi?" Even with her eyes closed she knew his mouth was nearly on hers.

"What?"

"What you're feeling scares you, doesn't it? That's where all this is coming from."

What do you mean by this? she could have asked, but she already knew the answer. She feared her body's reactions and responses when it came to Mike. Sex had never been like this with the other men in her life, not even Seth whom she'd believed she loved unconditionally when they'd gotten married. Seth was, what, a walk through a well-lit and patrolled park, while Mike put her in mind of clinging to the back of a wild horse galloping at full speed.

Pulling away from a mental image of her hair flying behind her and her fingers tightly gripping a thick mane, she all-too-quickly reconnected with her body. Mike's hand on her mons had stilled. His breath no longer feathered over her breast. Gathering her courage, she opened her eyes.

Yes, he was looking at her, intently studying her, if truth be told. Unless she was mistaken, he was searching for the same thing she was.

Understanding. Comprehension.

Frightened by their joint search, she forced herself to sit up. To her relief, he didn't try to stop her, but neither did he take his hand off her until she stood and twisted away. Not saying anything, not sure she had any words in her, she walked out of the sleeping quarters and headed for the barn entrance. Unless there was a need to keep livestock inside, her family didn't lock the metal gate, but although a large chunk of her wanted to pass through the opening and keep on walking, nudity and all, she stopped when she was still in the shadows. The day was hot, but a strong breeze kept her from breaking out in a sweat.

From here she could see much of the corral that held Fred

and her heifers but not the livestock and, beyond that, the home she'd been brought to when she was two days old. It was a bit lonely in there with her parents gone, and yet she'd needed the time to herself.

Now there was a man behind her, a man she didn't know what to do with.

"What are you seeing?" he asked. The strength of his voice told her he was only a few feet behind her.

"The sky. The incredible sky. All that open space. The first time I brought Seth here he called it a wasteland."

"How did you feel about that?"

"Hurt. Bothered because he couldn't see the same thing I did. How can anyone call something so free a wasteland? Just because the horizon isn't filled with skyscrapers is no reason—"

"You don't have to convince me. I was raised seeing the same views."

Oh god, that was part of what made Mike's impact nearly impossible to weather! How right he was. They'd both been nourished from the same source. Gripping the hinged end of the gate, she pulled in a deep drink of sage-scented air before looking back at him.

Naked. Gloriously and unabashedly naked. Lean and yet powerful with a farmer's tan and legs whose shape had changed over the years so he could sit astride a horse indefinitely. Her own legs tended to bow outward, making her wonder if he'd noticed the similarity. He saw his body as a tool, an extension of his intellect, not something to seduce women with. She couldn't say how she'd come to that conclusion, maybe because he wasn't trying to expand his chest or suck in his non-existent belly the way many men did. Wishing she could take her own body for granted, she hauled her gaze off him and back to the acres that were her world.

"I was desperate to see this again," she admitted. "The last few weeks I was away was like waiting for Christmas, only with an adult's comprehension of time's passage. I was so sick of traffic and buildings."

"There was a time when you could hardly wait to be in that traffic."

"I know. Funny how one's priorities change."

"Is it that or we finally get in touch with our personal priorities? Ourselves?"

She didn't want him to be perceptive any more than she wanted him to be so sexy that just thinking about what was between his legs floated her teeth. "Maybe that's it," she acknowledged. "All I know is that my wanting scared me." *Just as my need to feel your cock inside me did. Does.*

"I've been there, Wendi. I know what you're talking about."

If she pressed, would he be as nakedly honest as she'd just been? But much as she needed the answer, she remained silent. There'd been enough emotional and physical nudity for today, damn it. Time to end it

Time to regain her equilibrium.

She turned around.

8

He was too damn close. Too beautiful.

Digging her toes into the ground, she tried to remember how to lift her arms so she could cover her breasts, but the movement was so complex, and what did it matter? Not only had he seen everything her small breasts had to offer, he'd fondled and nibbled and licked them.

Heat flicked her core to distract her from what she'd been trying to accomplish. She wanted him to touch her almost as much as she needed to be left alone. Ached to bury herself in his strength, to drown in his warmth. To turn tail and run until she couldn't run anymore.

Now that she was facing him once again, the breeze caressed her back, and a heat she couldn't quite bring herself to acknowledge began crawling out from her core in all directions to lick at her thighs and buttocks, her belly and breasts.

Her mouth didn't want to stay shut. And now her hands—somehow they'd gathered enough strength that they were reaching for him instead of staying where they belonged. Unable to stop herself, maybe not wanting to, she lightly touched his chest. Like her, he'd sweated while they were having sex, which had left a film of dried moisture beneath the fine hairs sprinkled over his pectoral muscles and midsection. Of their own accord, her fingers caressed those hairs.

When he sucked in a breath, she felt superior, in control, but then she made the mistake of resting her fingertips on his chest so she could feel his expelled breath and she nearly lost it. She didn't have to look down to know his cock was coming to life.

"We're dangerous around each other, aren't we," she said.

"I'm not sure I'd call it dangerous." His voice was soft, in tune with the sound the breeze was making in the dry grasses. In contrast, the hands now closing around her waist telegraphed the strength it took to control a frightened or wild horse, lift bales of hay, or force a bull in and out of a trailer.

"What then?" she asked. His features were slightly blurred, not that it mattered, because her mind carried his imprint. As did her body.

"Exciting? Hell, I don't know. I'm a man; I'm not expected to be good with words, especially at times like this."

Although she wasn't sure how he defined *at times like this*, she didn't pursue the question. "All right," she tried. "You aren't buying 'dangerous' and I don't know if the word 'exciting' covers things. We aren't getting very far."

"Do we have to?"

Good question. Great question, in fact. However, answering it might well be beyond her for the less than simple reason that two naked bodies were within scant inches of touching and two pairs of hands had already made that connection. So many thoughts and emotions swirled through her: confusion and fear, raw hunger and the simple joy of being alive. "We could table it for the time being."

"I like your thinking." Leaning down, he touched his lips to her forehead. "Look, maybe it's a man thing—a man in the presence of a desirable woman thing—but I'm thinking you're asking too much of yourself."

How ridiculous they'd look to someone passing by, two naked-as-jaybirds adults standing flat-footed on a hay-strewn floor all but playing grab ass while carrying on, or trying to carry on, a conversation. "In what way?"

"Neither of us expected to see the other today. Can't we have a reunion without going through the whole psychological thing?"

"Reunion?" Hopefully spearing him with a stern expression, she slid her hands lower until fully extending her fingers would bring her in contact with his cock. "I don't recall hauling out our old yearbooks and thumbing through them wondering what became of former classmates."

"Then what would you call it?" With that, he arched his lower body toward her until his cock all but sealed itself to her belly in a challenge she couldn't begin to ignore—not that she wanted to. "This is one hell of a 'hi, how have you been,' handshake."

Despite the unmistakably wonderful message in the press of flesh against flesh, she couldn't help but chuckle. And she was careful to make sure her breath reached his throat when she spoke. "Think it'll catch on?"

"Only with nudists."

Her chuckle became a laugh, but instead of trying to come up with a quick-witted reply, she licked his throat. He jerked, shuddered. "Don't," he muttered.

"What? Touch you?"

"Not like that, yet. I want to be able to think."

His honesty both surprised and warmed her. Taking his request to heart, she dropped her hands to her sides and turned from him. Although he'd briefly released her while she was in motion, he settled his fingers over her waist again and stepped forward so they stood side by side in the barn entryway. She hadn't seen Fred when she'd last looked out, but now he trotted into view, hot in pursuit of one of her larger cows, who obviously wanted nothing to do with him. Fred's ability to effortlessly move his great bulk so easily had her nodding in approval. "Is he your prize stud?" she asked.

"Right now, yes. We'll see what shape he's in at the end of the breeding season. He was young enough last year that I gave him only limited service."

Standing next to Mike while talking about a subject they were both familiar with relaxed her a little. She was still acutely aware of him, of course, and keeping her hands off him took strength, but at least she no longer felt out of control. No longer a heifer in heat.

"I'm confused," she said. "You're not living on your folks' ranch and yet your bulls and their livestock have the same brand."

"Not quite. There's a lightning bolt under my W."

"Oh." With Fred zigzagging like he was going through an obstacle course as he kept after the unappreciative cow, she couldn't see his brand.

"I wanted my own identification and yet be true to my heritage."

"Good choice."

A few fat white clouds were building in the distance. From long experience she doubted they'd produce a thunderstorm, but they gave a sense of life and energy to the horizon, not that she needed more of either condition. Perhaps he'd tapped into her thoughts, because he drew her even closer so their hips touched. "Like your folks," he said, "mine are starting to cut back. I didn't want to risk sucking them into something they didn't have the energy for by leasing some of their land. Dad would want to get involved with the physical aspects and Mom—"

"Your mom would be cooking for everyone who came near the property as well as keeping your books."

"And good as she is with finances, I'm no longer her little boy."

Her mind might remember Mike as a constant-movement child, but her body was only interested in the adult he'd become. There was something timeless about him, as if he had one foot in the past that was this land while the other reached for the future. She wondered if the same could be said for her. "So where are you living?"

"Out of Pendleton," he said, naming the largest town in eastern Oregon, a still-rough and hearty cow town and home to one of the country's largest rodeos. It was also a good five-hour drive from here on narrow country roads. A wave of something dark and hollow ran through her.

"Pendleton," she repeated. "Because?"

"Several reasons. I was able to sign a land lease for a good price. I thought getting established in a more populated area would be easier. And until I bought my stock truck I kept having to rent one."

Those were good and practical reasons, so why couldn't she stop thinking about those five-hour long, tire-wearing trips between here and there? In an attempt to distract herself, she clenched her hands in front of her, but of course that brought her fingers close to her core. Her awakened core.

A bellowing roar caused both of them to look at the livestock enclosure. From what she could tell, the outcry had come not from Fred but her big cow. Fred had managed to corner the cow by herding her into the midst of a number of tightly bunched heifers, but instead of surrendering to her suitor, the object of his current affection was staring him down while pawing the ground. Oblivious to the pointed turn-down, Fred pushed another cow out of the way so he could sidle up to his intended.

"I wouldn't do that," she and Mike said almost at the same time.

True to their expectations, the big cow perfectly timed a sideways rear leg kick at Fred's underside. The solid thud of hoof against flesh made Wendi wince. Squalling like a lost calf, Fred jumped back.

"Oh no!" she exclaimed. "Did she get his penis?"

"Don't know."

Instead of taking off naked to check on Fred's welfare and thus his pocketbook, Mike stayed by her side, and if his hand now lightly massaging her shoulder was any indication, he wasn't overly concerned that his prize bull had been gelded. Fortunately, after shaking his great head, Fred tossed his head, flinging snot at the ungrateful beast who'd done him wrong. Then, whipping his great rear end around, he set his sights on the other cows.

Wendi couldn't help it. What started as a chuckle turned into a full laugh. "My kingdom for a camera. There's a male who can take rejection."

"Guess his ego's going to recover and his manhood's intact," Mike observed. His hand trailed down from her shoulder, slowly closing in on her breast. "For the record, one reason I bought Fred is because he has great eyesight."

"And bulls identify estrual cows by sight, not smell."

"You know that?"

"A farm girl? I should."

Although Mike chuckled, she sensed that his thoughts had gone beyond what she'd just said. Although technically they were within the barn's shade, the afternoon's heat circled around and into her, making her guess it was the same for him. Their clothes were behind them while what they each and separately had to accomplish today was ahead of them. They couldn't stand in this neutral place forever.

"I'll make you a deal," Mike said. "I won't sue you because your cows wore out my bull."

"How generous of you."

Not content with just reaching the swell of her breast, his fingers began a gentle but insistent press that reached deep. "I can't do any less for an old *friend*. And because I'm a generous man, I'll accept whatever your folks paid for frozen sperm as partial payment for Fred's services. However, because that doesn't resolve the matter of my not having a bull for the Thurston herd, I'm going to have to charge you for theft of services."

"Me? I'm not the one who let his damn bull run away."

"He wouldn't have taken off if you hadn't put all those horny cows in one place. What red-blooded bull could ignore all that bellowing?"

Continuing the silly argument called for her whirling on him and jutting her chin up at him while she gave him a piece of her mind. Unfortunately, or maybe fortunately, her body wasn't the slightest bit interested in making any kind of move. "Do what you feel you have to," she muttered with her lids at half mast. "I just want you to know that if you file a lawsuit, I'll file one of my own. Don't forget, Fred trespassed and what I've seen him do looks like intimidation and force to me. And I'll demand you pay all attorney fees *when* you lose."

"Hmm." By turning her slightly and curling his body down around her, he easily nibbled the side of her neck. "Hmm. Maybe we can work out a compromise."

9

All but purring, she locked her knees so she wouldn't collapse. "What kind of compromise?"

"How about the barter system?"

"Either that or services in trade."

"Services," he said with his mouth still on her. "What did you have in mind?"

Say it. Just say it. "Fred's trying to work his way through my herd in a single day, but because there's just one of me, you aren't going to be able to match his productivity."

"I should hope not. The effort would kill me."

"And then I'd be left with disposing of the body. Okay, maybe I can't expect you to keep up with your bull's pace but couldn't you give it the old college try?"

As she'd both hoped and feared he would, he pressed a forefinger under her chin, lifting her head. "This isn't something I want to joke about."

"I'm not." Although she tried to silence her sigh, it broke free. "Believe me, I'm serious."

"I want to believe you, Wendi. The way you talked and acted when we—"

"When we went after each other like animals in rut. Go on, say it."

Nodding, he started massaging her upper arms where he'd been gripping them. "I did and said things right before I left home that I'm not particularly proud of," he said. "I was so eager to be an adult. To be free of the responsibility that comes with being a ranch kid."

"I understand."

"Yes, I'm sure you do. We agreed to stay in touch, declared our love and talked about a future, but I didn't do my part."

"I know. You stopped calling and only wrote three letters." *Which I still have.*

"I was a bastard."

"No, you were smart." Before he could ask what she meant, she hurried on. "We were too young to know what we wanted out of life. Oh, I cried myself to sleep a few times when I stopped hearing from you, but a year later I was in the same position. All I wanted was to put my past behind me and take on the world."

"Do you think the world kicked our butts and that's why we're back where we are?"

Another perceptive question. Vital enough that when she wrapped her arms around his waist, she barely noted what she'd done. "Maybe."

"You sound as if you don't care."

"I don't, right now."

Strange, she thought as Mike chuckled, unless she was mistaken, she'd paid more attention to his laughter today than she ever had with any man before. There was a looseness, an ease to it that said he embraced lightness. Yes, he could be serious as witnessed by his decision to leave his job, but life wasn't a somber undertaking to him.

Impulsively, she wrapped her arms around his neck and rose onto her toes. The contact didn't go deep enough so she lifted her right leg and pressed it to his left. He helped anchor her leg in place by gripping her thigh, which left her free to concentrate on rubbing her breasts against his midsection. She was aroused, warm and soft and wet, but unlike the first time, now she could control her impulse to try to drive him to the ground under her.

She knew where this was heading; they both did. Only now the sex just didn't have to be rushed.

Rocking to one side and then the other allowed her to slide her body over his. His cock was caught between them, trapped and yet potent, giving rise to the fantasy of fucking standing up, but for that to happen, she'd have to stand on something.

What something?

Never mind. That wasn't what she wanted after all. In truth, she wanted nothing on earth because she had it all, him, against her, her body alive and real and simple. They could stand like this forever, speaking without words. The vital messages, the only ones that counted now, shot out from him, and her heart and pussy absorbed everything.

Holding on, skin against skin, dipping into a shared heat and finding it endless. Endless? No, because something unwanted was pushing its way into her consciousness. Afraid her mind was asking questions she couldn't answer, she tried to silence it, but it only grew stronger. "My leg!" she gasped.

His head tipping to the side, he lightly squeezed her thigh. "What about your leg and which one?"

"I'm getting a cramp."

"Well, we don't want that, do we?" Looking properly concerned, he released the leg he'd been holding. She slowly lowered it, running her inner thigh along his outer one. Her heel traced his calf during her descent. She made no attempt to pull her hands off his neck, and both of his hands were spread over her back, keeping her against him.

"You need to sit down," he said. "And for me to massage your muscle."

The prospect of a cramp had already faded, but she was no fool. Either that or so much a fool that she couldn't see it. Either way, as he lifted her in his arms, she rested her head against his shoulder and took in the scent of a cowboy. It wasn't pretty, no hint of culture or a manufactured aroma. Instead, Mike smelled like his world.

Just as she did.

Easily carrying her over to the bed, he lowered her onto it. If she hadn't been concerned that he might injure his back, she would have been tempted to continue to grip his neck, forcing him to lean low and vulnerable over her.

"What was it?" he asked when she was sitting cross-legged on the bed. "Thigh or calf?"

"Calf."

"My specialty. Roll onto your stomach."

Her mind suddenly on fire with the possibilities for rear delivery sex, she did as he ordered, taking care to leave enough room for him to sit next to her. Folding her arms under her cheek, she watched as he bent the leg closest to him and began stroking her calf. He hadn't asked which leg needed tending, but she didn't care. No, indeed, she didn't give a damn about anything in life except those strong yet gentle fingers of his. Not only was he lightly pressing her calf; his other hand held her foot, those fingers searching for sensitive spots in her instep.

She should tell him that every inch of flesh there was sensitive.

Should inform him that she was willing to return the favor, eventually.

Oh, heaven! Fingers that knew their job kneaded and stroked, turning firm and then gentle by turn, confusing her senses because she couldn't decide whether to concentrate on her calf or instep. Her buttocks were heating, the small of her back tingling, thigh muscles both taut and loose, fingers occasionally clenching, mouth hanging open and forehead and cheeks as hot as her buttocks.

So that's what melting meant. Going boneless and muscleless, becoming all nerves and beating heart, thinking with her cunt.

"That doing any good?" he asked.

Depends on your definition of good but lordy, I have no complaints. "You're starting to make progress, but this could take awhile.," she came up with. "I need to make sure I haven't suffered any crippling injury."

"No." His voice carried only a hint of mischief. "We certainly wouldn't want that." Using the side of his thumb, he stroked her foot from toes to heel. "One thing I've learned, just because a certain body part hurts doesn't mean that's where the injury is."

"Oh?"

"Oh indeed. If you don't mind, I'll give you a demonstration."

"I don't mind."

"Didn't think you would."

For a moment she was aware of nothing except more massaging and countless sensual messages running up her leg to her core and beyond. Then he leaned low over her. An instant later, he lightly bit her buttock. "Oh shit!" she gasped.

Another bite, sharper than the first. Electric.

Not making the mistake of trying to roll over or sit up, she nevertheless lifted her head so she could spear him with a mock stern look. "What the hell was that?"

"You don't know?" His grin was so damn beautiful it nearly

undid her. "About the connection between the ass and foot?" He demonstrated by grinding his thumb into her instep, instantly stripping her muscles of all strength. Sighing, she lowered her impossibly heavy head back onto her folded arms. Anticipating another bite, she couldn't relax.

"It's been well-documented," he continued. "Extensive studies done at the nation's leading research centers and fraternity and sorority houses have left no doubt of the ass-foot connection. I'm surprised you didn't read about it in the medical journals."

"That—that's all they concluded? That there's a direct line of communication between a person's ass and his or her feet?"

"Of course not. This was a far-reaching study focused on the whole pleasure-pain syndrome."

Pain? What—

Damn, he'd just nipped her buttocks again! There'd been an instant spark of sensation she didn't want, but it died almost instantly, to be replaced by a fresh infusion of heat starting with her pussy and traveling all the way up to the top of her head.

"Not fair," she started to protest. "I had—"

"Sometimes it takes more than one treatment to effect a cure." That said, he raked his teeth over the full length of the mound closest to him. Although she gasped and trembled, she managed to remain still. And when he lowered her leg and leaned even farther over her so he could give the other cheek the same treatment, she ground her teeth. She was falling apart, muscles disconnecting from bones and bones disintegrating. Maybe he'd be left with nothing more than a puddle to sop up.

What an insane image! She wasn't a melting block of ice. In fact, she was as far from being frozen as it was possible to be. On fire came close.

Now what?

Oh yes, he was stretching out next to her, lightly patting her poor *abused* buttocks while running his lips over her back, starting at her waist and traveling up to her shoulders. Kisses. Yes, that's what he was doing, kissing her.

Although she'd started drooling, she couldn't begin to think about stopping. Somewhere in there she'd pulled her arms out from under her head and tucked them under her breasts so her cheek rested on the bed. He was still kissing her, sometimes running his teeth over the back of her neck, sometimes using his tongue to paint her with his saliva. Staking his claim.

"Oh my god," she whispered.

"Good thing I learned to read, isn't it." His moist breath slid through the hair at the nape of her neck. "Otherwise, I wouldn't have learned about this medical advancement and would have to put you in traction."

"Traction? For a muscle cramp?"

"Of course. Established treatment technique. What kind of an education did you get?"

How could she possibly give a damn about responding when he'd gone back to nibbling the base of her neck while running his hand from her thighs to her shoulder blades? Fortunately he didn't appear to expect an answer, quite possibly because demonstrating treatment techniques was taking his total concentration. Relaxing was impossible of course, but there was nothing wrong with thinking only about his tongue, teeth, and lips as they claimed all he could reach of her upper body. He was so gentle now, treating her like a hothouse flower or beauty queen instead of a cowgirl capable of managing a small cattle operation on her own. Unable to tap into any part of the resourceful woman she took so much pride in being, she sent silent messages of appreciation to Mike. As she did, her inner tissues softened and expanded.

Her body was preparing itself for sex, plain and simple.

What about his? Was it too much to ask of him to dive head-first into a satisfying fuck when she'd barely touched him?

10

_____

"What's this about?" Mike asked a few seconds later. "You forget who's the heifer and who's the bull?"

"Oh," she said from her superior position on her elbow with Mike stretched out on his back on the narrow bed. "I know the difference between the sexes all right, both animal and human variety. And I'm a liberated woman so you're going to have to deal with it, cowboy."

"Deal how?"

Funny how vulnerable a man looked naked, with his lonely cock jutting toward a barn roof. Vulnerable and alone and yet still powerful. Maybe she should admit she wasn't entirely sure what she had in mind now that she'd maneuvered him into a less dominant position than he'd been in before. But if she said a word, he'd know she'd barely succeeded in tamping down her need for sex long enough to concentrate on him.

Concentrate she would. More than that, she was determined to give him some of the gifts he'd handed her.

"Granted," she said, sliding lower so her mouth was near his midsection, "I haven't done the extensive reading of medical research you have, but not only do I have several years of college under my non-existent belt, but I've also been to a goat roping."

"No you haven't."

"The hell I haven't. And I've lassoed a pig."

"A sleeping piglet probably. Don't forget, you weren't the only one who went the 4-H route."

If she hadn't been studying his reaction to having her teeth so close to the most valuable part of his anatomy, she might have believed he was relaxed and teasing, to say nothing of not being particularly interested in finishing what he'd begun. What *they'd* begun. "The point I was trying to make before your attempt at a put down—" Smiling her most evil smile, she dipped her stiff tongue into his navel. "—was that you aren't the only one who picked up some pointers along the way." She punctuated her comment with another quick but deep tongue prod.

"What the hell?"

"What's the matter, cowboy? Having the tables turned got you off balance?"

When she started to lower her head again, he grabbed her hair, stopping her. "No biting."

"Oh? So it's perfectly fine for you to gnaw on me, but I can't give you a taste of your medicine?" Waving her extended tongue at him, she pretended to be intent on continuing her assault on his navel. "Just like a man. You can dish it out, but you can't take it."

"The hell I can't."

"Then let go."

Going by his expression, he wasn't comfortable with her suggestion, but after giving her hair a warning tug, he released her. Instead of hurrying the assault that made her head spin and her juices flow, she rested a hand on his chest and lost herself in the rhythm of his breathing. How incredible that this man of

action and determination was lying naked on an old bed because of her. Of all the things he could and should be doing
today, he'd chosen to spend it with her. Grateful, she made his
pleasure her goal.

Her world.

When she kissed his belly, he again took hold of her hair, but
this time it was simply so he could track what she was doing.
The longer she spent tasting and testing, running her tongue
and lips over his pubic hair, the less regular his breathing became. Her own breaths stopped and started, stopped and started.
Even with so little of his body touching hers, it remembered when
they'd come together as one, making it difficult to concentrate
on her vow to place him first. Her pussy was empty and hungry,
flooding itself in anticipation of being fed. Her breasts ached,
begging her to stop what she was doing and tend to them.

Not now. Later. And *his* hands on her, not self-pleasure.

When her eyes closed, she stopped seeing him as a flesh and
blood man. He became something more, symbolic of what she
wanted from life. Adventure and challenge, clean clear morn-
ings and dark, hot nights. After days spent tending to their land
and livestock, they'd mount matching stallions and race into
the horizon. With their stallions running as one, they'd hold
hands and stare into each other's eyes until their horses could
no longer gallop. Pulling the steaming animals to a halt by a
quiet stream, they'd dismount, tear off their clothes, and sink to
the still sun-warm earth.

Panting from the image, she opened her eyes and focused on
the hard length of meat she hadn't yet touched.

She wanted to, oh god how she wanted! But once she had—

It didn't matter!

No more holding back, no putting off while she fought her
own hot demons.

Sliding even lower on the bed brought her head in alignment
with what she'd been seeking. Once there, she counted the sec-

onds until maybe a minute had passed. His fingers against her scalp twitched, and several times he ground his buttocks against the bed. Feeling as if they'd both passed some kind of test, she lifted herself over the masculine leg closest to her. Now nestled in the shelter of his gaping limbs, she ran her tongue over his tip.

"Oh, shit," he gasped.

"You want?"

"You know I do. It's just—oh shit," he repeated when she licked him again. "Oh boy, oh boy! Shit."

"That doesn't sound very much like a widely read college grad, more like an ignorant cowpoke."

"That's the best you're going to get from me." He had that wide-eyed look of an animal who'd like nothing better than to bolt but was trying to hold it together. Seeing it gave her a sense of power. It also made him sweeter, more honest with his emotions.

Parking her observation at the back of her mind, she lightly closed her fingers around his cock, leaving the tip exposed. "The first time I saw this," she admitted, "I was intimidated."

"I know." His voice was strained. "I'm sorry you were."

"That was one of those fleeting things, well nearly fleeting, something I pretty much put behind me once I'd gotten used to looking at it. And touching it, to say nothing of having it inside me." Lighthearted, she pretended to shake hands with his cock, followed by a chuckle when he gasped. "After the shock was over, I started having the most interesting thoughts. Thoughts that got between me and my studies more times than I care to admit."

Things were narrowing down in her mind, leaving her with no thought of her surroundings or what might happen after this time with him. In truth, her world revolved around what she held.

And she wasn't in charge after all.

Loving him, at least loving this part of his anatomy, she closed her lips over its head so she could shelter it within her moist warmth. This wasn't the same as taking him into her pussy, but the similarities were powerful. Her mouth became her gift to him.

Stretching out over him so her hair dragged over his hip and the hand that had been holding him rested on his belly, she sucked him deep into her throat. Although she couldn't sustain this position, it made her feel they were sharing something precious.

Pretending his cock was an ice-cream cone she was licking should have made her laugh. Instead, she dove into the experience, tasting and testing the hard sleek and living length. She loved his strength there. Loved the hard ridges and loose skin around his scrotum. Loved its smell and taste.

As long as she kept her movements slow and measured, she could control her responses, barely. But when she picked up the pace so she could watch him squirm, his anticipation became hers. That's when she had no choice but to press her legs together and suck in as much air as her lungs could hold to keep her personal wild beast at bay, when the knot in her belly threatened to take over. Wondering how close she could take not just him but herself to the edge without falling into space, she lightly, so lightly nibbled the side of his cock.

"Stop!"

"Stop what?" she asked with her lips against his soft-as-silk skin.

"Doing—that."

"You don't like?"

"I like too much."

His voice was rough, nearly raw. And his entire body was so taut she thought he might snap. "All right." After a final soothing lick that felt too much like good-bye when that was the last thing she wanted, she lifted her head. "Mike? I'd like to tell you something. I just don't want you making fun of me."

"I'd never make fun of you."

No, he wouldn't. "Back when we were kids—that's what we were, ignorant if horny kids—it never occurred to me to do what I just did. Fellatio? I'd hadn't even heard the word and if I had, I wouldn't have had the courage to try anything. The sex we had years ago, it was always missionary style. Did you know there were other positions? Maybe you didn't want to shock me."

He was relaxing a little, still tight and taut but hopefully feeling a little more in control of his body. "I had some inkling but not much. I figured—hell, I guess I figured that as long as you wanted to have sex with me, I wasn't going to push my luck." He shook his head. "Besides, I didn't want you making fun of me if I screwed up."

"How would I know if you did?"

"I didn't think about that."

"Because you were all wrapped up in performing?"

"Pretty much. Makes me glad as hell I'm not still eighteen."

"Me too," she agreed. Had she just promised herself not to get him all hot and bothered again and if so why had she made such an insane vow? However, a look at his guarded features told her she'd made the right decision, for now. He was male, a man, a true cowboy. There was no part of his heart or intellect that could surrender control of his body.

Fine. Good. Right. She'd take him as he was.

And take him she would.

11

Drawing up her legs, she knelt in the space his legs provided and slowly, thoroughly ran her gaze over him until his unspoken message reached her. Contrary to what she'd just decided, he was indeed offering himself to her, and not just his body but his thoughts and emotions too. He trusted her. That's what it all came down to, he trusted.

Could she do the same?

"You're beautiful," she said.

"Beautiful?" Neck straining, he looked down at himself. "Where?"

"Where it counts."

Obviously that hadn't answered his question as witnessed by his frown, but a further explanation would have to wait until a more rational moment, a time when their legs weren't pressing against each other and she couldn't easily reach out and touch his manhood.

Manhood? Maybe an old-fashioned and indirect term, but an honest one.

They weren't doing anything to each other at the moment,

not really. Granted, they were both nude and the promise of sex filled the air, but they weren't wrapped around each other. Yet. And a thousand thoughts continued to swirl through her. "I love looking at you," she admitted. "Once I was afraid to."

"When I was in the *all together*, that's what you're talking about isn't it? That's what you called it the day we went swimming naked in Beaver Creek."

Giving him a wry grin, she nodded. "I can't believe how uptight I was. Why did you put up with me?"

"Two reasons." Sitting up, he held a finger in front of her. "One, I was crazy about you. You were so sweet and honest and conservative and yes, uptight. Everything I thought a girl was suppose to be."

"And the other reason?"

"Simple. I was a teenage boy. You let me fuck you." He waved a second finger.

"Ow, okay."

"You didn't want to hear that?"

"No, I needed to. In other words, if I'd known how to, I could have wrapped you around my little finger."

The corners of his mouth twitching, he cupped his hands under her breasts. "I wasn't particularly interested in your finger."

"No, as I recall, you weren't." Using the momentum of her words, she shoved, knocking him back down. Before he could sit up again, if that's what he'd intended, she sprawled on top of him, making sure his cock slid between her legs. "So tell me, Mister Wagner, what part of my anatomy were you the most interested in?"

"Same as I still am."

Loving the feel of him under her, she concentrated on rubbing her breasts over his chest. Granted, her movement was severely limited, but too much friction wasn't safe, was dangerous, in fact. Planting her hands on either side of him, she lifted her upper body off him a few inches so she could run her hair over his shoulders. Perhaps she was tickling him, perhaps not. Either way, she reveled in the sense of power being on top gave her.

Even when he gripped her hips and maneuvered her so her legs were outside his and then helped her sit up, she continued to feel in charge. "There's a whole different world out there beyond these cattle ranches," she said. "Liberated, open, not always good but mind-expending. I learned to acknowledge and encourage my sexuality, not necessarily through personal involvement, but sex in all its manifestations was everywhere. I couldn't help but be impacted."

"Are you glad you were?"

"Yeah," she admitted, the heels of her hands on his rib cage, "I am." *And I hope you like the changes.*

"Same with me." His gaze never left her as he worked his way to the top of her thighs. Once there, he stroked her mons, a light yet possessive touch that sent fire spiraling everywhere until even her throat burned. "I didn't embrace a lot of it, drinking and drugs, a lot of the materialism I was seeing. I don't need possessions."

"Neither do I."

"I need to feel I'm doing something worthwhile," he said.

Even with the sensual distractions radiating from him to her, his words resonated. "So do I. I believe this land needs devoted shepherds. To be nurtured. I now know that's part of why I dropped out of college and changed jobs as many times as I did. I couldn't see a purpose to what I was doing."

He gave her a nod, just a nod. And yet she found a world of communication in the gesture. Eyes burning from sudden tears, she leaned down over his chest and pressed her mouth to his. Blood rushed to her head, warning that she couldn't sustain this position. Besides, she was flattening his cock between them. Just the same, she parted her lips and took in the tongue he offered in welcome.

Making the move as slow and sensual as her spine allowed, she brought herself upright again. His eyes had a smoky tinge to them, depth and layers she hadn't seen before. Her edges were being blunted, sanded away maybe. Once she no longer existed as a separate human being, would he seep into her pores and veins?

"No more waiting, Wendi," he whispered. "And no more talking."

Yes, oh yes, she could give both of them that!

Driven by her pussy's needs, she straightened. She hated losing touch with him, but it was only temporary, only until she'd filled herself with him. He gripped and stroked her thighs as she positioned his cock at her entrance, as she spread herself with her fingers, as she sucked his tip into her. Head back and eyes closed and crying a little, she settled back down, slow but barely controlled, hungry.

Filling her, expanding her, his cock stroked her swollen, hot tissues and set off tiny explosions. Rocking forward and then back, she found the alignment she needed to continue her descent. Her thighs burned and demanded release. Ignoring them, concentrating on the living rod nestling deeper and deeper in her, she eased herself into place.

Part of him. No longer separate. Sharing the same flesh and feeling the same heat.

When at last her buttocks rested on his thighs and his slightly bent knees assured that she could hold this position indefinitely, she opened her eyes again. She was beyond caring whether he saw her tears.

Breathing deep and strong, he caressed her thighs. Loving the gesture, she covered his forearms so she could walk her fingers over the deeply tanned flesh there.

Expanded. Filled. Sheltering him and yet being sheltered herself.

Now that her inner tissues had fully embraced the invasion,

she began rocking from side to side. Each move caused his cock to press against her pussy in a new way, a way that made her feel like a virgin again.

A wise, knowing, and hot-as-hell virgin.

Dragging one hand off him, she caressed her breasts. When he acknowledged what she was doing with a wink, she lightly clawed his chest. He responded by working a hand between their joined bodies.

A touch, quick and light. On her clit.

"Yes," she mouthed. "Yes."

"I can't—there's only so much I can do like this."

"I know," she told him although the truth was she hadn't considered his limited movements until now. "I'll try to be patient."

"I'm not sure I can be."

That made all the sense in the world, and yet she wasn't ready for change. Still scratching him while massaging her aching nipples, she commanded her vaginal muscles to suck him even farther into her. She'd semi-trained them to flutter during solitary sessions, and she'd learned that men liked being clutched this way, but she was no expert.

All she could give him was honesty.

Honesty and strength.

I need you deep, so deep maybe you'll never leave. I don't yet fully trust you because I don't trust myself, but the journey, yes, the journey!

"Oh shit," he gasped. "You're killing me."

"How?"

"Making me crazy." Arching his back and deeply bending his knees brought his buttocks off the bed. For a moment she thought she was astride a bucking horse. Then, muscles trembling, he fell back down. "I can't do—damn it, I can't just lie here."

"You—" She tightened her muscles down around his length. "don't like this?"

"Love it!" Again that gathering of muscles, again being pushed up and off balance as he bucked under her. "But it isn't enough. I need—"

"To ride me?"

"Yeah." Then as she tried to find her way through his still-smoky gaze to his core, he rolled onto his side, taking her with him.

They were side by side now, bodies still joined, arms gripping, legs intertwined. He continued to penetrate her, not as deep before, but still there, still part of her. With his mouth only inches from hers, she stroked the back of his neck. His hand over her buttocks kept her in place, kept her where she could feel his expelled breaths.

"We need to talk," he said, the words startling her.

"Now?"

"For just a minute. There's something I want to run by you."

She nodded because this was what he wanted, because his eyes were suddenly clear and her breasts were on his chest and her leg against his and he was running his foot over hers.

"The land lease in Pendleton is almost up. I can move my bulls wherever I want."

Don't tell me you'll be leaving Oregon, and don't tell me you want me to go with you. Not just when I've come home. "All right."

"I believe I can find land around here. And if I can't, I can lease from either my folks or yours."

"Oh."

"Do you know what I'm saying?"

This wasn't about acreage and trucking issues, about a business move. It had everything to do with joined and sharing bodies. Him and her. "I'd love that,"

"You're sure? Some of the things you said today, you aren't sure how things are going between us. If you aren't comfortable—"

"It's so new, Mike. Overwhelming. You have to know what I'm talking about."

"I do," he said somberly and kissed her cheek.

"We're more complicated than we were ten years ago."

"A hell of a lot more complicated. Relationships."

"Marriages."

"Divorces."

"Yes," she agreed, and although she wished this conversation could wait until they'd finished fucking, she understood its need. "If we're going to continue to see each other, we'll have to work through those things. I don't see how—if it's a long distance relationship—we'd ever get to where we need to be."

"Where we are right now isn't bad."

"No." She tightened muscles that had been aching to do just that. "In fact it's nearly perfect."

"Nearly. Not totally."

She sensed the gathering of muscles, but despite the momentary panic and terrible loss of him nestled inside her, she knew he wasn't going to leave her. And when he rolled her onto her back and sat up, she bent her knees so she could place her fingers where his cock had been. Sliding her middle and forefinger into her drenched core, she studied him.

"I'm going to fuck you," he announced. "Not like the first time. Slow and complete."

"Maybe I need fast. Hard."

"Trust me."

12

Strong hands, hands made for work, slid under her buttocks and lifted her. With him kneeling between her bent legs and her arms over her head, she became Mike Wagner's toy. She existed to please him and be pleased in turn. It seemed that they'd been fucking for hours and yet the actual act had only lasted a few moments. The rest of the time had been spent in talk and preparation.

No more talk. No more thoughts.

Sex.

Fucking.

Keeping her off balance with the bulk of her weight on her back and shoulders, he inched closer, slowly yet relentlessly killing the space between them. She sighed when his cock slid along her inner thigh, moaned when something both soft and hard pressed against her entrance. She welcomed him in.

Home.

Slow, long, gliding strokes, her cunt open and honest. He was the one in control here, the one who could move, who saw everything about her, her jiggling breasts and sweat-glistening throat, her gaping mouth and unfocused eyes. She was his, willing vagina and useless legs, her fingers sometimes clawing his forearm, sometimes reaching for his chest, often tearing at her hair or massaging her breasts.

His self control frightened her. How could he maintain that sleek, smooth, and languid pace? Was he strong enough to hold her like this forever, to work and work and work his thigh and back muscles? She couldn't be sure because her senses barely extended that far, but his breathing seemed measured and light.

He buried himself in her, withdrew until she began to fear loss, came at her again, always long, sleepy movements.

And although she wanted more, needed it hard and hot, his pace became hers. They were part of a whole, a single unit locked in life's oldest act. She was slipping, losing herself, seeping into him and loving the sensation.

Oh yes, lordy, yes!

A change. Not subtle. Coming from someplace deep and primitive in him. The unexpected power sent her sliding along the blanket and his cock yet deeper. Determined not to lose any part of his length, she anchored her fingers around his elbows. "Don't go," she begged.

"I'm just picking up the pace."

She could deal with that, wanted to. Now her eyes might now be closed, might still be open a bit, not that she cared. Neither was she sure whether his next thrust was any stronger than the one that had come before. Her pussy had been filled with him, continued to house him, and that's the only thing that mattered.

That and his hands on her and his body angled over hers.

Maybe because she'd spent her childhood in tune with the cadence of the horses under her, she easily caught on to the depth and length of his powered thrusts. His rhythm became hers. Became her.

She was trotting, sitting tall and bareback with a strong colt under her. Feeling the young animal's potential in untrained muscles. The colt's strides lengthened out to become a smooth canter. Her mount grew older, stronger, more sure of his ability. He now ran for the joy of it, the hard thud of hooves against packed earth, mane and tail streaming behind him.

Lifting her head to the wind, she urged her mount on, pushed him into a gallop. Felt the tremendous power, the single-minded drive for the finish line. In her mind she lay low over the straining back and sent her own strength into laboring muscles, willed him on with words and heels digging into his sides, even a whip against his flank.

Ride me! Ride me!

Yes, hooves attacking the earth, muscles screaming and burning, the rider feeling the same burn not just in her legs but her pussy as well. Mostly her pussy. Charging, racing, someone screaming, the world a blur and her cunt on fire. Her cunt and legs and breasts and throat, fingers and shoulders, back and buttocks.

"Yes! Yes!"

"Yes, damn it, yes!"

Ah, that was Mike again. The horse of her imagination gone. The man of her reality pushing against her with all his strength. He gasped, grunted, cried out, jerked.

She wanted to cry for him, for both of them, to acknowledge the gift filling her core, but she'd started to fly. To gasp and sob.

Unable to breathe or think or feel beyond her pussy, she laughed. Climaxing felt so damn good! And if her laughter was ragged and raw and primitive she didn't care.

Mike.

She'd fucked Mike.

And he'd fucked her.

"I have to start back," Mike said as he closed his cell phone. "Fortunately, old man Thurston's okay with my substituting another bull for Fred, but I'm going to have to get the replacement delivered as soon as possible."

She'd just come back from getting a bucket of water for Mike's horse so hadn't heard the conversation between Mike and Carl Thurston. It occurred to her that her romanticized notion of what it meant to be a cowboy would have to be altered to include cell phones. "How long will that take?"

Mike frowned. "Back to Pendleton tomorrow. Probably the next day spent catching up. I should be back by Friday."

Friday.

"I'll have to connect with Carl first," he said looking down at her as if guessing her thoughts. "Get my bull settled in and producing. But I could be out here by night."

"I'll have dinner ready." How casual and comfortable her offer sounded, an old married couple making familiar plans.

"I could take you out."

"Where? The nearest café is twenty miles away."

"Saturday, then, for our night on the town."

"Then Friday evening is for us?"

He'd removed his horse's bridle so she could drink. Taking it off his shoulder, he eased the bit back into the animal's mouth. "Us sounds good."

There didn't seem to be anything left to say after that. At least she couldn't think of a word that wouldn't revolve around the sex they'd no doubt dive into within minutes of his arrival. They'd talk, eventually. They'd work on resolving the issues that had complicated them during the years they'd spent apart, eventually.

But first fucking.

"I'll hold you to it," she told him, running her fingers under his shirt.

Before he could respond, a long, low bellow turned them toward the enclosure holding Fred and the heifers. Fred was standing alone and looking at the bunched and wary heifers.

No doubt the sound had come from him, but instead of taking off after his newly claimed harem, he stood on widely spread legs with his head dragging a bit. He bellowed again, something plaintive and weary.

Mike chuckled. "I know what he feels like. Worn out. You want me to feed him before I leave?"

She shook her head. "I'll take care of it, extra rations for a job well done."

"Is that why you're offering to feed me Friday night?" he asked. He winked and wrapped his arms around her. "So I can keep up with Fred."

"No way, cowboy. He might get a herd. All you're entitled to is me."

"I can live with that."

So can I. Maybe forever.

GETTING LUCKY

MELISSA MACNEAL

1

―――――――

Luke McGrew slammed the top of her desk and stood up so abruptly that his chair toppled backward. "You know what I like about you, Janie?" he demanded, glaring fiercely at her. "Not one fucking thing!"

Jane Cook inhaled sharply, not dropping his gaze. She stood up, too, rising slowly and deliberately as she composed her response. As the president of Enterprise, Wyoming's only bank, she never enjoyed rejecting anyone's loan application, but as a woman she craved justice for wounds this too-handsome man had inflicted long ago.

"Well, then," she murmured. "At least you won't be luring me into the back of your camper to screw me out of anything this time. *Will* you, Lucky?"

His eyes narrowed in a face that was way too striking—and way too famous. "Is that what this is about? A stupid stunt I pulled in high school?"

"Nope." Jane crossed her arms, lifting her breasts so the pale green lace of her camisole beneath her sage suit would taunt him. "This is about a financial statement that's gone too far in the hole for me to dig you out. It's about the feasibility—or lack of it—of making any profit from ranching on your mama's property. So unless you sell it—"

"Not an option!" he barked. "I've come home! I tell you, I can make this thing *work*, if you'd get your head out of your—"

"And how will you pay off your sisters' shares? Crystal and Tiffany have already been here, demanding I settle the estate and get them their money," she countered coolly. "I can't see them waiting for you to turn a profit, Luke. Not that it'll happen."

"You can't see *shit*—because you never shoveled any!" he rasped. He leaned across her desk, bracing himself with his hands . . . long, strong hands with manicured nails . . . his bared forearms tensing beneath the black knit turtleneck with the sleeves shoved up. "How nice for you, that you followed in your daddy's white-collar footsteps! Just because you took over his office here doesn't mean you know *squat* about ranch appraisals, or these figures you quoted me for replacing fence and reseeding the pastures and—"

"Go talk to Daddy, then. He'll tell you the same thing."

Just to annoy him—just because she could—Jane braced her hands on the desktop too, with her face mere inches in front of his. It was a dangerous move. It showed her just how flawless his complexion looked up close . . . clear pores and the closest shave she'd ever seen. His midnight hair was layered and sprayed, and his eyebrows and short sideburns had been waxed to accent those mean green eyes . . . eyes women around the globe fell into when they ogled his magazine and billboard ads for western wear. No doubt about it, Lucky Luke McGrew was a fine, fine piece of work these days.

Not that she was interested. She let her gaze fall to his chiseled lips and made a little kissy noise.

Luke's expression curdled. "Been there, done that," he finally spat. "He told me you were in charge now."

"I guess this conversation's over, then. The luck stops here." Jane stood up straight again and lowered her voice. "I'm truly sorry about your mother's passing, Luke. I wish we could make you this loan, but when I gathered your financial data I found no evidence you could repay—"

"Oh, save it! I'll go somewhere else for my money and you can just go screw yourself!" He turned on his heel, still muttering. "Should've known the minute I saw your name on the—"

Jane winced when he slammed her door. She turned to watch him out the window then, wondering how he'd latched on to that Lincoln Navigator . . . how he'd worked as a high-dollar model for all these years yet had less than nothing to show for it. And why on earth did he want to come back to this dusty little town, after fifteen years of living the high life in New York? When he spun out of the bank's lot, his tires squealed and a chunk of gravel pinged against her window.

"That didn't go well. I'm profoundly disappointed in your lack of vision and professionalism, Jane."

"Daddy, did you even *look* at—?" She grabbed the papers off her desk and waved them at the man in her doorway. Carter Cook was technically retired, but he came in most days rather than rattle around the house alone. "You *know* how I researched his credit history—debt out the wazoo! And you *know* I appraised Patsy's ranch twice, trying to fudge for him! Just like you know it would take a monetary miracle—an act of God—to make that poor old place turn a profit! The house is a wreck! The outbuildings are falling in, and the fences—"

"Invite him to dinner tonight. We'll grill something."

"*What?*" Jane fought the urge to throw her papers up in the air and walk out—which made her realize just how badly Luke McGrew had upset her. Where did he get off, using words like "fuck" and "screw" when he came begging? "Daddy, this was a business decision! Had *you* handled his app, you would never in a million years have—"

"Luke has lost his mother, Jane. Surely you recall what a painful ordeal that is." He gripped the lapels of his pinstriped suit then, fighting a frown. His face had aged considerably since his wife died. "His two sisters are circling like vultures—never had an ounce of class or compassion between them. We don't know *why* Luke's so strapped, or why he's coming back here to live, but we owe it to Patsy's memory to give him a better welcome than you just did. Let's show him some common courtesy and a good meal, now that you've rendered your *business* decision."

And where the hell had THAT come from? Jane stared after her father's retreating, rather stooped, figure. He hadn't trusted Luke McGrew any farther than he could've tossed him when she and Lucky were kids. And Patsy's memory, well . . . a lot of wives in Enterprise weren't sorry she was gone. She'd had more than her share of troubles, starting when her first husband disappeared—and she'd capitalized on every one of them. Patsy's ranching savvy hadn't paid her bills, that was for sure.

Jane stuffed the loan papers in a manila file folder. She rarely took work home, but having those cold, hard facts with her suddenly seemed like a good line of defense for when she paid Luke a visit.

And what are you afraid of, Plain Jane? Sticks and stones can break your bones but you swore off letting Lucky Luke hurt you anymore. Grow up! Move on!

Easier said than done, wasn't it? Luke had looked *so* damn good when she'd gone nose to nose with him. And for just a moment, hadn't she seen that old spark in his predatory eyes? But *she* was the top dog in this fight! *She* had all the control over his future in Enterprise, and she'd told him a big, fat no!

If you'd said that on prom night, this would be a helluva lot easier.

No sense in putting it off. Daddy would give her that *look* until she obeyed his suggestion to invite Luke to dinner.

When she got home, Jane entered the house from the garage as usual, yet something made her walk more slowly up the stairs to her room. The house looked the same; on the surface, so much had remained just as it was when her mom was alive. But the aromas of dinner and fresh bread no longer greeted her after a day's work . . . no cheery voice called out from the laundry room. The comfortable furniture and lace curtains maintained the appearance of the happy home she'd grown up in, but she and her father both knew it was a sad, fading illusion they hid behind. The place felt like a morgue without Miriam Cook.

Jane hurried upstairs, as if she could escape her mother's absence that way. She changed out of her pretty sage suit into jeans, tennies and a T-shirt, and grabbed that loan file again. No sense in making Luke think he deserved any special treatment or primping, on her part. While she couldn't take her eyes off striking features that had matured so well these past fifteen years, she also couldn't deny that Lucky Luke was a helluva lot prettier than she would ever be. And what woman wanted to deal with that?

Out the door she went, without calling first. Lucky would only cuss her out and tell her to stay the hell away . . . and this way, the element of surprise was in her favor. The ball was in her court and she intended to keep it that way.

2

"Where's your balls, little brother? You leave 'em in New York, or did that bank bitch whack 'em off?"

Luke swatted at Tiffany's cigarette smoke and then slid Mama's cracked red ashtray across the kitchen table at her. "Fat lot of good *you* did, when *you* went to talk to her!" he countered. "Then you let me go in there cold—not knowing she was the *president* of the damn bank—"

"Well, if you'd come home once in a blue moon, you'd've known that." Crystal, on the other side of him, smashed out her cigarette and stood up to go. "I've got a business to run. All I can say, Lucky, is that you damn well better find a way to pay us our shares. Not *our* fault you can't see the plain facts about ranching this place. At least Janie got that part right."

"Or maybe you got too caught up in starin' at her boobs to think straight," Tiffany joined in again. As she stubbed out her Kool, she blew smoke through her nostrils like a dragon. "But whatever it is, you better get over it, hear me? Crys and I looked after Mama all those years—especially after she got sick last winter—and we just want what's rightfully ours. I *told*

Mama it was a big mistake, makin' *you* the executor of her estate, but you were always her baby boy. Lucky could do no wrong! Sis and I took all the crap and got none of the glory."

"I never did one thing to make Mama favor me more than—"

"You never had to, dammit!" Tiffany stood up, glaring down through the cigarette haze. "You were a boy, grown to be a man. Mama always pandered to her men—even after they ran out on her."

"Not my fault none of them stuck around!" he protested. "And from what I can see, you and Crys didn't invest any time or money on her, either. So get back in your rig and take your damn attitude with you!"

"If that's the way you want it, I'll see ya in court!" Tiffany spun on the heel of her boot and stomped across the worn vinyl floor. She slammed the front door so hard the windows rattled.

Luke shook his head. Was it any wonder his sisters had never married? They smoked and drank and swore like mule skinners. Did nothing to improve their washed-out blond appearances, and wore cheap, outdated clothes. What guy in his right man would put up with them?

Mama loved you best 'cause you smelled better, honey-bunch.

His mother's voice came straight from his childhood, in that teasing, cheek-pinching way she had. And even though the little recollection made him miss her more, he had to smile. Mama had her reasons for favoring him, and she'd obviously never shared them with his twin sisters—just like he'd asked her not to. It had been her idea for him to get out of Enterprise and make something of himself, too, but his twin sisters would never in a million years understand that.

While his mother hadn't said anything about the checks he'd sent her, she obviously hadn't maintained the place—or herself—with his money, either. Where the hell had it gone?

About the only thing he knew for sure was that Mama hadn't spent it on her daughters: Crystal still ran the corner tap

210 / *Melissa MacNeal*

and Tiffany drove an eighteen-wheeler. Neither showed any sign of profiting from his generosity, or wising up by getting out of this nowhere little town.

And since they'd all three been in to speak with Jane Cook . . . and Jane had mentioned no deposits or accounts . . . .

Jane's the key to this whole frickin' business. Now that she's got the cleavage to make her pretty smile look like a come-on, how you gonna handle her, cowboy? She's way too good at turnin' you down . . . .

Luke exhaled harshly. He carried the ashtray full of butts out the back kitchen door and dumped it over the edge of the porch. Small consolation that it was the lumpy red Mother's Day present he'd made for Mama in fourth grade, and that it still held its place of honor after all these years. He sat down in the tired old swing to think about things, now that it was finally quiet. Nothing but the steady creak of the rusted swing chains and a view for miles: McGrew pastureland stretched as far as he could see.

And yeah, it was overgrazed and dried out, and the fences were falling over. The pump system was shot, so even if he refurbished the barns he couldn't water any livestock until he replaced about a mile of pipe. Janie and his sisters were probably right about never raising this ranch from the dead, but he wasn't ready to take three women's word for it. There had to be a way . . .

"Mama, what am I supposed to do now?" He sighed it as a prayer, but also as a regretful apology, too late to do either of them any good. He'd thought his reasons for not coming home much were perfectly valid—his mother's idea, mostly. But he'd missed the big picture, hadn't he?

And meanwhile, Jane Goody-Two-Shoes had gotten shed of her braces and grown out her thick auburn curls and lost her adolescent pudge. She looked the part of a successful business-woman—the only one in Enterprise, no doubt. Quiet pride had shone all over her face while she'd watched him sweat today.

That explains why you wanted to yank off her jacket and take her on that big-ass desk, right?

He planted both feet on the porch floor, making the swing wiggle crazily from side to side before it stopped. Much as he hated to admit it, Plain Jane Cook had done a *fine* job of maintaining herself and taking over her daddy's bank. He'd called her incompetent, but those certificates and degrees on her office wall looked legit—and they didn't have her daddy's name on them. She'd talked a good story, as far as quoting the costs of rebuilding fence and reseeding so many acres and operating a ranch at today's prices, too. He just wasn't in the mood to hear her at the time . . . too damn mad about the sorry state of Mama's house and how she'd done without so much—medical treatment included—while his twin sisters had watched her decline into poverty and illness.

It made no sense! It pissed him off! And here he sat on a damn porch that hadn't seen paint for years, unable to do a thing about it . . . because Tanya had done such a fine job of screwing him over, too.

Women! Jesus, but he was glad he didn't need one anymore!

So why did Jane's face keep coming to mind? Those pale green eyes, with long lashes that fluttered over the tops of those sweet, smooth cheeks . . . the dark coppery hair his fingers had itched to caress . . . the subtle scent of good perfume that belonged nowhere near the town of Enterprise, Wyoming—not to mention clothes that showed him exactly how she'd filled out since he left this life—and her—behind.

But she'd told him *no*. Again! He'd been so flummoxed about her loan rejection, after coming home to so many other nasty surprises, that he hadn't given the right answers. But any woman could be persuaded to do just about anything. He'd staked a career and a reputation on that, hadn't he?

Luke went to the kitchen and poured a stiff snort of Crown Royal into a green plastic glass. It looked tacky, sure, but it would keep him focused on this new reality and how to make Janie Cook see things his way. Starting *now*.

How can I make Lucky see things from my side of the desk? Jane wondered as she walked. *If Daddy thought inviting him to dinner was such a hot idea, HE should be coming to the McGrew place . . . .*

Jane stopped just outside of town, where the countryside gave way to the ranch in question. While the stroll had cleared her head, the bright rays of late-afternoon sunshine did nothing to improve the looks of this property. Barns and machine sheds sagged sadly, begging to be put out of their misery.

But wow, what a view! And since most of the loans she was making these days were for acreage in the country, for home-owners willing to lengthen their drive to work, to live away from urban sprawl and crime in the big cities . . . well, she had no trouble envisioning this tract by the roadside selling for *big* bucks. Maybe there was a way for Lucky to keep his home by turning loose of some pastureland—

She jumped back from the road to escape a rattletrap pickup truck that sped past her. *Stupid driver wasn't watching! Probably yacking on his cell phone—*

But then the truck skidded to a stop on the loose gravel. It backed up, coming right at her.

Warily, Jane stepped farther off the blacktop, clutching her file folder to her chest like a shield.

"Well, if it ain't Janie Cook! Fancy meetin' *you* here!" The rough voice coming out the window sounded familiar, and when the dusty red pickup stopped alongside her she recognized the two straggly haired blondes inside it. "We was just talkin' about you! Not surprised you didn't fork over that money Lucky wants, but hey—you better get real! We intend to get our share of Mama's money! And soon!"

"If I can't make him a loan and you can't convince him to

sell, that puts us between a rock and hard place," Jane replied quietly. "You both own your own businesses. I'm sure you understand my position—"

"You better put yourself in any position it takes, sister." Crystal, the heavier-set sister who was driving, leaned across her twin to make her point. "Tiff says she's gonna get a lawyer, and I'm goin' to court with her."

Jane sighed to herself. It was so like these two square-jawed McGrews to kick up a fight rather than think about the consequences of their actions. "I can't blame you—and I can't stop you," she replied. "But I'll warn you about how much of your inheritance those court costs and lawyer fees will eat up. While it's a fair-sized ranch, land like this isn't selling very fast, and it's not bringing what most folks want when it does."

"Yeah, well, we all know somethin's screwy about Luke not havin' enough money to buy and sell us *all*!" Tiffany chimed in. "Now that Mama's not around to stick up for her prodigal son, we'll see how long he holds out with *three* women ridin' his ass!"

Crystal brayed with laughter and gunned the truck.

Left in a swirling cloud of gravel dust, Jane closed her eyes against the flying grit and started walking toward the McGrew house again. How was it that some families just never got along? While she and her dad had become closer out of sheer necessity after her mom died, the three McGrew sibs were all out for themselves. It was common knowledge that Luke had a different absentee dad, which often became a bone of contention after moms died. But if the twins got a lawyer involved, at least it would take some of the heat from *her* shoulders . . .

And speaking of heat . . . how will you handle it? He's in that little house all alone now. Where'll you run to if he puts the moves on you?

"Like I'd run," she muttered.

3

Jane walked slowly up the unpaved lane toward the little house, saddened again by its appearance: the mailbox hung open like a gaping mouth and the driveway was two parallel ruts with an overgrown grassy patch down the middle. Peeling paint and bare spots on the shingled roof bespoke a major case of neglect . . . a desperation Patsy McGrew had camouflaged behind her colorful chunky jewelry and flirtatious ways. After all, the men coming here after dark didn't see those architectural problems—and didn't care.

Her footsteps echoed on the front porch, which had pulled away from the foundation. She held her breath and knocked firmly on the screen door.

Not a sound. As if the house, too, had passed on.

Jane knocked again, louder this time. "Luke?" she called through the baggy screen. "Hey in there! Daddy wants you to come over for dinner! He's grilling—does that sound good?"

"Depends on who he's lighting the fire under."

Jane clutched the files closer to her chest. "Now why would you think my dad—"

"He never liked me, Janie." Luke came to stand directly in front of her, with only the saggy screen between them. In those black clothes, he remained a part of the shadows, veiled from her vision except for his stunning face. But that low, penetrating voice vibrated in her soul . . . and lower. "He never thought any guy was good enough for you—and understandably so. But he thought I was trash, and that I'd drag you down with me."

"It didn't help that you spread such a nasty rumor about—"

"Hey." His sigh wrapped around her, sounding dangerously sensuous. "Some guy had to go first, right? I took the rap, and you were still a virgin after all the gossip died down. But we're adults now and the game's changed, Janie."

"H-how do you mean?" Like she didn't know.

"There's no ring on your finger. You're fair game," he replied smoothly. "But I know damn well you haven't been saving it for marriage."

She raised an eyebrow. "And what business it is of yours—why do you think—"

"You're too aware of your allure. And you know how to use it." He stepped closer, so his eyes were directly behind the screen. Large, dark pupils sucked her in while he took his time gazing at her. "You can't tell me nobody's proposed. Why didn't you say yes?"

How had this conversation gone so far around the bend? Jane cleared her throat, deciding to fight fire with fire. After all, they *were* adults now and he might as well know she'd decided her own destiny. Made her own choices.

"Derek was here from Australia as an exchange student. I—I wasn't ready to marry him, with the thought I'd rarely get to come home—"

"To *this*?" Luke's extended shrug encompassed all of Enterprise. "Man, I'd've taken the first plane out of Wyoming—"

"And you did. But I'm not made that way."

Luke let that sink in as he gazed through the dusty screen at her determined expression . . . a face that showed balance and good judgment and the ability to assess and analyze and take calculated risks. God knows he could've used some of Jane Cook's practicality a time or two in his life. But what a limited world view! She had no idea what she'd been missing!

And you're about to show her, right?

He cleared his throat. Even in jeans and a pink T-shirt, Janie Cook looked way too provocative . . . something he'd never anticipated, after living in New York, where the women dressed in sleek black and understated jewelry. "I'm just surprised you never ventured farther afield," he finally replied. "You always had so much more going for you than most of us."

Jane blinked. Now *there* was a change in bait if she'd ever heard one! Switching from piss and vinegar to honey. "Thank you. Maybe that's why I'm now the bank president—a big fish in a small pond—while you swam away, into a sea of humanity in New York. Different strokes for different folks."

As he considered this—dismissed the power play in her reply—Luke realized he'd spent the last few moments watching her lips move when she talked. He shifted his weight, carefully figuring out how to propel this opportunity forward . . . into his domain.

"I appreciate your dinner offer, even if it was your dad's idea. And I apologize for the way I behaved in your office today," he said with a sigh. "I wasn't expecting Mama's place to look so run-down, or sisters who circled like vultures. And I don't take it well when a woman turns me down."

"A guy with your looks hasn't had much practice at it." *Oh, nice one! Butter him up and make him think you're interested in—*

"My looks aren't why we're talking through the door this way."

"So ask me in! If you won't come over for—"

"I didn't say I wouldn't. I just know who's destined for the sacrificial fire." He exhaled slowly and placed a hand on the door handle. "Since you made up the rules in your office, you better believe I'll do the same, now that you're on my turf. Once you step through this door, sweetheart, you'd better be ready for whatever happens."

How blatant was *that?* Jane frowned and stepped back. No way would she let Lucky Luke McGrew take up where he'd left off after the prom! That would be like excusing—or forgiving—his adolescent prank, as though—

He swung the door open. Stood there in the shadow of the house watching her . . . a powerful puma assessing his prey. *'Come into my parlor,' said the spider to the fly*, those deep green eyes taunted.

"Maybe if I took another look at those loan papers, we could come to some sort of . . . agreement," he said softly. His knit shirt rippled as he leaned slightly closer.

"Oh, get real!"

"Oh, I'm very real, Janie," he breathed. "Real impressed with how you did your homework on this loan. Real aware of how *hot* you turned out while I was away. And real, real hungry, sweetheart. But it's got nothing to do with fixing dinner on the grill."

So how come I'm feeling a sizzle? Jane caught herself glancing at his fly and jerked her gaze up again.

Luke laughed low in his chest. He stepped aside, the Big Bad Wolf ogling Goldilocks as he gestured for her to enter.

If you don't go in, he'll think you're afraid of him. And if you do . . . .

Oh, if she did, she'd get devoured in two bites: his intentions were as dark as those formfitting clothes. "Truth or Dare" had always been his best game.

"Luke, I—you don't need to think I'm—"

"Neither one of us really needs to think, do we?" He held

the door with the patience of a man who had all damn day—or all night—to test her mettle. "You stated your case at the bank, and I'm stating mine. If you don't like the terms, well, we have nothing else to talk about, do we?"

This was insane! Out-and-out sabotage! "Why do you think I'm any likelier to fall for your come-ons now than—"

"Because I know what you want, Jane Cook. You have your plan and I have mine. Shall we see who wins?"

Her throat clicked when she swallowed. If she walked away, she would lose. He could go elsewhere for money. Or just move into his mama's house without anyone else's permission, to irk the shit out of his sisters—who would in turn pester her until somebody came up with their money. "Sexual leverage has never been—"

"Who said anything about *sex?*" His eyes widened with feigned innocence. "I was inviting you in for lemonade and polite conversation."

"Like I believe that!"

"And what was I supposed to believe when you stood there in my face today, making kissy noises?" he challenged, lowering his eyes to hers. "Is that how you soften loan rejections, Miss Cook? Like smooching a guy's boo-boos, after you've inflicted the ultimate shutdown by refusing his loan?"

"It was a business decision," she rasped. "Sometimes the answer has to be no!"

"Well, here's my response to that." His arm slipped quickly around her neck—

But it wasn't like she was going anywhere, was it? Jane's pulse skittered as Luke coaxed her against his taut body. It felt like prom night all over again . . . all the anticipation of being with the best-looking guy most likely to take advantage of her. Except now that they were adults—professionals—who knew the score, she had a whole new rep for him to wreck.

And what did she fear most? That he'd try for it—or that he wouldn't?

Jane closed her eyes as her breath escaped in a rush. She was no stranger to passion, after all, and it was clear Luke wanted— *He wants control. That's all this is about! If you let him*— "You smell like . . . booze," she stalled in a halting whisper.

"Crown Royal. Good thing Mama kept some around, in case of snake bites."

Jane gasped into his mouth as he opened her lips with his. She braced her hands against his hard chest, mentally prepared for the brutal, overwhelming kiss he was going to teach her a lesson with—

And then she sighed and let loose. God, he was smooth and easy and soft and . . . all the things he hadn't been when he'd coaxed her into his camper after the dance fifteen years ago. His lips teased at her, slick and warm, while he kept a maddening fraction of an inch of air space between their bodies. He tasted like whiskey, yes, but it was the tang of opportunity she fell for. Not since Derek Flaherty took his ring back to Australia had any man come on to her, because—well, this was Enterprise and the few eligible men didn't interest her. Or they were scared shitless of a woman who ran her daddy's bank.

Luke flicked his tongue lightly around her inner lips, teasing . . . testing. She was like a skittish filly—but a filly in heat. If he waited her out . . . .

When Jane moaned softly, he relaxed. She wasn't going to cry rape or put up a fake fight, because—

Jesus, this woman knew how to kiss! She pressed into him, standing on her toes for leverage like she'd done when they were kids. But this! This was beyond anything he'd expected! Sweet yet sly; feisty yet just submissive enough to let him think he'd make some headway, now that they'd gotten this little formality out of the way. She'd been dancing around this urge since the moment he'd entered her office. No, before that, when he'd called to announce he needed a loan: when she'd sucked air at the sound of his voice, it was wanting he heard more than resentment.

Luke slipped his fingers into her hair . . . held her head in his hand so he could give her something to think about tonight after she went to bed in that room above her daddy's. Thirty-three and she still lived at home. Maybe if he stuck around he could change that.

She broke away with a little gasp. Blinked a few times and stared up at him like she didn't know what had come over her. "Luke, that was—"

"No need to analyze everything," he murmured. "A kiss is just a kiss. A sigh is just a sigh—and all that other sentimental stuff."

Her eyebrow arched. "Like you believe that."

"And what do *you* believe?"

She exhaled, wishing he hadn't been so fast on the draw with that one. "I think you lured me in, and I let you. And now that we've gotten that behind us—reminded ourselves about the consequences of—"

Luke kissed her again before she could pronounce any judgments or make any rules. This was all about keeping the lady off-balance. All about backing her toward the wall, still kissing her as the screen door slammed. He lifted her chin, keeping his palm at her jaw . . . tasting, tempting her some more . . . rubbing lightly over that pink T-shirt that had two little hard spots now.

Jane wrapped her arms around his broad shoulders, knowing it was the wrong thing to do . . . knowing she'd already fallen too far. But wait! This was all Daddy's fault, for sending her here, wasn't it?

She giggled, surrendering to his luscious mouth. He had the smoothest, sexiest skin she'd ever felt.

"What's so funny?" He nuzzled her hair and then ran his tongue lightly around her ear. It was so damn good to hear a woman laugh, he hated to break it off.

"This is all my father's fault, you know," she murmured.

"Let's leave him out of it, shall we?" Looking her in the eye, challenging her to respond or retreat, he slipped his fingers under the hem of her soft T-shirt. "It's you I'm after, Janie. You made me hot and hard when I was a kid, and you haven't forgotten how."

"Like I knew what I was doing back then. Like anything female doesn't make you that way."

"True enough," he muttered, teasing her soft skin with his fingertips. "But I know what I'm doing now. What I'm after."

"Still can't give you that loan," she whispered breezily. Or did she sound breathless because his hands were advancing on her bra . . . dipping inside it to scoop her out?

"Farthest thing from my mind right now." He closed his eyes against the urge to yank off her shirt and take her on the floor . . . managed to remember that she was heading home soon, and that if he had any balls at all he was expected to show up with her. Looking like a man with more on his mind than dipping into Janie's goodies every chance he got.

Jane forced herself to stare him down; to get her act mentally together even while his smooth, warm hands were turning her to putty. "Lucky," she breathed, trying to sound like she meant this. "Making love to me right now will get you nowhere—except in deeper shit with my dad. And me."

"Who said anything about making love?" he taunted. But after another playful squeeze of her full, ripe breasts, he tucked her back into her bra. "Whatever happened to good old-fashioned fucking? There's a time and a place for that—and maybe we need to leave out the romance and expectations. Makes things a lot less complicated."

Jane tugged her T-shirt down, smiling demurely. "Ah, but

you said you didn't like one *fucking* thing about me, remember? Case closed. You coming? Or staying here to drown your sorrows?"

"So close to coming you were within a heartbeat of getting nailed," he replied in a hoarse whisper. "Now get on home. Tell your old man I like my steak medium rare. Pink and juicy in the middle, like your pussy."

Jane's jaw dropped. "Tell him that yourself, smart ass!" She shoved him away, ready to walk out before she fell for any more of his tricks—except there seemed to be papers scattered all over the floor.

She had no clue when she'd dropped them. And as Luke McGrew disappeared into a back bedroom, the soft laughter trailing behind him said she'd lose a whole lot more than her mind before he was finished with her.

4

Jane smiled out the kitchen window. Not only had Luke brought a bottle of wine, he'd had the horse sense to walk around back, to where her father stood beside the smoking Weber kettle grill, watching over steaks that smelled so heavenly her stomach rumbled.

Or was she really hungry for Luke McGrew? God, he looked fabulous in close-cut jeans and a clean cowboy shirt of blue and green plaid. It made him seem down-home, yet nobody around *here* had ever looked so sleek and sophisticated in a shirt like that. Nobody around here had those shoulders . . . .

"Mr. Cook, good to see you, sir," he said smoothly.

When he stuck out his hand, Daddy shook cordially . . . made small talk about how long it'd been, yada yada. Yet, as Luke had insinuated, her father was up to something. While she expected him to remain businesslike, Jane sensed a hidden agenda for this impromptu get-together with this local bad boy come home.

She busied herself with slicing tomatoes into their salads, so they wouldn't think she was eavesdropping on their guy talk.

And what *would* she say at the table? She'd made it clear the loan wouldn't be reconsidered, so—

"Next time I see you at a kitchen counter, I want you to be wearing an apron. With nothing under it."

Jane turned to gape at him, all cocky ego and presumption despite his quiet voice. He set the bottle of wine—a fancy merlot—beside her and stood closer than he was supposed to.

"Nice of you to bring that."

"Least I could do, since you two saved me from sipping my dinner all alone in Mama's poor little house." He glanced around nonchalantly, as though he, too, had ulterior motives. "Looks just like I remember it."

"Yeah, well, Daddy's not big on change since Mom died. It's like the house became a sacred shrine to her memory—"

"So get your own place. Then we could do it whenever we wanted."

Her salad tongs clattered against the cut glass bowl. Before she could turn to be sure her dad wasn't coming in, Luke caught her head in his hand.

"Just teasing," he whispered. "You know how I've always loved getting a rise out of you, pretty Jane."

"Yeah, well—" She sucked in some breath to keep from getting all woozy at the smell and feel of him. He'd showered. And up close, Luke McGrew was just *way* too good-looking for mere words. "I can remember a time when Plain Jane couldn't have turned your head with a crescent wrench—"

"And aren't we glad that's behind us now?" As though warned by a sixth sense, Luke stepped backward, still smiling. "I'm all for progress, Jane. Up for any ideas you might have about how I can keep Mama's ranch and get my sisters off my case."

"Creative financing. That's Jane's forté," her father said as he stepped in from the patio. "Three minutes on those steaks, dear."

"Okay, thanks." She sprinkled shredded cheddar over their salads, listening to his footsteps in the hallway . . . the creak of the bathroom door closing.

Luke moved in. Cupped her jaw and kissed her senseless—as though she had any smarts left after today's previous encounters.

She released him with a sigh that said way too much. "Look," she whispered, shaking the tongs at him, "you've got to stop this hanky-panky! I already got a suspicious looking-over when I came home from—"

He chuckled—and damned if he didn't kiss her again, stepping away only when the toilet flushed down the hall.

"So what sorts of creative deals have you made, Miss Cook?" he asked a little too loudly. "From what I can see, Enterprise needs to be dusted off and given a whole new reason for being, or it'll blow away with the tumbleweed. Mighty sad, to see so many storefront windows soaped over."

"I suspect your sister would be hurting, too, if she didn't own the only tavern in town." Her dad smiled as he reached into the cabinet for wine glasses. "But you're right on the money, Luke. We're not long for this world if we don't figure out a way to revitalize. Urban renewal on a small but intense scale—without all the big-city problems associated with that. Seems to me *you* might have some ideas along that line, since you've made such a name and face for yourself now."

"Thank you, sir. I take that as a compliment."

"As it was intended." Daddy popped the cork and poured three glasses of the dark, shimmering wine. "So I hope you won't mind if I pick your brain as we welcome you back—even though, having overheard the way you reacted to Jane's loan refusal today, I'm looking for a little sucking up tonight, as well. Nobody talks to my daughter that way, Mr. McGrew."

Go, Daddy, go! she thought. But again she stayed out of their conversation by carrying the salad bowls to the table in the dining room. Sucking up? When had Carter Cook ever used that terminology?

"I apologized to her at the house, yes, sir." Luke flashed her dad a dapper grin as they came to the table with the steaks. "Being upset about Mama's passing and my sisters' grabby attitude is no excuse for the language I used. It was totally inappropriate—especially considering how professionally and thoroughly Jane presented her data to me. It won't happen again."

Talk about sucking up . . . kissing up . . . She didn't miss the secretive grin on Lucky's face when he sat down across from her. She saw his intention to tease her and flirt all during dinner.

"Actually, I've had a neat idea about your mother's property," she began, passing him the bread basket. "And as I walked over this afternoon—admired the roll of the landscape and the view from your pasture gate—I envisioned a whole new complex. A sort of wellness and pampering retreat—with a spa and resort villas. Time-shares, even. Maybe a southwestern theme." She held the basket when he tried to take it. "But you said selling the place wasn't an option."

"Nope, it's not."

"Then how do you propose to pay off your sisters?" her father asked pointedly. "Frankly, we're both astounded at your financial situation, Luke. You've been well paid for those high-scale modeling jobs. Resistol and Gucci—not to mention pro rodeo and Marlboro—don't hire just anybody for their ads."

Luke cleared his throat and cut into his steak. "I'm sure even here in Enterprise you've heard of identity theft?"

Jane blinked, her bite of meat poised in front of her mouth. "Of course we have! But I can't imagine—"

"You can't imagine my talent for latching on to women who, as thieves in very pretty disguises, have stolen various parts of me over the years." McGrew looked from her to her father then, his expression guarded. "I haven't told my sisters this for obvious reasons, but you might as well know that I was married for a short while—until I found out she'd cleared out my accounts before she cleared out, period."

Her father's pale eyebrows rose as he considered this, chewing. "I hope you've taken legal recourse—"

"How? With her name on our joint accounts, it was easy pickings. Completely legal. But it won't happen again."

"Marriage? Or getting stiffed?" Jane gazed coolly across the table at him. If Daddy could dig around in this man's past, she saw it as her chance, too.

Luke smirked. "Like I said, I have this talent for attracting the down-and-dirty ones. Let's see, then there was the addict who kept faking her way through rehab—which I paid for out of the kindness of my naïve heart. And after that, an actress who needed a place to stay so she'd be off the streets until she got her big break—"

"Your famous face and generous nature make you a magnet for that sort," her dad replied.

Jane considered this. While her father often did the hard bargaining—local guys his age just couldn't bring themselves to talk money with her—she read people very quickly and accurately as they hammered out repayment details. Not only was Daddy sincerely listening to Luke's unfortunate story, McGrew seemed to be revealing a character flaw she hadn't expected. He'd lost that *tone*—that "you Jane, me Tarzan" attitude—and was actually confessing to a weakness.

That was a new one!

Without visibly moving above table level, Luke stretched his long legs to capture her ankles between his. So of course, with Daddy looking on, she couldn't react. "Yes, I've been told many times I'm way too nice. Just not by anyone around here," he added pointedly.

Daddy cleared his throat. Rose from his chair and opened the top drawer of the china closet, a man on a mission. "That comes as no surprise to me, Luke. And I, too, have kept a secret or two from your sisters, because your mother asked me to when I began managing her financial affairs."

Jane sat taller. What was *this* all about? That was a savings account passbook in her dad's hands.

"You see, Jane, while folks around here were busy faulting Luke for so seldom coming to see his mother, he was sending her money every month." Her father slipped the little book over to their guest, smiling benignly. "More times than I can count, I tried to convince Patsy to get a new roof, or to maintain her outbuildings, but she was too stubborn. Too proud to spend money from her boy, yet so damn proud that he'd sent it."

A gasp made her look up. Luke was staring at the book, blinking back tears. "She didn't use a dime of it. Deposited every last—"

"She told me once you might need it. She knew what a fickle life modeling could be, even for a famous face like her son's." Her father sat down again, moved by Luke's agonized expression. "It's yours, Luke. Not enough for a down payment, or to leverage a loan, but by the looks of your balance sheet you might be able to use it."

"I—thank you."

The room got tightly quiet for a moment. Why was she so taken by the grief on that handsome, well-known face when only moments ago Luke McGrew was on the make—the wolf at her door, howling to get into her pants? "I made us a chocolate pie," she murmured as she stood to stack their plates.

"Sounds good, honey. Then I have a little . . . dessert for you, too."

And what did *that* mean? Maybe, since her dad so rarely drank, the wine was making him loopy. Or maybe he was just so damn glad to have someone else to look at while they ate dinner. They'd rarely entertained since her mom died.

Quickly she cut the pie, grateful for quick-setting instant

pudding and Cool Whip to make it look a little festive. Grateful, too, for the chance to blink away a few tears of her own, after seeing Luke's face crumple. A mother was a huge person to lose, and even after seven years she still got choked up . . .

"My God—she's pasted—these go all the way back to my first shoots!"

Jane blinked. Luke sounded like a little kid at Christmas out there! The flipping of pages made her scurry for fresh forks and then back to the dining room.

"Your mother was way ahead of the scrapbooking craze," Daddy was saying. Damned if he hadn't scooted his chair around so he was sitting beside Luke as they looked at a large photo album. "Patsy scoured the racks—even went into Laramie and Cheyenne to get the classier magazines our stores don't carry, so she'd have the full progression of your career. Nobody prouder of a son than she was, that's for sure."

"That's why I came home so seldom," he said softly, gazing at another page of glossy ads. "Mama didn't want me to miss a single opportunity. She *told* me to travel wherever the work was, because she'd always known there was nothing for me around here. My sisters never understood that," he added in an edgier tone. "They always bitched that Mama *favored* me."

"I was younger than my sisters, too. And they were merciless about letting me know how spoiled I was," her dad remarked with a sad laugh. "Claimed our mother catered to my every whim while they had to toe the mark."

Jane raised her eyebrow at this one: Grandma Cook had never catered to *anyone*, that she could recall! And why was Daddy waxing so sentimental?

"There's something else you must know about your sisters, however," he said, glancing at her in a meaningful way. "Something Jane wasn't aware of when she researched your property and rejected your loan proposal. It changes the lay of the land, so to speak."

When he got up and went back into the hallway, Jane stared across the table at Luke, who was staring at her. He leaned toward her, and she did the same, as their hands reached the center of the table.

"What the hell is *this* all about?" he breathed.

"I have no idea—honest!" she whispered. She craved the warmth of his large hands wrapped around hers, yet wondered if it was wise to want him so much. "I had no clue about the passbook account—or your album—"

"Mama told me she kept it in her bedroom! Where my sisters wouldn't find it!"

And *that* made things more interesting, didn't it? Jane pulled her hands away and straightened in her chair, forking up a bite of the pie she couldn't taste. Luke, too, cut into his dessert. His flawless features looked ruddy with emotions she'd never seen on his face: Lucky Luke McGrew had never explained anything to anyone! *He* was always in the know and always right—at least when they were kids—and surprises like these didn't sit well.

As Daddy entered the room again, Jane watched him from the corner of her eye. He seemed composed enough, in control of this situation . . . but how had he known to fetch Patsy's scrapbook from her bedroom? He managed finances and estate details for several of his aging bank customers, because they'd been his friends for years and they trusted him to carry out their wishes. But *this*. This went above and beyond anything . . . unless . . .

Oh, surely not.

"Sorry it took me a moment. Several pages to account for." Her father smiled at them both again, yet Jane suspected he'd been . . . upset. Right now, Carter Cook was not the powerful banker coming down on the errant client for nonpayment or, God forbid, to initiate foreclosure.

Again he sat beside Luke, to spread out two sets of papers

that looked like . . . well, like legal documents. As her father took a moment to collect his thoughts, he slumped a little beneath whatever consequences he foresaw from what he was about to reveal.

"Another reason Jane cannot approve a loan to you, Luke, is that there's a lien on the property. A transaction she knew nothing about, because your dear mother hoped it wouldn't come to this. You see, she loaned your sisters—"

Luke's expression tensed.

"—a considerable amount a few years ago, when the refrigeration units at Crystal's Corner Café went out. Crys was already behind in paying her taxes, so she had no cash to cover this expense—or the updating of the dilapidated wiring that was at fault," he explained quietly. "And of course, because Patsy gave such an amount to one twin—"

"Tiffany got a chunk, too," Luke finished wearily.

"Precisely. To the tune of a new eighteen-wheeler, because she'd lost so much over-the-road time while her rig was in the shop." Her dad shuffled the top pages to reveal what looked like letters beneath them. "She intended to take a second mortgage on the ranch, but I encouraged her not to endanger her home and financial situation. I—I loaned her the money myself, with the stipulation that if it were repaid—as your sisters agreed, verbally, to do—the transaction need not be recorded."

Jane's eyes widened. She'd had some practice at reading documents upside down, and she was seeing five figures beneath each twin's name. "I can't believe—what if they never repaid—"

"Patsy knew her children well." Daddy's expression was indescribable . . . sad yet a bit sanctimonious. "She insisted we write up loan documents, in the event she passed on before the girls repaid her. Her signed statement confirms the twins' agreement to repay, and that any amount outstanding would be charged against the estate—"

"Which means Crys and Tiffany already *have* their shares of the ranch!" Luke blurted. "They borrowed against their inheritance, so they have no room to demand repayment from me!"

"That's part of the bottom line, yes. The rest of it is that these liens against the property are now repayable to First National Bank of Enterprise, because Patsy insisted—and I agreed—that I was to be repaid if the girls neglected this responsibility."

Jane watched Luke stare at the duplicate letters, written in his mother's pretty hand, and at the cold, hard facts on the loan papers Daddy had filled out and executed—without telling *her*.

And why would he do that? Jane mused, nipping her lower lip against an outburst. *What's he really keeping secret here?*

She didn't dare ask. Luke had enough to grapple with as he skimmed the documents.

"So you're telling me that while I don't have to pay my sisters—"

"I'll remind them of this myself, yes."

"—I don't have enough money to pay off the lien, either, so I can claim the ranch for myself?"

Daddy cleared his throat in a way that never boded well for his client. "The bank holds title to your mother's ranch now, Luke. Believe me, we never intended for this to happen. I'll do all in my power to convince your sisters—"

"Oh, this is rich." Luke stood up, raking a hand through his perfect hair. "My sisters have ignored their debt, believing I had enough money to hand them as their *shares*, so they could collect twice! They figured Mama would never inform me of this—"

"And frankly, I can't believe you loaned her the money." Jane gazed steadily at her father, more shaken that she cared to admit. "We've discussed the potential risk of becoming personally involved with our clients—even though they're our close friends—because—well, just because circumstances like *this* happen more often than anyone believes!"

She stood up, trembling. "Is there anything else you want to tell us, Daddy? Like why Patsy McGrew rated so much *personal* attention, above and beyond your duty as her—"

"Watch out, now." His face went annoyingly blank. "Better not ask questions you might not like the answers to, dear daughter. Not that I'd reveal anything that transpired between Patsy and me, because—as you know—client confidentiality becomes an issue."

"Oh, that *is* rich! Too rich for *my* blood!" she rasped.

And for the first time in her life, at the age of thirty-three, Jane Cook ran away from home.

5

Luke caught up with her as Jane was turning down one of the back alleys behind the storefronts along Main Street. She was walking very fast and very stiffly, and he knew exactly how she felt. Betrayed. Stunned. Appalled at the possibilities of what his mother and her dad might have shared.

"Janie, wait! I'll walk with you," he said as he rolled up alongside her.

"Whatever!" she muttered. But she didn't slow down.

He parked the Navigator at the curb—right behind Crystal's Corner, he noted. How ironic that his sister's place was throbbing to the beat of country boogie booming from the jukebox while his world was now quietly falling apart. He dashed down the alley, dodging a Dumpster to grab Jane's hand. "Honey, I'm sorry for what went on back there. I had no idea—"

"Me neither, but the pieces are falling into place." As she riveted her gaze on the uneven street ahead, tears glistened on her face. "I just can't picture Daddy stooping to—spending his evenings with—"

"Hey! For what it's worth, I can't picture Carter Cook getting naked with *anybody!* And maybe we're both jumping to conclusions. Maybe we need to compare notes, you and I."

With a loud sigh, Jane slowed her pace. When she reached the last building on the block she sagged against its old brick exterior. "That didn't come out the way I intended. About your mom, I mean."

"Mama was wired that way. Always trolling for it, and always able to catch some," he replied softly. "It was one of the reasons she wanted me to see the world, I think—so I didn't see so much of *her* world, once I was old enough to know the score." Luke slipped his arm around her trembling shoulders. "And if it makes any difference, maybe your dad was just really, really lonely. Without your mom—"

"Yeah, yeah, I know about all that. I've watched him drag himself from one day into the next—and my living at home and running his bank have probably limited his . . . social life." Jane shook her head, making her long auburn hair shimmer in the final light of dusk. "I just didn't think he'd do anything so blatant—like writing that loan for the twins—behind my back."

Nodding, Luke nudged her forward. He couldn't stand still—too damn keyed up about that passbook account and his deceitful sisters. And maybe too aware of how vulnerable and defenseless Janie Cook seemed right now. Putting the moves on her was totally inappropriate.

Or was it? Was she so professional—so far removed from the average man—that she couldn't share her outrage with—

Hey, who you calling average here? his ego rebelled.

Smiling wryly, Luke tightened his grip on Jane's slender shoulder. "But now the cards are on the table. It's a damn fine irony that my sisters get nothing from me! They'll have to endure your dad's little chat about repaying their loan, and pay interest on it, and handle all those official details that've come back to bite them now. Which leaves you and me on the same side, far as what to do about Mama's ranch. And about me staying there."

As he'd anticipated, this rational banking talk revived her. Jane straightened her shoulders, looking at him with catlike green eyes that glimmered as the street light flickered on.

"How do you mean, we're on the same side?" she asked warily.

He shrugged. "Doesn't take a rocket scientist to figure out that I'm still screwed. Maybe a change of attitude is in my best interest. Maybe I might listen more attentively now to your ideas about that spa."

She held his gaze, still assessing him—not that he blamed her, after the way he'd gone ballistic in her office this morning. "You serious? It'll mean huge changes in your property, Luke."

"Progress works that way. I can't honestly say I was looking forward to life without cable TV and no restaurants other than my sister's bar." Against his better judgment, he gently thumbed away two tears that dribbled from her bewildered eyes.

Jane relaxed and drifted against him. Buried her face in his shoulder—maybe to blot her eyes, but maybe because she was as needy as he was. It felt even better than he'd anticipated when she wrapped her arms around his waist. Never one to waste an opportunity, Luke pulled her close.

"I shouldn't be doing this," she mumbled. "It means I'm no different from Daddy, getting too familiar with a client who—"

"It means that, just like him, you need somebody to lean on. Somebody to talk to. Is it a breach of bank policy to be *human*, Janie?"

He felt her pulse thrumming in rhythm with his own. Warned himself not to fall for any tactical maneuvers she might pull as she tried to win him over to her argument. But when she looked up at him, his insides went soft and warm while something else got hot and hard. *Very* hard.

He lowered his face, watching for little signs of her rejection, but those long lashes fluttered against her cheeks in sweet surrender. Luke kissed her, softly at first, until her moan spurred him on.

Damn, but she knew how to push his buttons—on purpose now, he suspected, yet he went along with it. Her lips searched his for answers they both wished they knew, and in a rush of emotion, Luke hugged her tight...rubbed his body against hers as their mouths commiserated. A couple of cars went by and one of them honked.

Jane jerked and her eyes flew open. "This is a bad idea! It'll be all over town that I—"

"So let's take this home and put it to bed. Figure things out between us without any interference or interruption," he said in a ragged whisper. "It's going to happen, Janie. We might as well take the edge off."

It was the weakest come-on line she'd ever heard. Surely a guy fresh from the Big Apple knew more original, creative ways to coax a woman into bed!

But she fell for it—hard. Instead of cussing his situation or accusing her of a set-up or bemoaning the way Daddy had broadsided him, Luke McGrew was comforting her. She didn't like to admit she needed comfort, but maybe she had to roll with the punches in her changing world, just like Luke did. He made her too aware of how isolated her life felt. And frankly, she was damn tired of being held in such high esteem—and at such a social distance—because she ran the biggest bank in the county. Here was a man willing and eager to make her body purr—and gee, he just happened to be the best-looking hunk this town had ever seen!

Without even a token protest, Jane stepped up into his cushy SUV. She didn't swat away the hand that boosted her backside with a suggestive squeeze. And she didn't ask this man who was so far in the hole how he drove such a pricey vehicle, either: its tinted windows shielded her from any nosy locals they might drive past.

Luke took the bumps and curves faster than he should've, and when they hit the McGrew gravel lane just outside of town he sent up a shameless trail of dust in their wake. Without a word he escorted her through the back porch door. He slammed and locked it in one urgent move, and then pinned her against the wall with his body.

"If you want out of this, speak now," he muttered against her ear. He was raking his hand through her silky hair, gyrating against her with obvious intent. "Don't say later that I took you against your will or used sex to get what I wanted, Janie. It doesn't work that way now."

She snickered. "Oh, it *does* work that way, Lucky, but I won't run away from you this time. They say a good fight clears the air and hey, since we're not fighting each other, that energy will—"

"Shut up and kiss me within an inch of my life, woman."

Something went high and tight inside her. Derek, world-class adventurer that he was, had never challenged her this way, had never made her feel all feral and . . . *free*. "Fuck me like you mean it, Luke. Make me glad I held out back then and fell for you now."

"Yes, ma'am. Whatever you say."

He was all over her, kissing and squeezing and gasping for breath when she did. Jane fumbled with his shirt buttons to reach inside that close-cut plaid cotton and caress skin . . . hot, smooth skin that bespoke pampering like her own body never got. He felt muscular and fit. When her palms shaped themselves to his pecs, he sucked air.

"Let's go upstairs," he said, grabbing her hand. "If your daddy comes looking for you, this'll be the first place—"

"He has a key, you know. I thought he was just checking up

on your mama after she got sick, but—" Jane followed him with quick, short steps through the shadowy little living room toward the stairway. "—the way I feel right now, if he walks in on us, he'll see what he sees, dammit."

"You *are* pissed!" Luke pulled her against him for another kiss that made her head spin. "Something tells me this'll be a whole lot better than when I tried to trick you into it fifteen years ago."

"Damn straight. Back then I was protecting my reputation. Right now I'd welcome one."

At the top of the stairs they stopped, but this time it was Jane who launched into him with a ravenous kiss. He steered her into a small bedroom at the front of the house then, and without taking in many details, she surmised that Lucky Luke's room hadn't changed one bit since he'd moved away. She could imagine Patsy McGrew slipping into her son's domain any time she needed to remember the boy who'd left Enterprise—and his mama—behind for bigger and better things.

And as Luke peeled off that western shirt, Jane was ready for a bigger and better thing herself. She'd declined Derek's proposal nearly ten years ago; had dated sporadically since then. Even though this tryst was borderline sleazy—something she'd have turned up her nose at this morning—she had a different world view now.

And the view, when he yanked down his jeans, was magnificent.

He wore stretchy little briefs—black and red checked—but it was the way he filled them out that held her attention. Her hands stopped midway at peeling off her conservative shirt—because when this man of the world got a look at her panties, it might all be over.

"Does me good to have a woman like you gawk at me, Janie. Don't stop."

He found the edge of the twin-size bed with his backside so he could yank off his boots—and then Jane found herself between his knees. Helping him remove those boots, of course.

But his jeans weren't completely down his legs before she reached for that bulge between them. "I'm gonna suck this till you holler," she announced, and before he could think about dodging her, Jane scooped him out of his skivvies.

He didn't have any hair there, either—which meant his skin was sooo smooth and hot as her lips traveled quickly down to the root of him. He wasn't all that long, but he was the type who'd make the most of every inch.

"Jesus—Janie—"

She grasped him and moved her lips and tongue wetly around, up and down his shaft. Luke fell back on his elbows to let her play. He watched her closely, moaning low as his hips shifted with his arousal.

"Don't think for a minute you're gonna get away with making me explode in your mouth, and then calling it good, girlfriend. I've got fifteen years of wet dreams to make up for. I'm taking everything you've got."

Little shivers of electricity flashed inside her. Had he really wanted her all this time . . . dreamed of the girl who'd run from him so long ago? It made a good bedtime story, anyway. So she decided to buy into it and not ask too many questions.

With a final tight suck up the length of his cock, Jane looked him in the eye. "One snicker at my white panties and it's all over, cowboy."

His eyes glimmered in the shadows. "Maybe I like white panties. Maybe it fits with what we're bringing back from Memory Lane here. But I want to take them off you. Stand up."

Heart pounding, blouse hanging open, Jane rose before him. Luke deftly unzipped her khakis and tugged them over her hips, drank in the sight of her for a moment, and then hugged her to his face to inhale deeply.

"Oh God . . . oh God, I can't believe I've gotten this close," he breathed. "You smell like a real woman—none of that perfumy stuff—and I have to take what I want *now*."

He yanked her panties down and rubbed his clean-shaven face against her curls. A hand wedged between her legs and Jane yelped when his fingers slipped inside her. Her knees buckled and she balanced herself by grabbing his shoulders.

"I found something the lady likes," he murmured with a devilish chuckle. "Tell me how much."

Was that low, desperate moan coming from her own throat? Jane's head fell back and she gave in way too quickly to Luke's nimble, knowing fingers. She throbbed for him. Her body rocked to the rhythm he set so effortlessly, straining toward release.

And then he nailed her with his thumb, high and hard.

She screamed. Felt the rush of honey as her hips wiggled shamelessly in Luke's face. Not even undressed, and she'd succumbed to this man.

"Luke, I—we'd better—"

"You're not finished till I say you're finished, sweetheart." Effortlessly he wrestled her sideways, onto the bed beside him. "Last one with any clothes on has to do what the other one says."

As she yanked her khakis past her feet, Jane realized that losing this game wasn't such a bad thing . . . and right now she'd do anything Luke McGrew commanded. Never had she felt so driven by inner need: full speed ahead, and damn the guilt and the consequences! Beside her, Luke jostled the bed in his rush to be free of his clothes—

So Jane stalled. If he wanted to be the master and have her at his command, well, when might she ever get to play this game again? She toed off her shoes, getting her fill of his lithe movements: the way his whipcord body moved with such wild animal grace . . . the lust and eagerness in his gaze when he saw she was watching him.

"I hope you don't mind it hard and fast this time, Janie. I haven't felt this charged up in a long, long while."

And didn't *that* make her feel good? She'd barely gotten her pants off when he swung her sideways and angled himself over top of her. Luke pinned her to the mattress and gazed down at her with bottomless eyes that glowed in the fading light. He yanked open the nightstand drawer. Pulled out a condom and slipped it on so fast Jane knew it was a well-practiced move, yet she was fine with that. At least he was more responsible with sex than he was with his money.

"Take me deep inside your hot, luscious cunt," he commanded, "and then wrap those gorgeous legs around me and hold on tight. This cowboy's ready to ride."

He thrust inside her without ceremony and Jane got lost in the smooth, swift force of him. He wasn't rough, just urgent. Driven by the same demons she was when she began thrashing against him. His down-and-dirty talk and the way he expected her to comply without question had kicked an edginess into gear, and Jane rushed hellbent toward whatever madness or miracles this man could perform.

He stroked her hard, his corded arms bearing his weight on either side of her head. Luke's gaze never wavered: he looked directly into her eyes as his face and body tightened with his escalating excitement.

"God, Janie, you're so damn tight," he rasped. "I'm not gonna last. Gotta run with it and fuck you and fuck you and—"

They wailed together with his climax and then Jane surrendered to her own—so thoroughly caught up in Lucky's magic that she went mindless. Succumbed to a high-flying oblivion that made every inch of her body curl inward.

After several breathless moments, Luke rolled off her. He landed beside her in the narrow bed, still quivering.

Jane lay very still until her body came down from a high like she'd never imagined. Was that what an orgasm was *supposed* to feel like?

"I—I hope I wasn't too rough, or—"

"You were wonderful, Luke," she sighed. "Way more than I bargained for. Way more than anybody I've ever been with."

Should she have admitted that? He might think she was totally clueless about—

Talk about clueless! You should never have agreed to this! her conscience badgered her. *You have to go home now. Daddy'll know exactly what you've been doing—and you still have this property issue to settle, remember?*

"Something I said?" Lucky whispered. He propped himself on his elbow to watch her face. "If I was too—"

"It's me," she rasped. "Already wondering if the best bedding of my life is the worst thing I could've done. Why can't I just let go and enjoy myself? Enjoy *you*—"

"Because you're too damn grown up and buttoned-down." He kissed the tip of her nose and got out of bed with a reluctant sigh. "I might as well take you home, Janie. Your old man didn't come looking for you, but he just walked in on us, didn't he?"

6

Jane unlocked the bank Saturday morning with a sense of dread so heavy her head pounded. *What the hell was I thinking? Out of the frying pan into the fire—but I'm not nearly finished getting flamed.*

Her dad had cleaned up the dishes and gone to bed by the time she'd gotten home last night. He'd kept to himself this morning, but he'd be in his office within the hour. No doubt in her mind he'd play Twenty Questions—and no doubt Luke would show up to rub her nose in it, too . . . remind her how hot she'd been for him, and expect that to put him in a better position, as far as where the bank stood with his mama's property.

She'd show him a *position*, all right! She'd lean over and pat her ass so he could kiss it! And when his sisters came in, all pissy because Daddy had revealed their little secret, well— Daddy would be the one dealing with them, wouldn't he? Those McGrews were *not* going to take control of—

And that's what this was about, wasn't it? Control. The feeling that she could plan her destiny—and maybe Lucky's, too— and carry it through. The sensation of calm and competence she felt when she walked into her office and sat down behind her impressive desk.

She did that, and closed her eyes. Let the solidity of this old, reliable banking institution settle into her bones. By God, she'd weathered take-over attempts from larger banks, as well as fists shaken in anger when notes came due and crops didn't come in. This little blip on the radar screen was nothing, in comparison.

If Daddy had been in Patsy's pants, well—that was his way of moving on after her mom's death, wasn't it? Just like a man, to go sniffing after whoever batted her eyelashes at him. Despite Carter Cook's old-money white-collar ways, it was almost a relief to know he hadn't been totally dependent upon her for company. Hadn't been totally lonely—

Like you??

Jane sighed. Okay, so maybe her dad wasn't the only one who'd succumbed to the comfort of intimate contact. Like Luke had insisted, it wasn't against bank policy for her to be human—*not* that she'd fall for every little thing *he* said!

Much more confident now, Jane clicked into her computer to check her day's schedule . . . just another Saturday morning, with no appointments. She could clear away a few details on the Stoddard Livestock Auction's purchase of adjacent acreage and—

"Morning, Miss Jane."

"Good morning, Lacey." She smiled at the young intern who was spending her summer here earning experience toward her MBA. "If you'll take the window and the drive-up, I can finish some paperwork. I'm not expecting a soul. Don't know about Daddy, though."

"Yes, ma'am. I can handle that."

Jane dismissed her with a smile, envying her fresh face, stylish blond hair, and cute little figure. She'd started up the ladder the same way, and—

Was I ever that young? That fresh and eager?

"Damn straight I was!" she lectured herself. "And I'm the

top dog now because I've paid my dues and done my time. Not many women in Enterprise can say that!"

Satisfied, she clicked over to the Stoddard file and immersed herself in its figures and legal details. Nothing like black-and-white sale papers to clear away the murkiness of emotions and doubts.

"Miss Jane? There's uh, somebody here to see you. Says it's urgent."

Lacey's breathy voice made her look up. She couldn't miss the intern's flustered expression . . . the flush on those cheeks. "Who is it?"

The young blonde laughed nervously and lowered her voice. "The hottest damn cowboy I've ever seen. You call me if you need anything, hear?"

Before Jane could blink, she caught sight of a bold black hat and that smile known around the world. Except maybe by Lacey, who obviously didn't recognize their homegrown super-model from the magazines.

"Thank you, Miss Reese," Lucky cooed as he read the girl's name tag and shook her hand. "Miss Cook is expecting me."

Lacey all but passed out in the doorway before Jane dismissed her with a wave. Then Luke swept in, a man on a mission in his long black duster, wearing black tooled boots ornamented in silver and that black cowboy hat slung low over his eyes. He was Walker, Texas Ranger, Clint Eastwood, and Paladin all rolled into one. As he shut the door behind him, Jane reminded herself that he was on *her* turf now.

"Good morning, Miss Cook," he crooned, sounding like the class Romeo sweet-talking his teacher. "We need to talk."

"Do we now?" Jane stood up, leveling her gaze at him . . . trying her damnedest not to fall for his bad-boy charm. "I'll go first, then. If you think for a minute that last night changed anything—that I'll fall for your pathetic come-on lines—"

"Fall for this, Jane." A wicked grin slashed his handsome face as he whipped open his duster.

She blinked and her jaw dropped. "You're not wearing any—"

"Thought I'd make my *point*, right off. No beating around the bush—unless it's your bush, of course."

Her cheeks flamed and she giggled nervously. "You can't just come sashaying into my office without any—"

"Why not? I've got your attention, don't I?" he countered. "Thought you'd like to see that I've got plenty of balls, and I intend to have my way. You started this, little mama, and we're not through playing yet."

"Cocky sucker, aren't you?" she muttered, hoping her dad hadn't arrived in the office on the other side of her wall. Luke's cock was part of the picture, all right—and it was pointing right at her . . . daring her to drop her defenses and play his dirty little game. "No matter what surprises Daddy pulled out of his hat last night, you still can't have your loan, Lucky. The bank holds the title to—"

"And what was it you proposed? A spa resort? With a southwestern theme?" Luke stepped slowly toward her, oozing lust and an incredible physical presence. When he stopped, that shaft was still pointed at her like a pistol, just above her desktop as he placed his hands on his hips to hold the duster out of the way. His skin was smooth and tanned, and while his abs didn't resemble a body builder's, he didn't show an ounce of excess flesh, either. How well she remembered the feel of that firm, taut flesh teasing hers as he thrust into her—

"Actually," she wheezed, "I'm thinking a *cowboy* spa is just the ticket! After the way Lacey fell all over herself—assumed you wore pants, like a normal customer—"

"Nothing normal about me, Janie. I came on like a caveman last night, and I'm here to mend some fences and maybe—"

Something clicked then, and Jane crossed her arms to concentrate on the new idea taking shape very rapidly in her mind.

A cowboy spa! With hot male massage therapists and hair stylists tricked out in western wear and—and if Lucky Luke McGrew was here to mend fences, well, why couldn't he start on his mama's property? Build a few new ones and flash a little muscle and pour a little sweat—no, a *lot* of sweat—into this idea she was about to make a reality?

"Your body language says no, sweetheart, but that little grin is saying yes, yes, *yessssss.*"

"Say yes to my proposition, cowboy, and we'll both get what we really want. I just love a win-win situation, don't you?"

"I don't play if I can't win."

"Good." With quicksilver speed, she reached across the desk to shake with him—but it wasn't his hand she grabbed. "Come around here, so you can see the Web sites I've modeled my idea after. I think you'll agree we're at the perfect time and place to—"

"To fuck your pretty little brains out," he continued with a low growl. "I thought this desk would be the perfect spot to consummate our deal."

"*No way.*" She let go of him, then, to sit quickly in her chair and swivel it so her back was to him. "Daddy'll be in any minute, just on the other side of this wall."

"And don't I just love a challenge?" he whispered. He was leaning over her shoulder now, breathing against her ear as she feverishly clicked into the sites showing similar projects in Arizona and the Dakotas. "I'm sorry you retreated into your chair—acting all scared and coy—but I'm gonna fix that, Janie. Have a notion to just bend you over this desk and lift that pretty skirt—"

"See what these folks have done?" she demanded pointedly. "Rustic-looking cottages and condos scattered along the rim of that valley for the view, with a central facility for—"

"I know the view I want," he murmured against her ear. "I like this one, down the front of your blouse, but in the dark last

night I didn't get to see that ever-lovin' ass that does such wonderful things to a pair of pants. Show it to me now. Naked."

Jane swiveled to face him head-on. Luke dodged her chair,
but dammit, he was ready for her: he shrugged out of his duster,
to reveal his totally nude—and totally awesome—torso for her
inspection.

"I think you'll like my . . . bargaining tool," he quipped, thrusting it at her. "Come on, baby, what's one little lick gonna hurt?
Just to show me you can be a sport about all this spa develop-
ment stuff. You've got me by the financial balls and you know it."

Clad only in his black hat, boots, and a sly, sexy grin, Lucky
Luke McGrew had to be the most magnetic, most awesome
man she'd ever seen: smooth, bronzed body . . . a shaft that vibrated, just begging her to take it seriously—

*Good God, what else could you possibly want? He's offering
himself up like a sacrificial lamb.*

Well, maybe a sacrificial ram.

Exhaling forcefully, she focused on his sleek black hat. "Is
that a Resistol, Mr. McGrew? Something from one of your ad
shoots?"

"Yes, ma'am! Top of the line—"

On impulse she grabbed it and put it on her own head. It
slid back, way too big, but that didn't matter. "So now that I'm
wearing this, *I* can resist all. At least until I have my say about
this business proposition."

He rolled his eyes. "Lucky and I cannot believe you're being
such a hard-ass about—"

"Lucky?" Jane glanced at his cock, which still begged for attention only inches from her face. "You call it Lucky, do you?"

"That's usually the case for him, yes."

"Ah." With a giggle she stuck out her tongue to wiggle its
tip around his little hole. "As I was saying, I'm thinking we
could put our full-service spa facility just beyond that pasture
gate down from the house—"

He sucked air and caught her chin in his hand. Those deep green eyes blazed at her so fiercely her mouth fell open—

And then he nudged his cock between her lips. Or had she leaned forward to take him in? Jane closed her eyes, knowing she'd been bested—this time. Knowing she could no more sit here and talk business to this hot, naked cowboy than she could build and staff a new spa by herself.

Something else clicked and her eyes flew open. Luke was easing forward and back, savoring the sensation of her lips around his member, oblivious to any business but his own ... but he was just the man to help with other aspects of this project, wasn't he? He had to have hair stylists and massage therapists as friends out the wazoo back in New York—and Lord knows he had the charisma to lure them out here! How exotic was that, to advertise world-class services, right here in little old Enterprise?

With a moan, Jane sucked him harder. She gripped his hips, loving the feel of his firm ass as she slid her lips up and down the hot, hard length of him. Luke was panting now, tightening all over with desperation.

He pulled out of her mouth then, and raised her up out of her chair to kiss her, no holds barred. His tongue entered her mouth and Jane gasped, inviting it in to play with hers. She lost all sense of time and place—all fear about who might be listening through the wall or from behind her door—but she and Luke were being excruciatingly silent, weren't they? Wasn't that part of this little game, to get away with the unthinkable, here in this staid, sterile bank office?

Inhaling harshly, Luke shoved her chair out of the way. He was all fiery eyes and intent now, and one little nudge backed Jane against the edge of her desk.

"Spread 'em, cowgirl," he rasped. "We're gonna make some noise without making any noise. Then we'll see about this spa thing. Got it?"

She nodded mutely. What choice was there, really? He wasn't forcing her—but then, he didn't need to. His hat fell off her head as he tipped her backwards, balancing her on her blotter as he raised her denim skirt up her legs. Her pulse thundered. This was so wicked—so—so inappropriate!

"What if Lacey—or Daddy—walks in?"

"Then we'll have a three-way, won't we?" he murmured against her ear. "Tell me how bad you want this, Janie. I can feel your heat. I can smell how ready you are. Spell it out, now."

Words failed her. "Luke, I don't think—"

"Good. We said before it's better to leave that part out." He grabbed his hat from her desktop and damned if he didn't slip a foil packet out of its inner band. "Lucky here's a man of action. Likes to go with the moment. But he loves a little encouragement—even takes directions pretty well."

She held her breath as he sheathed himself in shiny black latex. God, but that thing looked wicked . . . capable of irreparable damage to hearts and reputations, same as it was fifteen years ago.

"I think you better just shove that cock inside me," she rasped. "You know damn well I want it in my—"

"Do you? Prove it," he taunted. "Maybe a little begging would be in order."

She curled her lip—more at her own surrendering than at his cheeky attitude. He was all man—and he was all hers if she let him do it his way. "Please, Lucky," she whispered, putting an extra little whine in it. "Please fuck me. Hard and fast—and swallow my screams in your white-hot kisses while you're at it."

His smile blazed like a summer afternoon. "Anything you want, Janie," he whispered sweetly.

He entered her swiftly and claimed her lips with his. Jane fell back onto the desk with the sheer, exhilarating force of him. She speared her fingers through his feathery hair and kissed him hard, humping upward to meet his thrusts. He was hunched slightly, angled to go deep into her most sensitive inner parts . . . against that elusive G-spot no man before had ever discovered.

Exhaling hard to keep from wailing, Jane buried her face against his bare shoulder and let him ride . . . hung on for dear life as the white fire spiraled within. Her desk was creaking, but there was no stopping such a storm once it blew up.

Luke grunted and began to pump with uncontrollable need. Jane rode it out, her own body soaring just ahead of his to a peak that left her mindless and tight with the effort of keeping it quiet.

He shuddered violently. Held her close for a moment. Caught his breath against her ear, where it tickled her sensitive neck.

"God, you're good," he murmured. "Worth coming home for."

She let out the breath she'd been holding and managed a grin. "Good thing that Resistol fell off when it did, or we'd still be fighting it."

"Oh, we'll fight it again. Real soon." He looked up, listening. "Don't move."

He reached for his hat again and this time pulled out a length of paper towel folded around a couple of packaged wet towelettes. Jane watched in sheer awe as he gently wiped her off and dried her before cleansing himself.

"Now you know why cowboys love these hats," he whispered with a devilish grin. He eased her skirt down and opened his arms.

Jane came up off the desk into a soft, sweet hug she wasn't expecting.

"Now then," Luke said as he picked his duster up from her office floor. "Tell me again about that cowboy spa."

7

An hour later, Luke buttoned his duster and gave her a final lingering kiss. "Hope you're happy now," he murmured. "It's a pleasure doing business with you, Janie."

After he opened the door to leave her office, he turned to give her a suggestive wink as he tipped his hat. "We'll get together about these details soon as I've called my buddies back east."

"Make them an offer they can't refuse," she said. "It's their chance to do world-class work and set everything up just the way they want it. Money's no object."

"Easy for *you* to say. I'll be the one busting my butt to pay them off." With a smile that made the wanting flare inside her all over again, Lucky left her office—no, he *swaggered* across the lobby to make that duster sway just right, knowing Lacey and her customers were watching him. His boots tapped a confident tattoo across the tile floor in a rhythm that caught up her heartbeat and asked it to dance.

As the Navigator purred to life outside her office window, Jane sat at her desk grinning. Her pulse thrummed and she was so damned excited she made a fist and pounded her desktop in victory.

"Yes! Yessss!" She swiveled her chair to gaze at that Dakota resort's home page again, envisioning her new spa's classy web presence . . . something sleek and sexy, classy yet playful . . . black leather with hot pink lace, maybe. A magnet for the women who'd pay big bucks to come here.

"You're shameless, Jane. Absolutely shameless."

Her breath caught in her throat and she composed her face carefully before she looked toward the door. There stood her father—all suit, white shirt, and elegant tie—wearing that stern, patriarchal expression that had always reminded her of Winston Churchill. When he closed the door, Jane braced herself for the lecture he'd probably been preparing since last night. As she straightened her shoulders, she saw a telltale damp spot on her blotter and reached for papers to shuffle over it.

"Good morning to you, too, Daddy." She folded her hands over those papers and acted the part of the cool, confident bank president—even though inside, she was quivering like pasta in hot water. She was getting away with nothing. Never had, with this man.

"Sounded like you two were . . . pounding out quite a proposal in here." Her father glanced pointedly at her desk and then reached into her waste basket.

Jane's face flared before he even fluttered the torn foil wrapper between his fingers.

"This is not how we conduct business at First National, Jane. Especially when we already hold all the financial cards," he said in a low voice.

Something snapped. She wasn't a child anymore, dammit! "Seems you don't have much room to talk, considering how—"

"No finger-pointing, young lady. I'm not going to stand you in the corner or ground you for what went on in here, because it's the opportunity I've been waiting for."

Oh, here we go! Reverend Cook's about to deliver his sermon. She did her best to remain unruffled and calm. After all, if her dad knew so much about what she and Luke were doing there was no point in avoiding this conversation. He had just as much to answer to as she did.

"I've never seen you look so beautiful—or so happy, dear. High time, too." His face softened as he tossed the condom wrapper back in the trash. "You look so much like your mother sometimes, it kills me. Except when she was your age she laughed a lot more and sparkled with the joy of living—of raising you."

Her mouth clapped shut and tears burned her eyes. Where had *this* come from? And where was he going with it?

"And while I had to express a bit of fatherly disgust just now about how you and Luke McGrew are setting each other on fire," he continued quietly, "at least you fell for a very successful man who knows how to knock you off your pedestal. It's icing on the cake that he happens to be good looking and that he's apparently come back to stay."

Her mouth drifted open, but no words came out—a fact her dad found extremely humorous, judging from his chuckle.

"I was worried you'd never find anybody—let alone someone who dazzled you. Because that's just what your mother was best at, Jane. She dazzled me every day of the forty-eight wonderful years we had together." He clasped his hands in front of him, gazing down at her with a deep wistfulness. "I didn't want you to miss out on that, tucked away in this nothing little town on the edge of nowhere. While I'm so damn proud that you followed in my footsteps—continued my legacy here in Enterprise—I never intended for you to sacrifice yourself. Life's too short, sweetheart."

Jane wiped away a stray tear. Once in a blue moon her father waxed this sentimental, and frankly, she didn't know how to respond. She'd always been so self-reliant and focused on business, she'd gotten little experience at this emotional give-and-take—especially with her dad. Mom had always been her corner-stone, the one she identified with and modeled herself after. And right now Jane missed her desperately.

"Thank you, Daddy," she murmured. "I never considered this position a sacrifice. It's all I ever wanted to do."

"And you're damn good at it. And I don't say that often enough." Her father cleared his throat then, with one eyebrow arched slightly. "And having stated all that, I want you to know how it was between Patsy McGrew and me when—"

"That's your business!" she protested, raising both her hands to stop him. "And if I overstepped by—"

"You're going to hear me out whether you want to or not. Luke's mother suffered enough from the wagging tongues in this town while she was alive, and I'm going to clear away this particular cloud out of respect for the woman she was. And the man I am."

Jane went limp. Sat back in her chair. Better to hear him out and decide later what she'd really learned, and what she would believe.

"It's no secret that Patsy McGrew had a certain . . . magnetism. An aura of forbidden fruit that made her attractive—fascinating—despite her run-down ranch." A little grin played on her father's face. "She liked to make people feel special. Liked to spoil them and please them. I got to know her better when Doctor Dale hinted that she wasn't filling her prescriptions because she couldn't afford to, because I knew Luke had been sending her money for years."

"He's appalled about the condition of the ranch—and about how she probably died of treatable conditions." Jane shook her head sadly, recalling how bedraggled and anemic Luke's mother had looked last time she saw Patsy alive. "He also said she sent him away after graduation. Probably so he wouldn't see how much . . . company she had."

"Always took care of everybody else first. Believed it was

her fault that Luke's shiftless father just never came home one night," Daddy added sadly. "So Patsy felt worthless as a person. Poured her emotional and financial energy into insuring that Crystal and Tiffany would always have a living, whether or not they had men in their lives."

"And that . . . vulnerability—the safety of knowing she wanted no further attachments—was what made Patsy attractive, wasn't it?" Jane murmured. "That aura of need gave men something noble and honorable to justify the attention they paid her."

Was that what Luke saw when he looked at *her*? Someone who needed to feel better about herself, rather than a woman who made him so hot he couldn't wear clothes under his duster? Jane had never thought of herself as needful or lacking, but maybe perceptive men saw things she didn't.

"That was part of it, yes." Her father shifted his weight, yet he didn't seem apologetic or nervous. "But mostly, I just liked her. She knew how to be a friend, and she was a wonderful, sympathetic listener. I needed that after your mother died, even though I denied it for quite a long while. Trying to protect you, I suppose."

Jane knew damn well what kind of friendship Luke's mama had offered up in Daddy's grieving need. Looking back, she could connect the return of his confident walk and sense of purpose to evenings and afternoons when he'd been away . . . golf games that never really got played and maybe even meetings with other Wyoming bank officials that never got attended. Or hadn't even existed, except as his alibis.

But was that so horrible? She'd felt great relief when her father's hangdog expression had finally disappeared, because she hadn't been capable of fixing it. If Patsy McGrew had done that for Daddy, well, why couldn't she just be grateful that consenting, lonely adults had found comfort together?

"I obviously didn't change Patsy's mind about how she handled her financial affairs, however. And it's no secret that none of her children are good at managing their money, either. Nor are they adept at forming solid, lasting relationships."

Her father focused on her with that unflinching gaze that had always made her squirm. "I strongly advise you to check into Luke's reasons for leaving New York as thoroughly as you researched his credit history and assets," he insisted. "He's a disaster waiting to happen, and I don't want you getting sucked into an emotional maelstrom. Our stability and closeness as a family hasn't given you much experience with—or defense against—dysfunctional relationships."

Dysfunctional? Jane couldn't think of a single thing about Luke McGrew that didn't function! "Point well taken, Daddy. I've been curious about his homecoming myself, and I intend to dig deeper before I commit our resources to this spa project."

"Good girl. I knew you'd remain practical and levelheaded."

Practical? Levelheaded? As her father left her with a smile, *stable* was the *last* way Jane felt when she thought about Lucky Luke McGrew. As she gathered up the papers on her desk, that dark, damp spot on her blotter made her grin with the recollection of how it got there. Never in a million years had she imagined succumbing to a naked cowboy here in her office—just as she'd never anticipated the dizzying peaks Luke drove her to so effortlessly.

She glanced at her computer screen again, sighing pensively. If she was going to make her spa resort come true, she couldn't do it alone. And it wouldn't get done by just sitting here wishing for it.

Her gaze wandered to the data on Luke's loan app . . . to the phone numbers of modeling agencies he'd worked for, and his personal references.

She picked up the phone. Time to find out just what they thought of Lucky Luke McGrew in the Big Apple, and why he'd left them behind.

8

"Josh? Josh, it's Luke McGrew. Hey, man, I've got the opp of a lifetime out here, but you've got to move fast!"

Luke paced the sagging back porch, surging with energy as he gazed out over the pastures that had held so little promise only yesterday. He might've swept Jane off her feet with his big, bad cowboy act this morning but if he was to make good on his side of this deal, he had to come up with a whole lot more than Lucky.

"Your ass is in so much trouble I shouldn't even be talking to you," the stylist replied in a waspish whisper. "Tanya dished the dirt about you to some bank bitch this morning, and she's spreading the word around New York, too. If she has her way, the Feds'll be breathing down your neck any minute now, dragging you back here where you belong."

Luke winced. If Jane had already spoken to his agent—*ex* agent—he'd have some tall explaining to do. He glanced toward the road, even though no squad cars would show up any time soon. "So Tanya misses me, does she? Well, I'm done with her, Josh. I fulfilled all my contracts and I'm a free man—if you can overlook my being in hock up to my eyeballs, thanks to her."

"She doesn't see it that way."

"She can't see anything but her next fix and her next big deal. I'm finished living that way, Josh. Finished tiptoeing around her damn mood swings."

His friend sighed over the phone. "Yeah, well it's been crazy here without you. Marlboro and Resistol are steamed because they'd planned their new campaigns around your ugly face—"

"Their mistake."

"—and Tanya's whirling around here like a hurricane in heat—"

"Another reason—the *main* reason—I left," Luke insisted.

"—so if you don't get your ass on a plane today, there won't be much left of anybody," the salon owner finished with an exasperated sigh. "She'll have bitten all our heads off."

"Listen to yourself. Is that the way you really want to live?" Luke smiled, damn proud that he could assume the confident tone of a man with all the answers . . . a man who'd seen that the world was spinning out of kilter and had gotten the hell out of Dodge before it blew up in his face.

"I've gotten us a sweet new deal, Josh," he went on. Again he looked out over the dried-up pastures, seeing them in a shiny new light. "Brand new spa resort, starting from the ground up, and we're in charge! I need somebody to hire and manage the personnel—that would be *you*, guy—and somebody to make quick, spot-on decisions about floor plans and decor and all the equipment acquisitions. My partner's drawn up the financing and I'm already . . . hip deep. But we can't do it by ourselves."

There was a pensive pause. "How's the money? I mean, if I'm supposed to just drop my entire life to come running out— where is this new venture, anyway?"

"Enterprise, Wyoming. Clean air, fresh start, sky-high opportunity—and no Tanya," Luke added triumphantly. "I feel like a new man—like a junkie come clean! I wake up each morning without *fear* of what's going to go wrong!"

Another pause. "What're you on, McGrew?"

Luke laughed out loud, loving the way it carried out over the ranch—soon to be *his* ranch again! "That's my little secret! But I promise you'll feel just as fantastic after you see what I'm cooking up out here. Money's no object, but the lower tax base and cost of living means—"

"Where the hell is Enterprise, Wyoming?" Josh interjected. "Just Googled it and I didn't bring up a single hit."

"And you can change that! You can be the man with all the savvy for this new cowboy spa—"

"*Cowboy* spa? You've gotta be kidding—"

"—and you can bring your pick of stylists and massage therapists! Bring your chef friends and whoever the hell you want!" Luke continued exuberantly. "Think of it as world-building, except it's not Second Life on your damn computer. It's the real deal, Josh."

"Hold on a minute."

Luke could picture Josh Honn covering his cell phone with a perfectly manicured hand as he walked away from his reception area. Honn Salon would be a frenzy of egos and high-strung stylists and their temperamental clientele at this hour, so if Josh was escaping to his private balcony to talk, it was a sign he might get serious about such a devil-get-screwed proposition.

"Okay, I'm back." Without the whine of hair dryers in the background, Josh sounded more focused—and ready to rumble. "So you're hooked up with another damn woman and she's already worked you over? Are you fucking *crazy*, Luke?"

McGrew chuckled. It amazed him, how comfortable he felt with this whole thing in such a short time. "Partly right on that. But calling my professional friends from New York to staff this place was *her* idea. It's not just a resort and a cutesy cowboy spa, Josh—it's a new lifestyle for the locals. A way to keep our town on the map. And it's such a damn fine idea, I wish I'd thought of it myself."

"I thought you'd sworn off women who fuck you once and then expect you to support them forever," Honn countered. "I'm really worried about you getting into—"

"Relax. I've got this totally under control."

"You say that every time!"

"But this time, the woman in question knows exactly how deep in the hole I am. We've leveraged my debt into a . . . unique bargaining position. Using her bank's money."

There was a pause and then Josh coughed. "Come again? Somebody else's money is behind this?"

"Yep. That bank bitch who called Tanya? She holds the purse strings here—and since you're one of the references on my loan app, she'll probably call you, too," he replied. "I'm giving you this heads-up so you can say *yes* like you mean it."

"Waaaait a minute, buddy. What's really going on here?" Josh sounded wary now; ready to run the other way. "I own a business—a big, successful business, remember? You're not making any sense here."

Luke's thoughts raced as he looked out over the rolling pasture again for inspiration. Honn sounded ready to hang up: he was in the middle of his business day, after all, and didn't have time to talk about screwball ventures that made no sense to him.

And then Luke spotted a graceful horse and rider in the distance.

His heart sped up. He recognized Jane Cook's pretty silhouette: she was visualizing the layout for this new resort . . . obviously something dear to her heart, or she'd never have proposed it to him. She'd have shut him down with that loan rejection and let him storm out of her office—out of her life—yesterday . . . could've found a way to foreclose on the ranch so she could proceed with the project on her own.

He swallowed hard, realizing what he would've missed out on between now and then. Jane urged her horse into a canter that looked so damn free—so damn beautiful—he knew he'd better make his case with Josh right now. In a matter of minutes she'd be heading for the house, to get the low-down on Tanya and why he'd parted ways with her.

"Okay, here's the deal," Luke insisted. "When I came back home, I had no idea my twin sisters had borrowed against Mama's ranch, so the bank holds the title to it. I also had no idea that the bank owner's daughter was now the president—or that she'd changed from a gawky, freckle-faced redhead with braces into the most gorgeous, sophisticated—"

"So you *are* hung up on a woman again, only this time she's floating *you*," Honn interrupted. "Hey, thanks for asking, buddy, but this sounds like an arrangement I can live without. Gotta go, Luke. Talk to you later." *Click.*

Luke winced. His gaze hadn't wavered from Jane . . . the way she looked so damn perfect sitting a horse and riding across the ranch, backlit by endless blue sky and sunshine. This was more than just a business venture to her: it was a personal investment. A dream that would bring this entire town back to life.

As the breeze caressed his cheek like his mother had so many years ago, he could hear Mama's smoky voice: *You can take me from rags to riches with this project, Lucky. It's my big chance to be Cinderella.*

Luke glanced around, half expecting her to materialize beside him. Spooky, the way he'd had no sense of Mama's presence until he came home. And he couldn't ignore it.

So he had no choice, did he? With two powerful women like Patsy McGrew and Janie Cook urging him along, he had to make this dream come true.

9

Jane saw him standing on the sad old porch and her heart skittered like a new foal on its first frolic. Even without that bad-ass black duster and hat, Lucky Luke McGrew looked lean and mean as he stood with his shoulder against the support post. He was watching her as though he'd expected her to ride up this way . . . as though he was getting ideas that didn't include laying out a resort facility.

And what should she believe about this cowboy-come-home? He'd grown up riding horses and bucking bales like all the local boys, but becoming a supermodel in New York—appearing in ads with the Marlboro and Resistol names behind him—changed a man.

Obviously—if you can believe a word Tanya Valdez said.

"Easy, Tucker," she murmured to her mount. "We've got to plan our strategy, because that's exactly what Luke's doing."

Her palomino gelding tossed his head and whickered softly, eager to be out running again. When she'd given him his head first thing, before slowing down to assess the lay of this ranch again, the sheer joy in his flawless gait had reminded her that she took him out far too seldom these days.

All work and no play makes Janie a dull girl, she prodded herself.

But right now she had to press Luke for the truth . . . the down-and-dirty answers to questions his airheaded agent had raised during her rant on the phone. If her Web site was accurate, Ms. Valdez managed some *very* impressive talent, but sheesh, what a lot of *static* that woman put out! She wanted Luke McGrew back because his face was worth millions, but Jane wasn't so sure about the information she'd heard between the lines. Some of it just didn't jive with the Lucky she knew.

Or had he changed beyond recognition? Had he covered his ass with so many convoluted stories that he didn't recognize the truth anymore? She'd listened with her libido instead of her brain, and that had to stop.

As she got within yards of the ramshackle house, Jane composed herself. No more falling backward with her legs spread. No more falling head-over-heels for the bad-boy prodigal son who'd left a string of broken hearts in his dust, including hers fifteen years ago. *She* was in charge, and he needed to remember that this project went nowhere without her full approval.

A slow, sexy smile spread over his face as she eased Tucker to a halt in front of him. "Good afternoon, Luke. Your agent, Tanya—"

"*Ex* agent," he insisted.

"—Valdez dished up some pretty heavy dirt about you when I called her this morning," she continued firmly. "If I don't get some straight answers, this deal's dead in the water."

"I can understand why you'd say that. And before I agree to anything further myself, I insist we call the place Patsy's Ranch. Not the hottest promotional hook, maybe, but Mama just told me she'd give us her blessing if I'd name it for her."

266 / Melissa MacNeal

Jane blinked. From atop Tucker's sturdy back she looked down at Luke, but this psychological advantage didn't really give her any emotional distance. If he was pulling his mama's memory into this—playing on how much she missed her own mother—well, that tactic wouldn't work! And from what she'd known, Patsy McGrew wasn't the sort of woman who'd cared about her name being in prominent places. She was just looking for a way to get her bills paid.

"Let's not put the cart in front of the horse," she replied. "Tanya told me you skipped out on some contractual obligations and left her in a bind. You might be the modern-day Marlboro man wearing the black Resistol hat, but I can't have you fronting for my resort if you won't honor your promises and—"

"Tanya's the reason I got the hell out of New York. She's always just a snort away from total destruction, Jane." Luke looked her straight in the eye. "She'll say anything to keep the money coming. Steals it when she can't earn it fast enough."

Jane's brow furrowed. "Was she stealing from you?"

"Damn straight she was! Set me up with those credit cards you saw on my loan app, so I could track my travel expenses, and then she bought her damn cocaine with my ATM cards!"

Luke shifted, clearly uncomfortable with these recollections. "I could've—should've—prosecuted, but it involved dragging her high-dollar dealers into court. Not fuckin' likely!" he added with a sad laugh. "By the time I saw through all her phony stories—realized that when I couldn't reach Tanya by phone, it meant she'd disappeared into a coke haze—my name was on some overdrafts that would fund a third world country."

She'd researched that part . . . had wondered about so many large withdrawals from banks around Manhattan and the Bronx. "Do you suppose she did that to her other clients, as well?"

"Maybe. But I'm guessing the other ones caught on to her

sooner—or handled their own expense accounts. Like I should have."

"She was your lover, wasn't she?"

Jane braced herself for his answer, watching his expression closely. No doubt in her mind, by the tone and content of Ms. Valdez's frenetic diatribe, that while Tanya was dipping into Luke's accounts, he was dipping into her. It shouldn't matter: a hunk like Luke McGrew wouldn't be without a woman. Yet Jane blinked a couple times, as though preparing her eyes for a major crying jag she couldn't let Luke see.

Why not? Haven't you hidden from your emotions—yourself—long enough? Luke's not the only one who needs to come clean here. He needs to know how good he is at hurting you.

Sighing, Luke shifted his weight. "You've seen how it is with me, Janie," he confessed ruefully. "I'm a sucker for a pretty woman and sometimes Lucky does my thinking for me."

"Ah. So it was all Lucky's doing that you took me to bed and then took me in my office and—"

"NO!" He grabbed her arm, his face tight with regret. "I was so damn glad to be with a genuine person—somebody whose head wasn't messed up with all the drugs and the lies and—well . . . I've always been sweet on you, Janie. Even if I made that stupid bet about whether you'd let me into your panties after prom."

He gazed into her face, looking more vulnerable than she'd ever seen him. "It's a moment I'm not terribly proud of," he admitted, "and I totally understood why you weren't happy to see me in your office requesting a loan. I'm sorry, Janie. When word got around about that prom dare, Mama laid into me. Told me if I couldn't behave better than that, well—I might as well just leave home, because she'd kick me out anyway."

Jane raised an eyebrow. She hadn't heard that version of Luke's going-away story. But it still stung that everyone in Enterprise knew what he'd tried, on a dare from a drunk buddy that night.

It's time to let go of that. You've got bigger fish to fry.

Even as she had this thought about releasing her past demons, Jane didn't like it when Luke let go of her arm . . . hadn't realized how his touch affected her, even when they were fully clothed and having a serious talk.

"Let's keep your mother out of it for now," she said in the most resolute voice she could muster. "If I'm to believe what Tanya told me, she's on her way out here to haul you back to New York for—"

"Yeah, well she's full of hot air! I wouldn't go with her, anyway! Hard as this may be to believe, I'm home for good, Janie." His volume rose, along with the swarthy color in his cheeks. "I see this resort as something worth investing myself in. Something, finally, that would make Mama proud of me and keep me connected to my roots. Such as they are."

She softened slightly and then reminded herself not to. "No doubt in my mind your mother thought the sun rose and set with you, Luke. That scrapbook she kept was a clear indication of—"

"Yeah, well, I didn't respect her enough to take her advice, did I?" he asked in a ragged whisper. "She told me to go find myself, and I used that as my excuse to only come home a handful of times in fifteen years. Maybe a dose of her down-home reality could've helped me avoid barracudas like Tanya Valdez!"

Janie shrugged. Didn't want to declare victory until they finished this chat, even though her hopes made her stomach flutter. "I can see why you fell for her," she murmured. "Tanya's a fashionably tiny blonde who wields a lot of power—"

"She dyes it. Seldom eats because her system's so messed up," he refuted. "And her power? It's mostly in her head. She has some very effective, efficient employees covering for her."

"So how does she conduct such a highly visible business? Don't the suits from those huge ad agencies know she's unreliable?"

Luke sighed tiredly. "Tanya has an amazing way of appearing quaintly eccentric and helplessly blonde. It makes people—"

"Meaning men? Meaning you?"

"—overlook her destructive habits," Luke continued with a sigh. "Hell, I'm guessing the heads of those ad agencies might've been snorting right along with her. So, to them it wasn't an issue!"

"Was any of that cocaine for you, Luke?" It wasn't a question she wanted to ask, but in a town like Enterprise, rumors of a drug habit would get the resort shut down before they even broke ground. No matter who'd financed it.

"Absolutely not." Once again he stepped forward to grasp her, this time at the knee. "I know how bad all this sounds. And I'm sorry Tanya ran you through her ringer. But I'd've been less than honest if I hadn't listed her on my loan app, right?"

Luke's eyes looked clear and green . . . that deep green of a peaceful forest in full shade, inviting her to explore its cool depths. No evidence of substance abuse. No mannerisms or diverting his gaze because he was being insincere. "Yeah, I guess that's right," she murmured.

"So why don't you come inside? We'll put pencil and paper to your ideas about Patsy's Ranch, and I'll tell you about the guy who wants to come run it." He smiled that gotta-have-it smile and added, "I made lemonade, too. Squeezed the lemons myself, hoping you'd come over."

10

Jane exhaled slowly as his gaze dropped to her breasts. Luke wanted to squeeze those, too. And if she went inside with him, prying eyes wouldn't witness it. She was on his turf again—

Hell, he took control in your office this morning! You're a fool to believe any place is safe!

Safe. She'd worked hard for personal security and financial independence, but when she was with this gorgeous New York cowboy nothing was sacred or secure. So what was a girl to do?

He falls for powerful women with money, remember? Play him for all he's worth! If the resort doesn't work out, the money's still yours—and so's your pride this time. Have some fun with this!

Jane grinned wickedly. It was a potent idea . . . an idea so right for this moment. "Seems like a good time to talk about ways you can . . . work off the bank's investment in your ranch," she purred. She unfastened her top button with a come-on sigh. "After all, a viable repayment plan has to be in place or we can sketch out plans all day and they won't mean a thing."

"I don't push a pencil all day for anybody." Luke's growl

was the masculine version of hers. He was getting into this little game very nicely.

"So we need to set a value on your physical labor. Clearing out brush and rotted fence, for starters, and then construction work, once the . . . erection's underway," she quipped. "Sweat equity, we'll call it."

His breath escaped from narrowed nostrils. "You saying I'll earn repayment points by sweating over you, too, Janie? Didn't think you were that kind of girl."

"We'll think of that as servicing the loan—and the loan officer," she murmured. "My official accounting will begin once we've signed on the line—but you could persuade me to consider these initial . . . *consultations* as payments, too. Retroactively."

Slowly Jane dismounted, taking full advantage of the way Luke was watching her body. She took her sweet time stroking Tucker's muzzle and telling him he was a good boy as she wrapped the reins around the porch post. When she turned toward Luke again, her heart was pounding. "I could sure use a long, tall drink of that lemonade while we discuss our business."

He grasped the front of her shirt, between her breasts, and led her inside. "I think you'll be amazed at how fast I get this loan paid off, Ms. Cook. Of course, we need to clarify who owns the resort and spa properties and who owns the land they're sitting on."

"Details! I suspect we can hammer them out with no trouble at all, if we keep ourselves . . . open to opportunities." She laughed as the screen door slammed behind her and Luke pulled her into his embrace. "Now tell me about this personnel manager. Josh Honn, is it?"

Luke kissed her senseless for several long, lovely moments and Jane let herself fall into it head-first.

"Josh who?" her cowboy murmured. "Right now it's just you and me, sugar, and I intend to take full advantage."

"No, *I* do. Pull down your pants and sit your ass over there," she said, pointing to a chair beside the old chrome dinette. "I gave Tucker his exercise this morning, so now I'm gonna ride *you*, Luke."

The surprise in his eyes made her feel bad and bold—like a woman from the wild west who had horses and cowboys alike eating from her hand. Luke's zipper sang a randy song, and when he lowered his jeans, Jane chuckled.

"Did Tanya leech from your accounts to the point you can't afford undies?" she teased. "You seldom wear any."

"I like to stay ready for *you*, Janie. Tanya's in New York—history now—and we're gonna leave her there, all right?" He shoved the denim below his knees. Landed in the chair with his legs spread and a come-on smile that wouldn't quit. "Lucky's ready to earn his keep now—see? I can't wait for you to straddle my lap and just riiiiide, Janie, ride!"

Something about Luke's happy song and his blatantly male face sent her pulse into overdrive—not to mention the ripping of foil and his swift sheathing of that high, hard cock. A bright red one this time. And then there was the sight of that tanned, luscious body above his half-mast jeans and western boots. Quickly Jane stripped off her own jeans and shoes, leaving her blouse open.

Time to be the woman on top. Time to sate this man and herself once more, so they could get down to the real business of planning Patsy's Ranch.

"Your name for the place has grown on me," she confessed as she swung a leg over his lap. "Has a sort of retro sound that'll appeal to the folks around here and from the cities. I'm thinking they'll be our core clientele—at least until we get your face into some national ads."

"You think too much." Luke's hands spanned her waist as he challenged her with those deep green eyes. "Right now, a good lap dance'll go a long way toward starting my repayment plan."

When he coaxed her against his erection, Jane undulated so her breasts would tease him, too. She felt way too wayward and free when this man handled her! Lucky was hard and insistent, poking her midsection. And when Luke burrowed into her bra with hot kisses, she knew it was all over. Any sense of control she'd had was all an illusion, wasn't it? When she felt all steamy inside, like a sexy volcano about to erupt, who *cared* about control, as long as all their itches got scratched?

"Gonna ride you now, Bronco Boy," she rasped against his ear. "I hope you're ready."

He lifted her, and when the tip of him brushed her damp pussy she sucked air. "And I'm gonna put you in your place now, Janie," he responded with a randy laugh. "We'll see who rides and who gets ridden."

He lowered her with a playful roughness and thrust high and hard inside her. Jane cried out with the sudden sensations—with the joy of making love where they could make all the noise they wanted.

Luke slipped lower in the chair—the better to angle himself inside her. God, she was hot and playful today, and he was every inch her fool. He thrust into her warm wetness, clenching his eyes shut against the need to release so soon. She did that to him, in a way no other woman had. They were all after his money as they gazed at his face—and Janie was, too, but he could consider this an investment in his future. Her payback plan seemed endlessly appealing . . . just as Jane Cook did.

Again he inhaled her fresh fragrance and then nuzzled the soft skin of her breasts. She quivered in his grasp, letting out raspy little moans that spurred him on. It was a far cry from Tanya's cool, quiet distance, as though she endured him until it was over so it could be all about her again.

She's behind you. Pissed because you closed those credit card accounts and ducked out.

Luke smiled with that realization. Holding Janie close, feeling her hot cunt sliding up and down the length of him with her accelerating need, felt far more satisfying than anything he'd known in years.

She drew up and held herself there to tease him. "Your mind's a million miles away, Luke," she whispered. Her warm breath tickled his ear; made him wiggle beneath her. "I'm gonna make you shoot so hard you won't be able to think about anything else, ever again. You'll be my slave, Luke. My cowboy toy. You'll be giving these command performances at the drop of your bad-ass black hat, whenever I say so."

"You're my willing victim and you know it. Take *this!*"

As he arched up to nail her in that spot that left her brainless with her mouth hanging slack, Jane closed her eyes with the sheer joy of it. For so many years she'd wondered if any man would want her this way—for something besides her position at the bank—and it felt damn good to inspire such unadulterated lust in a man as handsome as Luke McGrew. As the spasms began, she wrapped her arms around his shoulders and turned herself loose to ride his quickening thrusts.

"Take it home, Luke," she urged him. "Make me scream and holler with—"

"Squeeze it out of me," he countered. "Make me come so hard I won't see straight for the rest of the—"

Her hoarse cry triggered a surge that left him utterly mindless. Utterly awed as he writhed in her merciless grip around his cock. Her hips wiggled in his grasp as he ground against her to release every last drop. Maybe then he'd be able to concentrate on the drawings they needed to do.

"God, Luke that was the most—"

"That was the most revolting thing I've ever seen," replied a female voice behind them.

And then a similar one chimed in. "Yeah, but at least we're not the only ones gettin' screwed over by the bank! Frankly, I'm glad we witnessed this!"

Jane closed her eyes. Froze in place as Luke kept his hands spread over her bare ass.

He cleared his throat. How long had the twins been watching? Not that it mattered: their careless hair and bovine expressions were so far removed from the woman he had in his arms—a far cry from their mother's sense of dignity, too—that he came down from his euphoric high fully focused. Ready to put a couple other women in their place.

"Wait in the front room, girls," he muttered. "Seems like a real good time to discuss how *you* screwed Mama over! If you hadn't compromised her finances, none of us would be in this position."

Tiffany's lip curled. "Don't give me that bullshit! You're falling for the line Jane and her daddy are—"

"Out!" Luke ordered, pointing toward the front room. "We'll talk when I'm damn good and ready!"

11

"Imagine our embarrassment when Carter Cook called us in to say the bank took over our ranch!" Crystal raked her fake fingernails through her hair, leaving it even more like a bedraggled rat's nest than before. "I have no intention of—"

"This spa thing is *not* what Mama would've wanted, and you know it, Luke!" Tiffany chimed in. "Whatever strings you think you're pulling here—like a noose around our necks—"

"Sorry, ladies, but we saw your signatures on those loans—and on the notarized documents turning the debts over to the bank if you didn't pay your mama back," Jane said firmly. "So don't accuse my father of any dirty dealing. This was between you and your mother before the bank ever got involved, and you both know it."

"And you can't come whining to *me*, because while you were sponging off Mama, thinking she'd forgive and forget that money for tavern upgrades and a new truck, *I* was sending her money every month. *Every fuckin' month* for all these years!" Luke stood in the front room, facing the blonde twins who looked as dull and faded as the sofa they sat on. And while Jane admired him from her stance a couple of yards away, she had no desire to be in the middle of this family feud.

"Then why the hell didn't Mama loan us the money from *that* account?" Crystal whined. "It made no sense for her to put the place in hock if she had the cash!"

"We'll never know that, will we?" Luke came back at her.

"I can't presume to answer for your mother," Jane chimed in, "but I suspect she kept her dealings with her children separated—easily accounted for—so Daddy, as her financial manager, would know exactly where the chips should fall after her death. He knew about Luke's passbook account, after all. And when he notarized that note your mother drew up, he hoped you'd repay her before she died. First National makes it a policy not to interfere with—or make assumptions about—the wishes of deceased clients. It's not good for the families involved, and it's not good business."

They rolled their eyes, but at least they were quiet. Then Tiffany, always a few notches sharper than her sister, cleared her throat. "So what this means is that we don't get our shares of the ranch—"

"Already got 'em!" Luke crowed, though he sounded none too happy. "And in order for me to claim my share, I'm having to work off another loan. Which is progressing nicely, by the way."

Jane could foresee this squabble going on and on, and she wanted no part of it. But since the twins had been crass enough to watch them make love, she wasn't above having some fun. "Maybe your sisters would sign on for the same sort of repayment plan we worked out for you. Luke. That's totally your call, though."

His face furrowed as he thought back to the sexual part of that plan, but then the light bulb flashed on. "Sweat equity?" he murmured. "Servicing the loan by working at an agreed-upon wage? I can't see my sisters tearing out fence or—"

"No, but we'll need materials hauled to the work site, which takes a truck. And our construction crew will need meals catered onsite until the spa's up and running. Just a thought," she added breezily. "I'm going to let you three work that out. Or not."

Jane walked out through the kitchen, well aware Luke would follow her.

"Hey—you're a genius, you know that?"

She turned, basking in his grin. "They might not go for it. And *I* will be keeping track of their payments and hours, and they need to know that up front. They're not going to wiggle out of a dime they owe the bank, Luke."

"And if they don't take the bait—a generous offer on your part—they'll start a monthly repayment plan that *I* set up, because I sure as hell won't let them ride on *my* labor!"

"I like the sound of that," she murmured. "Seeya later, cowboy."

"Don't think for a minute that I'm going along with anything that bitch says!" Crystal glared at him over the cigarette she'd just lit, while her sister was mirroring her irritation by lighting her own smoke from her twin's.

Birds of a feather they'd always been, and growing up with these older sisters had taught him a lot about the psychology of the female species. He'd been their errand boy and the butt of their jokes and the unwilling pawn in their childhood pranks— and he was finished saying "how high?" when they ordered him to jump.

Luke shrugged. Took a chair across the small front room so he didn't have to inhale their smoke. "Do what you want. You always have," he added with an edge in his voice. "But once Patsy's Ranch is up and running, you won't own the only eatery in town, Crys. I'm guessing the spa will feature a healthful café, and I wouldn't be surprised if the resort included a full-service restaurant with delivery and catering, or—"

"You can't believe folks around here will come running to chichi new restaurants to snarf sushi, or to sample food they've never seen before!" Tiffany said with a snort. She exhaled smoke through her nose—a trick he'd always found as irritating as the way she always, always sided with her sister. "These people want three squares—meat and potatoes and—"

"People will flock to the spa complex out of curiosity, first thing," Luke interrupted. "And I predict they'll try the food— welcome something besides burgers and fries and pale iceberg salads—before they relax themselves in the spa."

He leaned forward in his chair, focusing intently on sisters who were, frankly, showing their age in ungraceful ways. "Are you ready for the competition, Crys?" he demanded. "Like it or not, *change* is coming to Enterprise in a big way. It's up to you, whether you capitalize on the opportunity or hole up in your tavern drinking up your profits."

Crystal scowled, about to spout back at him, when his cell phone jingled the tune to "I Feel Lucky."

Luke smiled at how the old Mary Chapin Carpenter song reflected his mood so perfectly: damn the nay-sayers and traditionalists! He was up to his eyeballs in a whole new vision and he'd never felt more in sync with life. It was a sweet feeling, too!

He glanced at the number on his cell screen. "Josh!" he said. "You've called to say yes. I just know it!"

His stylist friend chuckled wryly. "Well, *maybe*. Seems you're more psychic than I ever imagined, getting your butt out of here like a rat jumping a sinking ship."

His sisters looked irked that he was talking on his phone and making them listen, but Luke really didn't care. He sensed an important point was about to be made—and Crys and Tiff needed that point driven home in a very direct way. "What sinking ship you talking about?"

"Tanya just got busted. Looks to me like somebody set her

up for the fall, and she's copping a plea for psychiatric evalua-
tion and rehab to get out of the heavier charges."

"Holy shit." Luke paused, picturing Tanya's drama queen
talents in full sway as she tried to talk the cops out of incarcer-
ating her. "So what happens next?"

"Well, it puts a lot of her pending deals and contracts on
hold, and—" Josh paused, as effective during dead air as he was
when he spoke. "Seeing her go down in a cloud of white pow-
der has made me rethink my situation. She's losing everything
she built up over the years—losing you, and then falling like a
domino in an elaborate shakedown pattern you started when
you walked out on her. I'm guessing the brass from Resistol
initiated this."

"It's the best thing for her, if she'll truly undergo the treatment," Luke murmured. "Before the coke, there was no better-
respected agent than Tanya Valdez. Everything she touched
turned to gold."

"But her career's gone down like a house of cards. My salon
won't be affected all that much, but . . . I hope your offer's still
open?"

"Damn straight it is, buddy!" Luke grinned at how all the
right pieces were falling into place now—as though destiny was
kicking in with the brilliance of Jane Cook's sexy smile. "Let
me know when to fetch you at the airport. You're going to love
what you see, Josh. You'll take this ball and run with it, big-
time."

When he clapped his phone shut, he snickered at his sisters'
identical expressions. "There you have it," he said smugly. "Josh
Honn, world-class stylist, is about to take command of Patsy's
Ranch—"

"I can't believe you're calling it that!" Tiffany grunted.

"—and you still have time to get in on the ground floor,"
Luke finished firmly. "One way or another, you *will* repay
those outrageous loans you stuck Mama with.

"Now if you'll excuse me—" He stood up, dismissing them with a nod toward the door. "—I have an ad campaign to engineer. People to see and places to take this new business venture."

And didn't it feel just dandy, telling his sisters where to get off?

12

"What do you think, Daddy? Isn't this the most incredible thing you've ever seen?" Jane grinned proudly at the blueprints and artists' renditions of the landscaped buildings that would soon transform Luke McGrew's home place. In the past three weeks the plans for Patsy's Ranch had taken shape in wonderful ways even she couldn't have anticipated.

"I wouldn't believe it if I hadn't watched it myself. Who would've thought such talent from New York would find its way *here*?" he replied with a chuckle. "I've got to think Patsy is mighty happy about all this, even if Luke didn't come home to stay until she passed on."

Jane considered this a moment. "If she were still alive, this wouldn't be happening, though. Just goes to show how much one life affects us all—how a twist in the kaleidoscope changes the entire landscape."

"And speaking of landscape—check out the billboards that just went up. I think you'll like what you see." Luke was leaning against her office door, wearing that bad-ass black cowboy hat and a smile that said he wanted to show her those billboards personally.

"It *is* time for lunch," she teased as she gawked at her watch. "My, how time flies when you're having fun!"

Her dad rolled his eyes. "I know an escape plan when I hear one. I'll see you two later."

Jane wasn't even settled in the seat of Luke's Navigator before he was hooking an arm around her, pulling her close for a white-lightning kiss. "You get prettier by the day, you know it?" he murmured. "Is my vision changing, or has Josh been working on you?"

She widened her eyes flirtatiously, loving the way his hungry gaze made her feel even better than her new eye shadow and highlights. "Yes—and yes," she replied pointedly. "As the local spokeswoman for Patsy's Ranch, I have to look the part, right?"

"I'm glad you're having fun with this, honey. Gives you a whole new shine." He pulled out of the bank's parking lot with a sense of purpose that made butterflies flutter in her stomach . . . like he was up to something. "And now that Ross Honn's got the Web site almost together—"

"Looking way better than anyone around here could've designed it," she remarked emphatically.

"—and the promo is rolling, we'll have to mush the construction along," he said in a husky, happy voice. "Something tells me folks are going to book resort space and spa time as soon as they see our ads."

She smacked his cheek with a wet, exuberant kiss—and then her mouth fell open. "As soon as they see *you*, you mean! Holy shit, cowboy! That's so hot it'll burn down the town!"

The billboard, right where the main road came into Enterprise, featured a full-size head shot of Luke in his black hat, with that direct gaze and sexy, sexy grin. PATSY'S RANCH the text said in bold Western lettering. SCENIC RESORT PROPERTIES. FULL SERVICE SPA & SALON. JUST WAIT TILL OUR COWBOYS GET THEIR HANDS ON YOU!

Seeing Luke on that larger-than-life surface, looking so damn sure of himself, did something wild to her insides. His gaze, and the camera angle, made it seem like those hypnotic green eyes could look right through to where she was getting way too warm . . . and very wet. "What if I can't wait?" she whispered.

McGrew's head lolled back as his laughter filled the SUV's plush leather interior. "Why do you think my rear seats fold down flat, little lady?" he asked in a lecherous tone. "And why do you think my ride's got tinted glass?"

She squirmed in spite of her best intentions to get some real work done this afternoon . . . work that might have to take a back seat while she got naked in the space behind them. It was déjà vu of prom night, almost—except they were both consenting adults now. No drunken dares from a buddy. No modesty or virginal reputation to protect.

"We've come a long way from your rusted-out camper days," she murmured.

"But we're not nearly there yet, sugar. This cowboy has no plans to ride into the sunset any time soon." He assessed her with a come-on look that made her melt. "Let's find someplace to park this thing and celebrate our success, shall we? I feel like working off a *big* chunk of that loan."

His expression waxed urgent as he put the Navigator in gear again. He headed back toward town . . . turned in where the pasture gate had once been—where he'd torn down the rusty barbed-wire fences so the heavy equipment could get in to dig out foundations and doze the complex's roads. Luke eased past the trucks with their rolling striped concrete mixers, waving at the guys who poured footings for the rec center and spa. They nodded and waved back as though seeing his famous face was an everyday thing—

And thank goodness it is, Jane mused. It was a sure bet these brawny construction guys took orders more seriously from Luke McGrew than they would from her.

"But you look sooooo much better naked to the waist, sweating in the sun, than any of these locals," she murmured.

"Huh?"

Jane laughed, realizing that she'd been talking to herself about him again . . . couldn't seem to go a moment without thinking about Lucky Luke McGrew. *Wanting* him, just like she did right now. "Don't mind me! I'm just a girl living out her finest fantasies with a world-class cowboy," she remarked breezily.

His lecherous grin made her giggle, yet as she silently admired the way he navigated past mounds of earth and dozed-over outbuildings, Jane was still curious about something. "You've got to solve a little mystery for me, Luke."

"What's that?"

How did she say this without sounding crass—without ruining his fine, feisty mood? "This vehicle starts at fifty thousand dollars," she said, truly awed because she'd never owned anything so posh. "Yet you came to my bank needing money—credit card debt out the wazoo. But nowhere in your loan workup did I see any record of car payments or—"

"That's 'cause I stole it."

A sick feeling rushed through her gut. He sounded deadly serious, and it would be just her luck to find out *now* that he was wanted for grand theft auto, or that Tanya Valdez had masterminded some crooked-ass scheme to—

Luke snickered richly as he halted the vehicle behind a windbreak of thick bushes. "Let's clarify—before you keel over in a dead faint—that I got a good deal because it was used in some shoots, but that I also paid cash for it. Drove it away free and clear."

"And how'd you do *that*?"

He grinned, opening his door as heat flared in his eyes.

"They don't call me Lucky for nothing, sweetheart. But just so you'll know—because I care about getting the details right this time—I collected a paycheck I suspected might be my last before I walked out on Tanya. Cashed it, and bought this fine machine as my last memento of the high life in New York. For all I knew, I'd be sleeping in it, if the bank didn't make my loan. And then when I saw *you* were the loan officer—"

"You figured I had an old debt to settle."

"Damn straight. I wouldn't have given me the loan, either, considering the circumstances and my lousy credit record. But I had to go for it, didn't I?" he asked in a low whisper. "What sort of a son would I be if I let my sisters claim Mama's ranch by default? Or if I let a cokehead agent screw me out of my future?"

A smile spread over her face and Jane got out of the car . . . climbed into the rear door he held open for her and over the console to reach the back cargo area formed when the rear seats folded down to the floor. It was a little cramped, but cozy and very private with the tinted windows. He'd spread an old quilt back there, as though he'd figured on this little tryst all along.

"That's what I've always liked about you, Luke. You were so bad you were good. Refused to live by anybody else's rules or expectations," she said wistfully. "Took off for New York and made yourself a star, while I stayed here—still living at home like a sheltered little—"

"You're a damn fine woman, Janie—and a smart one, too. And I'm grateful that you've forgiven me." Luke crawled over the console and knelt before her . . . a man on his knees and wanting something a lot more exciting than her pardon or her bank's money. "The question is . . . do you feel lucky?"

Snickering, Jane slipped her hand between his thighs. "Yes, I do. He feels very, very large. And hard." And wasn't *that* wonderful, to know she'd made such a gorgeous cowboy horny—for *her?*

"Take him out. He loves it when a pretty woman oohs and ahhs over him."

Jane fumbled with the stiff zipper in his jeans, almost as awkward as that high school girl with the braces and the splotchy complexion and—

But, no, that girl had grown up! Now she was feisty enough to do it in the back of a luxury SUV, without having to run off in tears because her date was only cashing in on a dare. *She* was taking matters in hand, calling the shots this time!

"How much are you worth, big boy?" she whispered, grinning at him. His cock jutted out now, between the sides of tight jeans she'd shoved past his ass. "What's the going rate to fuck a famous cowboy come home?"

"Keep talking dirty, and I'll have to wash your mouth out with—"

He came at her then, catching her head in his hand to claim a kiss where his tongue took the lead—and took her breath away. Jane gasped and grabbed him with the hand that didn't have hold of Lucky, to keep her balance while he kissed all rational thought from her head.

Luke's passion fueled hers. No longer was she shy about giving as good as she got and then issuing her own randy challenge. Their lips and tongues dueled as they opened each other's shirts. Then they squirmed onto their sides to yank down each other's pants.

"This was easier when I was a kid," Luke rasped.

"I wouldn't know. Nobody but you ever tried to take me in a vehicle."

"High time that happened, then. Roll onto your back, baby," he whispered, grinning in the dimness. "I'm gonna set those long legs free so I can kneel between them. Then I'm gonna grab your sweet ass and give you a piece that'll have you screaming."

"Did you set the emergency brake? If we get to rocking this thing too hard, it might roll down—"

"Too fucking late to worry about that, isn't it? I'm *not* letting you get up to look!"

Jane's giggle turned into a groan of sheer need when he pegged her with with his hot cock. Luke penetrated deeply, two or three times to drive her absolutely nuts for it. Then he held her hard against his hips.

He gazed into her face. Kept her in suspense as he thought about how to say something. "I've got protection, but it's in the glove compartment—"

"Too fucking late to worry about that, isn't it?" Jane echoed. Her pulse thundered in her ears as potential consequences raced through her mind, yet she grabbed his shoulders to keep him from shifting away. "I've been on the pill for a couple years to keep my body in better rhythm, so hey—why not rely on what they're really intended for?"

He sucked air, holding her gaze. "It's not like I've ever been celibate, Jane. I'll understand if—"

"It's a calculated risk, yes," she replied quietly. And at that moment she realized just how calm and absolutely certain she felt about this whole situation—Luke, as well as this devil-get-screwed spa project she was taking on. "But after all," she went on, "even if you were a monk stuck away in monastery somewhere, you'd never be *safe*, Luke. Any woman in your path would fall prey."

"What if I want that woman to be you?"

Jane's heart did cartwheels and she giggled again. "I'd say you've wised up a *lot* since you got home, cowboy! Shut up and ride, will ya? You've got a lot of proving up to do!"

With a low growl he lit into her again, teasing her high and hard with the wand that made him quite a magician indeed. As though he'd entranced her, all her anxiety and loneliness and concern about falling too hard too fast simply dissipated. Jane entered that mindless madness and reveled in the way his body drove hers to a peak of desperate need. As the spirals of heat began deep inside her, she reached for him.

Luke wrapped his powerful arms around her and brought them both to a climax that shattered all the doubts between them. He released his seed and she welcomed the feel of him without the latex coming between his hot sex and hers.

It was way better than being a senior on prom night, too young to handle the responsibilities—or the emotional connection—of lovemaking. Now that sex was more than a sum of body parts covertly coming together, Jane realized how much growing up she'd done in the past few weeks. While sure, her appearance had improved since that awful night, she'd never felt this beautiful . . . this free. And it was because of the way Luke looked at her, rather than the way she looked.

They collapsed on the rumpled quilt, grinning at each other.

"Why do I suddenly have this notion I should get a place of my own?" she whispered. Her fingers followed their urge to linger on the smooth, warm skin of his face.

"Funny you should mention that. I know of an apartment above the resort's rec center that's just looking for somebody to make it a home."

Jane swallowed hard. Closed her eyes and said the words before she lost her nerve. "Will you join me there? I—I'm not expecting you to marry—"

"No need to plan everything out right now, is there?" he whispered. He kissed her so gently she almost cried. "We can handle the details when the time's right, sugar. Right now, I want to work that loan down to a manageable amount—to prove to you and your daddy and my sisters just how serious Luke McGrew is about this whole proposition. High time I was more than just a pretty face."

She almost made a smart remark, but swallowed it—partly because he was making such a fine effort to be serious, and partly because he was struggling so hard with his pants in this cramped space.

And wasn't it nice, not to have the last word just because she could? Liberating . . . sweet and free, to just lie here and watch his body and his facial expressions.

Do you feel lucky? her inner voice quipped.

She grinned. Things were heating up better than she'd ever anticipated. It was going to be a fine, feisty summer, wasn't it?

13

Half an hour before the ribbon-cutting ceremony, Jane wandered slowly through the salon. Amazing, what the last few months had brought forth from dusty old ranch land. Her fingers lingered on sleek black leather and cool chrome; black granite work stations and floor tile resonated a richness she hadn't imagined—and the deep pink walls vibrated with an energy all their own! Josh Honn had left no detail untended, and the result was a full-service spa the sleepy little town of Enterprise, Wyoming could *never* have envisioned! She could imagine Patsy McGrew grinning proudly as she held out her hands for a manicure here!

"Everything to your satisfaction, Ms. Cook?"

She turned to grin at her facility's manager. "It's perfect, Josh. We couldn't have done this without you."

"We did all right, didn't we?" He adjusted his designer eyeglasses as he gazed around the gleaming, spacious room. "Even I never expected it to come out *this* well—but your idea found the right place at the right time, and *poof!* We made it happen whether Enterprise was ready or not! Congratulations."

He kissed her in that chichi way big-city stylists had, and then gave her upswept hair a final assessment. "I confess I had some reservations about the uniforms, though." Josh raked back glossy brown hair that hung a lot longer on one side, cut at a rakish angle to his slender face. "When you insisted on pink shirts—"

"The tight black jeans and western detailing on that shirt keep you from looking like a girl. Trust me," she said in a husky voice.

"Yeah, well you won't catch *me* in a pink shirt!" Luke sauntered in, so damn hot in his black suit and hat that she felt her crepe dress puckering from his heat. "You ready, sugar? You won't believe the crowd out there. Good thing our staff's all hired, because they'll be showing off model condos and the digs here until the cows come home."

Josh rolled his eyes, but Jane laughed. "And aren't you glad you don't have any cows on Patsy's Ranch anymore—except for this big ole cash cow we dreamed up?"

"Sure beats stepping in it," Josh remarked as he headed for the door. "Guess we'd better get ourselves to the rec center for the ribbon snipping."

"We'll be right there," Luke called after him, but his gaze remained fixed on Jane. He inhaled deeply, and his smile got tight. "Damn, you look good! I might just have to steer you into the nearest massage room and—"

"Not right now you're not!" Her face flushed with pleasure. At one time such a remark would've upset her: only a *man* would think about a quickie without considering the *mess* he'd make. But being with a man who couldn't keep his eyes—or his hands—off her had changed her attitude about guys who wanted it all the time.

"Yeah, all dressed up and no place to come," he remarked as he crooked his arm.

"Why do I suspect you'll find one before the afternoon's out?"

"I like the way you think, Janie." He kissed her quickly, knowing better than to smear her lipstick—or to start something he couldn't finish right now.

Jane took his arm and stepped outside. Was there anything more glorious than seeing this sea of people? So many excited faces . . . lots of happy chatter—some of it from realtors and photographers who'd followed the complex's progress since word first got out. And didn't Crystal and Tiffany clean up nice? They were mingling with trays of canapés and champagne, easy to spot in those deep pink western shirts and black jeans.

As she and Luke crossed to the rustic lodge-style recreation center, her heart fluttered: Lucky looked so natural, so right, glad-handing the press and politicians here to celebrate this opening. Such a man of the world he was—and he'd brought her up to his level of sophistication in many ways this summer. Who would've expected *that*, on the day he stormed out of her office cussing her?

When they reached the front door, her father looked proud enough to pop. As a hush settled over the crowd and he made a few opening remarks, Jane's mind entered that surreal state of being so damn happy she couldn't handle it all at once. In a slo-mo haze, she accepted an oversize pair of sheers . . .used both hands to snip the huge pink ribbon tied around the door handles . . . basked in the applause and the popping of flashbulbs. Luke was probably so used to all this hoopla, he wasn't giving a thought to—

His gaze made her heart stop. He seemed so intent on not kissing her, here in front of all these people, she could see the flaring of his nostrils and the effort it took not to scoop her body against his.

Jane licked her lips. He was figuring out a place to lift her dress and take her. His eyes smoldered with that purpose, and the crotch of her pantyhose went wet—or it would've, had she been wearing any. She gave him a catlike smile.

"I know what you want, cowboy," she murmured beneath the blaring of the high school's band.

"You want it, too," he whispered, oblivious to the well-wishers who approached them. "Tell me how much."

She widened her eyes mischievously. "Find out."

Then she turned, assuming her bank president personna again, taking her place beside her father to shake hands. Luke McGrew did the same, but he stood closely enough that his body brushed against hers. Guests entered the recreation center to get a good look around the meeting rooms, pool, and party facilities their little town had never thought it needed. Already, however, three wedding receptions, a family reunion, and a number of small conferences from Casper, Laramie, and Cheyenne were booked, and their concierge—Josh's brother, Ross—was at the desk inside to drum up more business.

As the crowd thinned, Jane noticed how Luke was edging away from the rec center toward the salon, eyeing her every chance he got as he kept talking to visitors. Her pulse pounded. It felt so improper—so damn dirty!—to be looking for a chance to escape, yet as soon as Daddy's cronies from the banking association in Casper had surrounded him to clap him on the back, she was off at a quick, purposeful stride.

"I'd better be sure someone's at the salon to show it off," she explained to a reporter known for being long-winded. "Be sure to get some cake and punch in the rec center lobby! Daddy's waiting to talk to you!"

Heart pounding, she somehow kept her walk to a brisk, businesslike gait. She entered the salon—heard a few voices asking Josh questions back in a massage room, and then the firm, steady tread of cowboy boots came around from behind her. Without a word, Luke took her hand and led her away from the voices, toward the restroom—

And then he opened the louvered linen closet door and steered her inside.

Jane sucked air. While the U-shaped walk-in allowed them plenty of room to maneuver, she'd never felt so vulnerable or—

"Luke, there's no lock!" she whispered frantically.

He growled and shoved his hat toward a shelf of folded towels. "Hike up your dress and lean forward, elbows on that shelf," he said in a guttural whisper.

Spurred by his desire—by that need to push the envelope in a big, bad way—Jane did as she was told. She grinned when he took his turn at sucking air.

"You little—!" He swatted her bare ass, chuckling. "Should've known you had a reason for wearing this dress instead of a suit."

"We'd better hurry, or—"

The jingle of his belt buckle . . . the swift swish of fabric down his thighs—

"Let me worry about that. I'll be behind you, so the first thing anybody sees'll be my—"

She inhaled sharply as he took her from behind, spreading her thighs farther with his hot, insistent hands. A finger wandered over to stroke her clit, and she jerked with the intense sensation.

"God, but you're so tight and so—"

"I can't believe we're—"

"—damn wet already . . . all I could think about out there was getting inside you to—"

Jane swiveled her head to kiss him over her shoulder. He slid in and out of her rapidly, driving them with a secretive need, moaning into her mouth. Her breath came rapidly as the spasms began. Half of her wanted to stop this ridiculous, risky rendezvous before Josh threw open the door to show this closet to a guest, while the rest of her was speeding toward orgasm.

And of course, that part of her won: Luke clutched her suddenly, thrusting into her with rapid little slapping noises. She curled inward . . . bit back the need to scream, and then wrenched her mouth from his to bury it against the fresh, fluffy towels stacked in front of her. He gripped her hard to empty himself, panting next to her ear and muttering, "Jesus, Janie . . . Janie . . ."

Her name had never sounded so sweet. She'd never in her life felt so decadent, or so daring. Through the louvers came the sounds of footsteps and conversations . . . Luke pulled away, swiping a small towel for himself and one for her. Silently they wiped off and refastened their clothing . . . patted their hair back in place, checking each other in the dimness to be sure it didn't look obvious, what they'd been doing in here.

"Ready?" he whispered.

She nodded, her eyes wide. "You go first, and when the coast is clear—"

But when Luke cautiously twisted the knob and eased the door open, a roar of applause and raucous laughter greeted them. Josh was standing there, extending flutes of champagne, while a couple dozen locals gaped and gawked and kept clapping.

Jane felt her face go ten shades of red.

Luke, however, stepped confidently out and put his hat back on. "Guess we can consider this place officially christened now," he teased as he took the bubbly. He handed a glass to Jane, beckoning her with those eyes. "And no ceremony would be complete without a toast to the lady who made all this happen. Nobody cooks up a deal like Jane Cook. *Nobody*!"

"Hear, hear!" Josh chimed in.

Laughing and crying—and yes, wanting to slam the closet door and hide herself forever—Jane came out. These people thought it was one huge joke that they'd caught her and Luke going at it. How would she ever face them again when they came in to set up CDs or pay down their loans? Every time

they looked at her from here on out, they'd be thinking about the sounds coming from behind this slatted door, and the way she'd shamed her daddy by—

And yet, as she glanced up over the rim of her graceful glass, she saw only good-natured smiles.

"We were wonderin' if Lucky'd ever make good on that old dare," one of the guys piped up. "Back in school, McGrew was the only one who didn't realize how bad he wanted you. 'Bout time you made an honest man of him, Janie!"

As laughter filled the salon again, she blinked. That was Steve Kirby. The guy who'd dared Luke to take her in the back of his camper. He was wearing a suit, standing with a group of investment brokers from Casper . . .

The champagne tickled her throat and she laughed—downright giggled at the absurdity of this situation. Sure, these folks had caught her in a compromising position, but what could they do to her? It was *her* salon, wasn't it?

"Never let it be said that I let a debt—or a dare—go unsettled," she remarked breezily. "If any of you thought I was just another stuffed-shirt bank president, well, I guess you'll have a different opinion now. And you'll realize I settle for nothing less than perfection. Enjoy your tour—and I look forward to seeing you here at Patsy's Ranch often!"

"Nice comeback," Luke murmured as the crowd broke up.

"Yeah, I did all right." Jane drained her glass, watching him through its refraction. The sparkle in her eyes made the champagne seem flat by comparison. "But it was *your* comeback that got this whole ball rolling. Sure, I had a few stray ideas about what I could do if the bank took over your mama's land, but—"

"You needed me to make it go. I like the sound of that. It means we're a team." He cupped her chin to kiss her softly, and even though a few people were still watching them, Jane kissed him back. Like she meant it.

"Know what I like about you, Janie?"

She raised an eyebrow. Hadn't they had this conversation a few months ago? "What would that be, Luke? I'll need awhile to listen to your list, right?"

"Yep. Because I like every little thing, sugar," he crooned as he nuzzled her ear. "Every fucking little thing."